"This was adorable and heartwarming from page one… low angst, full of warm families, cute dates, crazy best friends and steamy nights and car rides.... I was smiling all the way through."

— JENN, THE BOOK REFUGE

"It's clear that Juliette Cross can write anything she wants. Because this book? Unreal….*Parks and Provocation* was swoony, sexy, steamy and hilarious all at the same time."

— ANNA READS HERE

"This story is one that is going to stay with me for a long time to come. It's just brilliant!"

— BELLA READS ROMANCE

Praise for Juliette Cross & PARKS AND PROVOCATION

“Juliette Cross became a favorite author of mine fr the moment I was 2 chapters in to her paranorı romance WOLF GONE WILD. I have loved every thi of hers I've read and have come to see her as a comf author.”

— CRYSTAL’S BOOKISH LI

"Sweet crackerjacks, Juliette Cross builds worlds th you absolutely want to live in!"

— SUZANNE, GOODREAD

“Juliette Cross has imagined, created and executed on of the most magnificent, all-consuming, profoundly arousing, contemporary love stories that I’ve ever had the pleasure to get lost in.”

— EMERALD BOOK REVIEWS

“Oh, sweet snickerdoodles. This story got me right in the feels.”

— LAUREN, GOODREADS

Bright Like Wildfire

JULIETTE CROSS

Cover Design by Najla Qamber, Qamber Designs

Cover Image by Wander Aguiar

For Lindsey Duga,
You're awesome and amazing and I love you.

Glossary of Cajun Names & Words

1. Bayou Teche—*By-YOO TESH*—A bayou of south-central Louisiana flowing about 200 km (125 mi) south to the Atchafalaya River near the Gulf of Mexico.

2. Beauville—BO-vil—fictional town based on a small town in south-central Louisiana, the heart of Cajun country.

3. Bon Creole—*BOHN Kree-OHL*—Bon Creole is a real restaurant in a small Cajun town noted for having the best po-boys and Best Gumbo from the local Gumbo Cookoff.

4. Breaux—*BRO*

5. Doucet—*DOO-set*

6. Dugas—*DOO-gah*

7. Fontenot—*FAHNT-ih-no*

8. Mouton—*MOO-tohn*

9. Poirier—*POUR-ee-yay*

10. Theriot—*TAIR-ee-o*

11. Zydeco—*ZY-duh-KO*—A music genre that evolved in southwest Louisiana by French Creole speakers which blends blues, rhythm and blues, and music indigenous to the

Louisiana Creoles and the Native American people of Louisiana.

Chapter One

~BETTY~

"Dangit!"

I flipped the coffee pot on with as much frustration I could manage without breaking it, then hurried back to my bedroom. I'd accidentally programmed it for 6 p.m. instead of a.m. on top of hitting the snooze button twice.

Welcome to Monday morning.

After stripping off my sleep shirt in my walk-in closet and pulling on a pair of pants, blousy tank, and requisite cardigan —*thank you, inventor of wrinkle-free clothes*—I rounded the bed toward my bathroom.

"Ow!"

Jerking my foot off the floor, I hopped to my bed, rubbing my heel where I'd just stepped on…

"There you are."

I picked up the earring I'd lost over the weekend after my sister Emma and I had done a *Schitt's Creek* marathon with a pitcher of margaritas. In expected tipsy fashion, I'd undressed

—jewelry and all—en route to my bed, dropping them as I went.

Giving myself 2.5 seconds to recover from the earring injury because that's all I could spare, I rushed into the bathroom, got one glimpse of my hair and realized it was a messy bun day.

That was pretty much every day, truth be told. Even when I wasn't running twenty minutes behind. But until my principal complained, this was part of my uniform.

After brushing my teeth, putting on deodorant, then applying minimal make-up so I wouldn't terrify the teenagers I taught—or hear, *what's wrong, Ms. Mouton, are you sick* on loop all day—I slipped into a pair of flats and grabbed my laptop bag.

After quickly pouring a cup of coffee into my favorite travel mug that read *Tears of My Students*—thank you, teacher appreciation day gift card—I grabbed my lunch from the fridge and headed out the door.

The nippy breeze coming off the sugarcane field across the road from my new house lightened my mood just a tad. We'd gotten an early cool front. Of course, a Louisiana fall and winter was like an old junker. It took several starts and stops before it finally got going.

Right when I smiled at the break in the heat, I spilled a drop of coffee on my pants as I slid into my car.

"Ugh." Grabbing a napkin from my glovebox, I tried rubbing it, only to spread the brown stain wider on my khakis. "This day can't get any worse," I muttered.

Note to self: never say things like this. The fact that I did, opening up the universe to further kick me in the twat was proof that I deserved to be.

I sped my Toyota sedan the short distance into town, then suddenly had to brake when I was still a mile out. I was now sitting in bumper-to-bumper traffic on a country road that never, *ever* had traffic.

"What now?"

Did a sugarcane truck fall in the ditch?

As I rounded the curve, I could see a commotion about a half-mile up ahead at the intersection onto Evangeline Drive. Whatever it was, the traffic thinned out at Evangeline.

I shot off a text to Finn to tell him to let my hall buddy Lily know I might be late. We were supposed to be standing at the door in the hallway at the bell each morning. One of Principal Burke's rules to prevent students from dragging ass, PDA, and so on.

It didn't prevent it. It forced us to yell a lot and witness teenage hormones in full force, all before 7:30 a.m.

"Finally."

The cars were moving again. When I eased closer to the corner, I craned my neck like everyone else holding up traffic and gaped at the packed parking lot on the corner with banners and balloons flying. It was then that I saw *him*.

Bennett Broussard stood in front of his brand-new store, Broussard's Fresh Market. He wasn't hard to miss since he stood taller than just about everyone in the crowd, his radiant smile charming his captive audience. The wind tousled his wavy, chestnut hair, making him look like a hair model stepping off set. The morning sun caught him in a single golden ray, like a freaking spotlight from the heavens. Even the sun showered him with love and adoration. It was ridiculous.

Look, there were a number of reasons Bennett annoyed the hell out of me. He was conceited and bossy, and everything in life was served to him on a silver platter. He was the perfect prince and could do no wrong in the eyes of the whole damn town.

Then, of course, there was the *real* reason he'd become one of my least favorite people.

The glitter booby bomb.

Yes, I realized it happened twelve years ago, but it still got me angry.

And here he was, further ruining my Monday morning. Why was I even remotely surprised?

I slammed on my brakes as a slew of Beauville High cheerleaders ran toward the crowded parking lot of the new supermarket in front of my car. *Was that Heather Doucet?* She better not be late for my homeroom because I wasn't going to excuse her for attending the newest Broussard store ribbon-cutting.

So aggravating. Bennett's family already owned half the town. Now, he needed to add a bougie supermarket to the list?

The cheerleaders did a cutesy little routine in front of the giant ribbon, where they'd ended on their knees, shaking their pom-poms at Bennett. The crowd cheered and clapped as he waved to his ravenous fans.

Gah!

Wanting to escape the scene as fast as possible, I sped around the corner and hauled ass to BHS. Five seconds after I barreled through a red light, I saw the blue lights flash in my rearview mirror.

This cannot be happening to me.

I checked my speed as I braked, realizing I was going twelve miles over the speed limit. Then I swerved over to the shoulder.

The officer who stepped out of the patrol car was tall, lean, and fit as one might expect—or hope for—while getting a speeding ticket. His mirrored sunglasses were in place, a serious expression completing the hot cop look.

Exhaling a heavy sigh, I rummaged for my driver's license from my purse and registration out of the glove compartment, then rolled the window down right as he appeared.

He took the documents and removed his sunglasses, looking at my driver's license first. "In a hurry, Ms. Mouton?"

I glanced at his nametag and offered a bright smile. "Sorry, Officer Dugas. I'm a teacher at BHS and running super late because of this traffic jam back at the grand opening."

He grunted assent. "The Broussard grocery."

He didn't ask a question, just sort of confirmed the cause of my speeding like a maniac this morning.

"Yep." I exhaled a quick breath as he checked my registration. "Look, I'm very sorry. It's just been a really bad morning. Is there *any* way you can cut me some slack? I did tell you I was a teacher, right? We aren't exactly rolling in dough."

He made another grunt-like sound and looked at me. "I'm a cop."

Wowza. Nice baby blues, officer.

"Exactly! Public servants and all that. So you get it. If you gave me a ticket, it would be like breaking the public servant code, right?"

His wide mouth ticked up a smidgeon on one side. I was a little afraid of what a full-blown smile could do on a hot and serious and seriously hot man like him.

After another five seconds, he handed my documents back to me. "Watch the speed limit, Ms. Mouton. Have a nice day."

What? That actually worked?

"Have a nice day, Officer Dugas!"

Making sure to use my blinker and not take off from the shoulder like a bat out of hell, I made the last few miles to BHS.

Only Ms. Wellman was in the parking lot when I pulled up, tottering slowly to the faculty entrance.

She should've retired a hundred years ago, but who was I to tell anyone what was best for them. She also hated help of any kind, so I had stopped asking if she wanted me to carry her art bag.

Live and let live. That was my motto.

After parking, I shouldered my lunch and laptop bags and checked my watch as I took off.

"Morning, Ms. Wellman," I called as I speed-walked past her.

"Morning, Betsy."

My name wasn't Betsy. Never has been. It was Betty. Short for Beatrice, my grandmother's name. But Ms. Wellman made up her own rules, and I stopped trying to correct her long ago.

Dashing down the hallway, I crossed the crowded commons area where the students hung out before the bell, which according to my watch, would be in thirty seconds. By some miracle, I didn't catch either principal on duty as I zipped down the English/Language Arts wing to my classroom at the end of the hallway.

Finn was draped against my doorjamb, arms and ankles crossed, looking handsome as the devil in his crisply ironed attire and arrogant grin.

"What?" I snapped as I bypassed him to march over and dump my stuff in my desk chair.

"Tsk, tsk. Second time this week you're late, Miss Mouton."

"Stop hissing at me. You're supposed to be my best friend."

"That's why I'm warning you. I know how you get your panties in a bunch when Mr. Burke reprimands you. Of course, I think he just likes to get you in his office so he can check out your rack."

"Shut up. Don't remind me of that. It was *one* time."

He chuckled.

"Asshat," I muttered.

Mr. Burke was a married man, but that didn't prevent him from being a close-talker or chronic-ogler to all the attractive women on campus. Actually, the only one who wasn't a victim of his lechery was Ms. Wellman. One advantage of being born in prehistoric times.

The bell rang.

"Thank you for watching my door." I physically shoved him gently out of my doorway. "Now go to class."

"I don't have a homeroom. You know this. And why were you late anyway?"

"I don't even want to talk about it." I nodded to two boys in my homeroom and first period class as they walked between Finn and me since we now framed the doorway like two very mismatched sentinels. His tall, lean physique was the opposite of my shorter curvy self. Curvy in the ass and hips, at least.

I wasn't short-short. Not like my mom and grandmother. They were elf-sized. I was practically a giant at five-five next to both of them. But Finn was a good six-one-ish.

"Good morning!" came my perky hall buddy, Lily Breaux. "Did y'all see the *amazing* new grocery store, Broussard Fresh Market? I got a sneak peek inside before the ribbon-cutting this morning, and it is *amazing*."

We were opposite personalities, but I liked Lily. Even when she was outshining me with her door decorations, perfectly polished classroom, and fresh-as-a-daisy self. Which was basically all the time since I was seriously low-maintenance when it came to stuff like that.

Now, my classes and curriculum I took very seriously, almost too seriously. I had super high expectations for my students as I did with myself.

This was only Lily's second year of teaching, and she was bursting with inspiration and excitement. Not that I didn't enjoy teaching too. I loved it. Lily simply wore the persona of an excitable first-grade teacher. Unlike the rest of us jaded, heartless souls who taught high school English.

"Ohhh. That's right." Finn grinned wider. "I forgot it was opening day of the new store. So that's why you were late."

The tardy bell rang.

"Bye." I waved, giving him another shove down the hallway.

"See you at lunch," he called over his shoulder as he marched back to the Arts and Electives wing.

Finn—Finley Fontenot—taught Drama here at BHS and has

been since he graduated from the University of Louisiana at Lafayette six years ago. We'd been close friends in high school but parted ways after graduation when I'd crossed the Atchafalaya Basin to attend LSU in Baton Rouge.

After graduating in Education, I stayed in the city, taking a teaching position in Baton Rouge for a few years. But I discovered something quickly about myself. While I loved going to college there, I didn't want to live there. I had few friends and no family who stayed in the city. And quite frankly, I missed Beauville.

I loved getting anywhere I needed to go—grocery store, bank, work, gym—in five to ten minutes. And if I wanted something the bigger cities offered like the theater, concerts, or museums, Lafayette was a thirty-minute drive away. New Orleans only two. Easy day trip.

So when Finn had told me there was an English position opening up at our alma mater, I jumped on it. And hell yes, I shamelessly smiled till my face cracked during my interview with Mr. Burke to get the job. I didn't even care that his eyes kept roaming. Let him get a good, long look because I wanted that damn job.

Of course, I'd break his fingers if he ever tried to touch me. Not exaggerating. After inquiring with a few other teachers, I discovered he was harmless. Just a horndog. An obvious one anyway. Most men were, but they knew how to hide it well.

"Okay, guys," I said to the class after the pledge and morning announcements were over, "take an index card and pass it around. We'll do our reading check quiz first."

I passed the stack to the first row. Only a few grumblings as they handed them back to the rest of the students. Then Heather Doucet burst into the room, a beaming smile on her pretty face.

"I am *so* sorry, Ms. Mouton." She handed me an office memo marked excused.

Not wanting to think about *him* for another second of my crappy Monday morning, I focused on better things. Literature.

"It's fine. Just get seated, Heather. We have a lot to cover on last night's homework reading of *Jane Eyre*."

When she sat, her friend Naomi giggled and whispered something to her. Heather giggled right back.

"Do you ladies want to share what's so amusing?"

They both stiffened and faced forward.

"No, ma'am," said Naomi.

Trace, one of my favorite students in the whole wide world, rolled his eyes and said, "They were talking about how hot Mr. Broussard is who opened that new grocery store."

"Trace!" squealed Naomi, reaching over to swat his arm.

He inched away, grinning like a fiend.

Sarah in the front row snorted. "Like that's new news." She turned to her friend Caroline. "Did you see him in the BPAL production of *Chicago* last year?"

"Omigod. Did I." Caroline pretended to wipe away drool from her chin.

Time to move on.

"Question number *one*," I snapped.

Everyone jumped and straightened, pencils up and ready for the quiz.

I did *not* need the reminder that Bennett Broussard was, in fact, quite drool-worthy. Especially when there was a chance—a slight one, but still there—that I might be spending a lot of one-on-one time with him very soon.

A millennium later, my lunch break arrived. I met Finn in his office next to the auditorium, as always. As the Fine Arts Department chairperson and the director of all the school plays, he earned a ten-by-eight-foot room that could barely fit a desk, much less the wall-to-wall coat hanger where costumes were hung.

I plopped down on the loveseat across from him. It had been donated for one of his first shows but became part of his office décor. Such is the glamorous life of a public-school teacher.

Opening my lunch bag, I pulled out my turkey sandwich on wheat and tore into it, then heaved a sigh while I chewed.

Finn stared at me with wry amusement. I was accustomed to receiving this expression, so I ignored him and kept chewing.

"So," he said, pulling his container from the mini-fridge squeezed in behind his desk. He opened his container of cold pasta salad. "Bad Monday?"

"I don't want to talk about it." Then I took another huge bite of my sandwich to prove my point.

"Nonsense. Tell Uncle Finn. I'll give you the advice you need to remove that demonic scowl from your face."

I took another bite of my sandwich.

"Is it that you're still unpacking in the new house? Couldn't find a clean bra or something?" he asked in all seriousness while taking another bite of pasta salad.

Heaving a the-world-is-ending sigh, I let my hand with my sandwich fall to my lap and took a big swig from my water bottle.

"It's that Bennett Broussard."

Finn grinned.

I glared.

"His stupid ribbon-cutting made me late."

"Actually, if you'd leave ten minutes earlier to counteract any catastrophic Beauville traffic, then you wouldn't have this problem."

"I know, I know." I took another bite before adding, "I was already running late before the grocery store debacle," I admitted sullenly. "And then I was pulled over for a speeding ticket."

"Shit."

"But the officer let me off with a warning."

"Nice."

"You would've liked him. Tall, dark, and broody." I winked.

"Sounds like you had a fantastic morning. I don't know what you're complaining about. And you still made it before the tardy bell." He read my expression while I chewed and rolled my eyes. "What is it exactly that bothers you so much about Bennett Broussard again? Besides the fact that he's rich and gorgeous and totally fuckworthy?"

"Have you forgotten the glitter bomb catastrophe?"

"No one will ever forget that."

"Don't remind me."

"Kidding. That was so long ago, Bea. You were a child."

"Fifteen."

"Still, you can't hold a grudge that long."

Finn had no idea. I still held a grudge against my piece-of-trash father, and he'd walked out on us eighteen years ago.

But back to Bennett.

"He's arrogant and conceited and he just...bothers me."

Then I frowned at my own statement because he hadn't seemed conceited as he waved to the crowd in front of his grocery store. He appeared...grateful. I could also admit—only to myself—that him having a life so easy just reminded me of how I'd had to fight tooth and nail for everything I ever had. I'd be paying off student loans till I was probably in my coffin.

My phone buzzed on the cushion next to my leg. I checked the screen to see that it was from Peter.

"Omigod." I clicked it open and read the message. "Holy shit, Finn."

"What? Did something happen?"

It was my turn to grin like the Cheshire Cat. "I've got a callback."

"For the *lead*?"

Laughing, I said, "Of course! It's not like I could play fifty-year-old Ethel Banks." Then I frowned. "Well, I guess I could. But yes, for Corie Bratter. The lead!" I texted the director back in a rush and agreed to be at the theater at five this afternoon. "I can't believe it."

"I can. You're phenomenal on stage."

I couldn't wipe the smile off my face, realizing I had a good chance at the lead of Neil Simon's *Barefoot in the Park*. It had always been one of my favorite plays. While I was growing up, Mom and I watched the movie dozens of times together. The witty banter and tempestuous chemistry between Robert Redford and Jane Fonda on film always made me smile.

Then suddenly, my stomach plummeted.

"What now?" Finn's expression morphed to concern.

I licked my suddenly dry lips, finding there wasn't a speck of saliva left in my mouth. My voice rose to screechy fear levels as I said, "You know who's going to get the male lead in the play, don't you?"

Finn let out a bark of laughter. Then he shook his head at me, merriment in those traitorous eyes. "Bennett fuckworthy Broussard."

Chapter Two

~BETTY~

I HURRIED INTO THE THEATER AT PRECISELY FIVE O'CLOCK. OUR community theater, the Beauville Performing Arts League building, was originally built as a movie theater downtown in the fifties. The front reception area was tiny compared to modern-day movie theaters, and there was only one cinema, which seated a maximum of three hundred.

It had been renovated at the founding of BPAL with a proper ticket booth in the reception before theater-goers stepped through a large arched doorway into the concessions area.

For performances, they served snacks and sodas as well as wine and beer. On both sides of the concessions area—a horseshoe-shaped glass counter on a dais—were the curtained-off arched entrances into the theater. Where the movie screen once stood was now a stage.

The reception area was completely empty, as expected when I passed through. Voices carried from beyond the curtains. I swooped in to see a few people milling about on and off the stage. That buzz of excitement I always got when I stepped into the theater hummed under my skin. It lit a spark inside me I couldn't explain.

Walking down the slight incline past the rows of cushioned seats, I took it all in. A few people in their forties and fifties stood around, the call-backs for the lead's mother, Ethel Banks, and her romantic interest, Mr. Velasco. I only saw one other person around my age who I knew had auditioned for the female lead—Mandy Harper. She was busy gesturing wildly and talking a mile a minute to the assistant director, Trish.

Mandy played the lead for nearly every play that BPAL put on, and she was my top competitor for this role. She was not one of my favorite people. Not because she was my competition, but because she was annoyingly conceited.

Of course, I was a harsh judge of people, in general. They were typically disappointing to me in one way or another. But Mandy's personality reminded me of that one sweater in your closet—tiresome, clingy, and loud—that you kept around for some unknown reason.

Expelling a big breath, I let my gaze wander to the stage where the director Peter stood next to Bennett, showing him something in the script. Bennett had changed since this morning, no longer in a starched shirt, pants, and tie. His faded Levi's and navy-blue T-shirt outlined his shape to perfection. Not that I needed to be reminded that he had a broad chest and a tight ass.

He was chewing gum, which made his chiseled jaw look ridiculously amazing. I frowned as I rounded the front row and stepped toward Trish, the assistant director. She had that dazed look that one gets after being caught in the trap called Mandy Harper for too long. Her eyes brightened when she caught sight of me over Mandy's shoulder.

"Betty! So glad you're here. Excuse me, Mandy." She then zipped over to me.

I ignored the offended look on Mandy's face and smiled at Trish. I knew Trish fairly well. She'd been assistant director for *Moon Over Buffalo* last summer.

Honestly, it was Finn's way of luring me back to Beauville for the summer but also for good. It had worked. Not only did it make me miss home, but I'd also gotten bitten by the theater bug again. I ended up spending the whole summer living at my mom's and wasting rent money on an apartment in Baton Rouge that I didn't use.

It had been worth it. Being back in Beauville and back on stage had felt so right. Reconnecting with Finn and my family after living away so long had filled something in my life I didn't even know I was missing. That was when I started planning to find a teaching position back home.

Fortunately, neither Bennett nor Mandy was in Moon Over Buffalo since they'd just finished starring in the spring musical, *The Producers*. They were both amazing, I had to grudgingly admit. I was hoping they might not audition for this play since this year's musical *Guys and Dolls,* in which they'd both starred again, had just finished.

But here we all were. Lucky me.

"Hey, Trish. What scenes are we doing?"

She stepped up beside me with a script, showing me the highlighted lines of Corie Bratter's character. "We're going to do this opening scene where Paul arrives home on the first day at the apartment." She flipped a few pages. "Then we'll do part of the dinner party with Ethel and Mr. Velasco."

"The knichi scene?"

Trish laughed pleasantly, making me smile. "Yes. My favorite." She surreptitiously glanced in Mandy's direction, who had accosted the stage manager, Brittany. Trish whispered, "You're going to kill it and get this part."

Grinning, I whispered back conspiratorially, "I hope so."

"Ah, Betty! Glad you made it," bellowed Peter from the stage before leaving Bennett to hurry down the steps. "David and Pam," he called to the group of four call-backs for Ethel Banks and Mr. Velasco. "You two will go first. And Mandy, why don't you come on up here?"

"Break a leg," murmured Trish before returning to the front row, where she sat with her clipboard.

I sat on the end as Mandy practically flew with invisible fairy wings onto the stage next to Bennett. The nauseating smile she wore for him reminded me of some stalker movie I couldn't quite remember the name of.

"Alright, everyone. We'll try that first scene after Paul gets home, starting on page twelve. Then we'll jump forward to the dinner party scene. Mandy and Bennett, whenever you're ready."

Mandy inhaled a deep breath, then dove in, like a gumdrop splashing into a pool of chocolate. Her interpretation of Corie Bratter was so syrupy sweet; it was creepier than the fan-girly smile she'd laid on Bennett when she first marched up onto the stage.

I mean, she was actually a decent actress. I'd seen her pull off some challenging roles, but her version of the young newlywed Corie wasn't how I thought she should be.

Suddenly, I was questioning if my version of Corie was the right way to go, doubting myself already. Mandy had been in far more plays than I had. Was I going to get this all wrong?

Bennett was nailing Paul—the uptight, anxious attorney making next to no money and living in a drafty, top-floor New York apartment. I couldn't help but snicker to myself at Bennett's portrayal of Paul, audibly winded as he climbed to their apartment on the top floor and frowning in utter disgust at his wife's optimistic view of their new place.

As they came to the end of the scene, I felt nervous. I

glanced over at Peter and Trish. They both wore poker faces, not responding to the performance at all except to jot down notes.

Personally, I saw Corie in a different light. Maybe Mandy was the kind of Corie they wanted. Optimistic, yes. But also intelligent and persuasive. Not a simpering, saccharine wife, which is what I was getting from Mandy.

"Okay, good," snapped Peter. "Now the dinner party scene."

Frank, another veteran of BPAL who'd played numerous roles for the middle-aged characters, sidled over and sat near me. Meredith, the receptionist at my dentist's office, looked a little nervous, fumbling with the script pages in her lap. I wasn't sure how many BPAL productions she'd been in, but I crossed my fingers for her. She was so nice.

After the first scene, which went pretty well if you prefer your leading female to be a gushing sugar stick, Peter twisted toward me. "Let's go, Betty. Get on up there. Then we'll have Meredith and Frank try for Ethel and Velasco this time."

As I passed Mandy, she said, "This doesn't seem your sort of role, Betty. Kind of chipper for you, isn't it?"

"That's why it's called *acting*, Mandy," I snapped right back and took my place on stage while the others shuffled places.

After avoiding eye contact with Bennett ever since I'd stepped into the theater, I finally chanced a glance. He was smiling down at his script, still chewing that damn gum. Annoyingly, his jaw looked fantastic. Bet those chompers could do some serious damage to a steak...or a pair of panties.

Where the hell did that thought come from?

"What are you grinning about?" I asked him, looking up and not remembering him being quite that tall. "Sold all your fifty-dollar cheese platters on opening day?"

He smiled wide, toppling the charm-proof wall I'd erected just for him. "*And* the seventy-dollar charcuterie platters," he added playfully.

"Your little theatrical opening made me late for school. And I almost got a speeding ticket."

"Sorry about that." His stupid-fine grin was affecting my heart rate.

"No, you're not."

He huffed out a laugh, shaking his head and chewing the fuck out of that gum. How did it not get in the way of his reading a minute ago?

"You know, it's a rule you shouldn't chew gum on stage."

"Who's rule?" His brow furrowed, but there was pure amusement in those hazel eyes that hadn't left me since I'd stepped onstage.

"*The* rules. You know...theater rules. Just like you don't say 'Macbeth' on stage or you curse the play."

"You just said 'Macbeth.' On stage."

I rolled my eyes. "I don't believe in that superstitious stuff."

"We have something in common. I don't believe in the no gum-chewing rules."

"It'll get in the way of your performance," I snapped, seriously irritated.

He leaned closer as if to whisper something. I didn't move as he dropped his head near my ear, where I could get a good whiff of fresh, minty breath and some other masculine, woodsy scent.

"Don't worry," he crooned. "I have perfect control of my tongue."

"Let's go, thespians!" shouted Peter. "I'd like to get take-out from Bon Creole before they close tonight."

I straightened and shifted away, refusing to acknowledge that *the* Bennett Broussard was, in fact, flirting with me. I also refused to recognize that my body liked it very, very much.

When I heard his low chuckle, the glitter bomb incident instantly flashed to mind.

Twelve years ago, we were both in the summer teen

production of "A Midsummer Night's Dream" at BPAL. He was playing the leading role of Puck, though, in my opinion, he should've played Bottom, the Ass. Anyway, I played one of the minor fairies.

There was this one scene where he had a glitter bomb on a rope which he was supposed to pop and explode right as Bottom transformed onstage. He had a bad habit of swinging the damn thing in rehearsals, and I'd told him a hundred times he'd better not or he'd hit someone with it.

Well dammit. He did hit someone. Me! Right in the boobs. In front of a sold-out audience, which included my mom and sister and this boy Evan I had a huge crush on. The bomb exploded all over my tits, and I do mean exploded. Everyone in the audience laughed, thinking it was part of the show since it was a comedy after all.

And what did Bennet do? He laughed! Until he caught my death-glare backstage. Then he apologized, but he could barely get it out with a straight face, while I was standing there with tissue trying to wipe the glitter off my black costume and teeny-tiny cleavage. I told him he could shove his apology where the sun don't shine.

Fortunately, he'd just graduated high school and went off to college out of state at the end of the summer. He was a senior when I was a freshman at Beauville High School. So the rest of my summer plays at BPAL were Bennett-free. After I'd gone to college at LSU, I heard he'd returned home and was doing plays again. Mom had even dragged me to see him in an annoyingly flawless performance as Billy Flynn in *Chicago the Musical* last fall.

"Are you ready, Betty?" asked Peter, dragging me back to where I was...onstage again with the bane of my existence.

"Yep." I cleared my throat, looking down at the script pages. "Ready."

We launched into the scene, and I didn't let Mandy's

performance sway my decision on how I'd interpret Corie's character. I allowed some sarcasm to seep into the lines when she defended their new home to her grouchy husband. I'd sassed back with a less obsequious air toward my new husband while also giving him an affectionate smile here and there.

I felt good about sticking to my guns when Peter chuckled after one of my lines.

Then we went right into the dinner party scene, one of the funniest ones in the whole play. That time, we had more than Peter chuckling in the audience. Even though we were reading from the script and pantomiming parts of the scene like "popping" the knichi—some unknown eel-based delicacy Mr. Velasco brings over—the stage chemistry was totally there.

"Terrific," said Peter. "Frank and Meredith, you can come down. Nice job, thank you. Now, Betty and Bennett, can you go to"—he flipped through his script much farther ahead —"page fifty-two? This is a fight scene between the couple. I want to see how that works with you two together."

Without glancing at my scene partner, I flipped to the right page. "Ready?" I asked him.

"Whenever you are." His smooth rumble irritated me. It was a deep, pleasant sound. He shouldn't have a delicious voice on top of everything else. It simply wasn't fair.

I jumped into the scene, my character letting his have it. I even turned to face him and screamed the lines, layered with an extra dose of sarcasm and perhaps over-the-top anger.

Maybe I was letting my true feelings out, my annoyance with Mr. Perfect and how he was partly responsible for ruining my Monday, and then had the audacity to flirt with me on top of that.

The thing was, he gave it right back to me, delivering the lines with impeccable emphasis and timing that had everyone in the audience outright laughing, except for Mandy.

I couldn't *not* be impressed by him. He was impressive, okay?

"Good, good!" Peter cut us off after Corie's character stormed into a different room.

Someone actually clapped. I let out a breath of laughter, peering over at Bennett.

And wished I hadn't.

Those hazel eyes were fixed on me with undisguised admiration shining in the pretty depths. He wasn't chewing his gum, but his jaw clenched three times before breaking away from flat-out staring at me.

I stopped at the edge of the stage, thinking Peter might have a few comments. But then he waved us down and leaned in to talk to Trish. I glanced over my shoulder.

Bennett's head was down, that amusing smile quirking his lips, as he murmured, "Nice job, Mouton."

Then he tapped my leg with his script as he passed me by, leaving me in a wake of mint and masculine soap and rattled nerves.

Let's be more precise. He tapped me on the side of my upper thigh, extremely close to an ass-tap, which also felt... flirty? Deliciously so.

Then again, he probably flirted with everyone.

What was I thinking? He most definitely did. That was how he charmed and enchanted his flock to do his bidding.

Never mind. I pushed those vexing thoughts away as I headed for the steps, wondering, hoping I did well enough to out-act the glorious Mandy Harper.

When Trish gave me a subtle wink before turning and collecting all the scripts, I exhaled a happy breath. *I think I got the lead.*

Oh, fuck.

I think I got the lead.

Chapter Three

~BENNETT~

"SOMEBODY GOT A HOT DATE?"

Miss Lucille quirked a gray eyebrow over her cat-eye glasses with pink trim. She might be pushing seventy, but she was feisty. And nosy. But I loved her.

She'd been working for my dad and his small chain of appliance stores for forty years. Since I'd wanted some experienced employees to open the new store—the first one that was genuinely mine, not just a Broussard store I slaved at to "pay my dues," as Dad liked to say—she came over to help me out for the first month or two.

Of course, I'd had to sit through an hour of one of Dad's lectures, but it was worth it. Not even the thought of my father's overbearing control issues could dampen my mood today.

"Nope. Play rehearsal." I bagged the French Malbec that I'd snatched from our newest imports.

"That's an awful fancy bottle of wine for rehearsal."

"It's an apology." And perhaps bribery.

That tiniest of smiles that Betty had shot my way after our final audition scene three days ago had me in knots. I wanted more of her smiles. I wanted more of Betty. The problem was, she hated me.

I swiped my credit card and put it back in my wallet.

"Mmhmm. For a man or a woman."

"Goodnight, Miss Lucille. Thank you."

I double-timed out of there before someone tried to stop me with another problem to handle. I'd been putting in ten-to-twelve-hour days for months, and I wasn't going to feel an ounce of guilt for cutting out a little early.

I couldn't remember the last time I was this excited about a new play. I'd like to tell myself that it was because this play had a challenging role with more lines than I'd ever had, that it was playwright Neil Simon's genius or that I simply needed a damn break from the endless problems of opening Broussard's Fresh Market. But I wasn't a liar, especially to myself.

It was that spit-fire redhead, Betty Mouton, that had me practically jogging to my truck. I hadn't bothered changing clothes today because I knew I'd be back at the store after rehearsal tonight.

The bookkeeper I'd hired was able to manage things only when they were running smoothly. Well, hell. Those days were few and far between for a small business. Especially a new one. I had to step in every night to manage some inventory issues.

If I didn't check in after rehearsal to ensure everything went well at the end of the day, I wouldn't be able to sleep. So far, I have been managing the stress well. This new play was the pleasant distraction I needed to take my mind off the store.

I couldn't help smiling as I started my truck with my favorite escape in front of me. And a gorgeous scene partner to work with. I pulled out of the parking lot onto Evangeline and headed downtown.

I had barely been able to contain myself when Peter called about the casting. He'd asked if I minded.

"Why are you asking me?" I'd been surprised since he'd never asked my advice before.

"Only that you and Mandy have been leading together for a long time. But I think you and Betty are going to set that stage on fire. You had terrific stage chemistry at the call-back."

"I agree," I'd told him, swallowing hard against straying thoughts of what we could set on fire offstage.

I'd seen her perform in last summer's *Moon Over Buffalo*. No matter that she had a small role, she lit up the stage. Why wouldn't she? She was fucking beautiful. And talented.

I was excited to see she had come back to work in BPAL productions last summer. When I'd asked Peter about her, he'd told me she was returning to Baton Rouge. Disappointed, I'd tried to put her out of my mind.

When I'd walked into auditions for *Barefoot in the Park* and caught sight of her flaming hair, I'd tripped on my own damn feet coming down the incline toward the front of the theater. While stunned, confused, and aroused, I'd discovered from Peter that she'd recently moved back to Beauville and wanted to become more involved with BPAL.

I swear, I thought she could hear my own heart thudding in my chest as we read some lines together during the audition. She'd been just as aloof and annoyed with me as always, to my displeasure.

If I were honest, it usually wasn't difficult for me to meet and talk to women, to get their attention. Except for Betty who I really wanted to notice me. And didn't.

She didn't simply look at me with indifference but with annoyance and aggravation. Good thing I was a tenacious bastard.

I glanced down at the bottle of expensive Malbec as I slowed to a red light on Main Street.

Tonight was the first read-through when the whole cast would sit together and read the entire play from beginning to end. We had a minimal cast, only five of us. Six if you count the non-speaking role of Delivery Guy.

Frank and Meredith had gotten the supporting roles of Ethel Banks and Mr. Velasco. I loved those two, both veterans who'd been in multiple BPAL performances. And David would be the smallest speaking role of Phone Repairman who appeared twice.

I crossed one of the drawbridges over Bayou Teche; glad the bridge wasn't up since I was running a little late. The afternoon light reflected orange on the sleepy bayou that twisted and turned throughout Beauville like the snake that gave it its name. It was a small town, but one with a long history. My family goes back many generations here.

Pop used to tell me stories about the French trappers and the Native Americans who lived here first, long before the Acadians settled here from Nova Scotia. My favorite story was the one about the Chitimacha warriors who were plagued by a giant serpent, killing their people. So they banded together and slayed the behemoth snake. In its death thrall, the snake writhed and sank into the mud, leaving behind a pathway that filled with rainwater and became our bayou.

It's one of the many folktales I grew up with living in the heart of Cajun country. And though lots of my friends graduated and went off to live in larger cities, I never wanted to leave. That's why I came up with my plan for my store, to find a viable way to start my own business here in Beauville, apart from my father.

Pulling into the small parking lot behind the BPAL theater, I could hear the bar across the street kicking it on a Thursday night. As usual. The Drunk Pelican was one of the local favorites, customers pouring out onto the tables outside. Even on a weekday.

Combing a hand through my hair, I walked at a quick clip up the narrow alleyway from the back parking lot to the front of the building. Once inside, voices beyond the reception area curtain pumped my heart a little faster. As I swept inside the theater, I heard her voice before I saw her. And the resulting shot of adrenaline firing through my blood nearly made me laugh.

What was it about this woman that had me sniffing around her like a dog on the hunt?

Was it that she didn't like me? I didn't think I was that vain. Maybe I was.

Then she laughed at something Trish was telling her, and my whole body jerked to full alert.

There was something about her that drew me beyond reason.

Fire-red hair, sarcastic mouth, unwavering confidence, and gut-punching blue eyes that could cut a guy to his knees or incinerate him with a glance.

I fucking *wanted* her.

"Hey, Bennett," called Frank in his friendly way.

Frank was a bit of an eccentric. He'd spent the majority of his adulthood as a successful local attorney then retired to work at the town museum, whose main source of business was elementary students on field trips. Now, he was a member of the BPAL Board, enjoying retirement as a patron and performer of the theatrical arts.

"Hey!" I replied, my voice a little overloud and excited.

A few heads turned my way, including Betty's. She simply arched an accusing eyebrow at me rather than greet me with a polite smile like most women did.

Hell, while most women shot fuck-me eyes my way, Betty only gave me fuck-*you* eyes.

Yep. My cock was hard now.

"Looks like we're all here," called Peter from the stage

where he had a circle of chairs set up for us. "Let's get going, *Barefoot*."

This was typical of Peter. He always shortened the cast's name to one central word of the play. As everyone headed up the steps, I walked over and brushed Betty's forearm, noting the silky softness of her fair skin.

It always shocked me how petite she was, too. Her personality could beat the shit out of an NFL football team. But the woman herself was pint-sized next to me, the top of her head barely coming to my chin.

"What?" she asked.

Not rudely, but definitely not politely.

"I brought this for you." I handed over the paper-wrapped bottle, trying to be subtle while the others were chatting onstage.

When she gripped the neck of the bottle, my brain went sideways, imagining those slender fingers wrapping around other long, cylindrical things.

"What is this?" she asked, frowning at the French wine.

"An apology."

"For what?"

"You said I made you late for work the other day."

"So you swiped a free bottle of your fancy wine off the shelf and thought that would be a good apology?"

Laughing at her complete disdain, I shook my head. "What makes you think it was free?"

She snorted. "You own the store."

"And yet, I actually want my business to make a profit, so I don't go around swiping *free* goods and handing them out as presents."

Her eyes widened in surprise and perhaps even a touch of regret. "You paid for this?"

"Shocking as it seems, yes."

She pressed her full lips together, barely thinning out her

luscious mouth. "Well, thank you." She actually winced like it had been painful.

"Did I offend you in another lifetime that I'm not aware of?"

She didn't answer, her blank face telling me nothing as she held the bottle away from her body like it might bite her.

Then it hit me. "Wait a minute. This can't possibly be about what happened back then?"

Her blue eyes rounded. "Back when what?"

"Is this about the glitter bomb?"

She scoffed. Then blew out a breath. And then rolled her eyes. "As if."

"It is." I stepped closer, realization hitting, then I lowered my voice to say, "You're still mad about a glitter bomb hitting you *accidentally* on stage. Over ten years ago."

Her snarky indifference turned to narrow-eyed accusation. "You embarrassed me in front of the whole town," she hissed.

"The whole town? The theater barely holds two hundred."

"Three hundred."

"I apologized for that."

"You didn't mean it."

Choking on a laugh because this woman was a ball-buster.

"I'm sorry, again." I gestured toward the wine in her hand. "I seem to be apologizing a lot to you."

She glanced at the wine, then frowned but didn't say anything.

"Do you accept my apology?"

Her eyes shot upward like she was thinking really hard about it.

"Come on, you two," shouted Peter. "No time to waste."

After pulling the script out of my back pocket where I'd been carrying it all day to memorize lines while I worked, I stepped closer, inhaling a delicious citrus scent.

"Look. I honestly felt bad about your shitty Monday. And

I'm sorry you're mad at me for something I did when I was a stupid, clumsy teenager. I bought a bottle of wine for you. Take it. Smash it against the side of the building. Pretend it's my head if it helps tamp down the simmering rage you've got for me. Or drink it, which is my advice. Preferably with some chocolate or a medium-rare ribeye. Whatever makes you feel better. It was just a gesture of goodwill."

And there, for the very first time, the redheaded witch—who'd been starring in my daily fantasies all week—smiled. At me.

Something cataclysmic cracked and broke loose inside my chest. Like icebergs calving off a giant chunk of glacial mass, her smile dislodged an oppressive weight I didn't know I was carrying. Strange.

"Rare," she said with a sensuous smile that shot like lightning straight to my dick.

"What?"

"I like my steak nice and bloody, Broussard."

"Of course you do."

Then she sashayed up the steps, waving her sassy words and curvy ass like a red flag in a bull's face.

And I was fully ready to charge.

Chapter Four

~BETTY~

WALKING THROUGH MY LIVING ROOM TO THE FRONT DOOR OF MY new home, I tossed another empty box on the front porch and exhaled a lovely, happy sigh. With a hand on my hip, I stared out across the street, which was nothing but sugarcane fields, the tall green stalks waving in the afternoon breeze.

It was harvesting season, so it would be chopped down to the dirt before long, then they'd replant and start all over. I'd thought of buying a house in a neighborhood, maybe close to the park where my mom lived. But I loved the solitude out here on this country road and the faint breeze that seemed to always be blowing.

Glancing at my barren porch, except for the leaning tower of cardboard boxes, I made a mental note to look for some front porch furniture. Maybe I'd buy a rocking chair like Mom bought from that guy Country at the Tractor Supply store.

There was so much to do.

"Tomorrow," I mumbled to myself.

Today, I had to get my kitchen fully unpacked. I'd been in my new house for over a month and still had boxes stacked in different rooms.

Glancing at the bottle of Malbec that I hadn't yet opened, I remembered my encounter with Bennett before the read-through of the script yesterday. He was sincere in his apology. So *why* was I still butt-hurt when it came to this guy? I couldn't even figure it out myself, but every time I saw the man, my defenses shot up, ready to battle.

"Better get over it," I muttered to myself since we'd be working closely together for the next few weeks.

Huffing a sigh, I settled on the tile next to the box of hand-me-down pots and pans from my mother and grandmother. Mom had also included some weird tools to help me eat healthier.

"What *is* this?" I snort-laughed at the zucchini noodle maker, trying to figure which way was up. Then I reached for the box dedicated to donations to Goodwill. Because there would never be an occasion where I was going to be making zoodles.

"Sorry, Mom," I muttered, noticing movement out of the corner of my eye as I put it back in the box.

My heart dropped because I sure as hell saw something dark move by the doorway leading to the sunroom. An animal was definitely moving around in there.

"Holy shit!" I jumped up with a pan in my hand, ready to swing at whatever mongrel dog had managed to get in my house.

"Baaaa!" came a bleating noise, then the animal clip-clopped into my kitchen, proud as you please.

"A goat? Where the hell did you come from?"

"Baaa!"

He was a teeny, tiny thing. All black with a white diamond on his forehead and two white socks on his back feet. Hooves.

Whatever.

"Baby goat, aren't ya?"

It flipped its floppy ears when I stepped closer and hightailed it out through my sunroom.

"Hey!"

He squeezed through a crack in the screen door, left open because it had snagged on one of the boxes I'd been stacking near the entrance. I had empty boxes everywhere.

I chased the little hellion into the yard, wondering where the baby goat came from. He zig-zagged all the way to my back fence, then squeezed his little ass under a broken bottom panel of the wooden fencing.

My trifold stepladder was leaning against the patio where I'd used it to screw in hooks for my hanging plants. I hauled it to the back fence and walked up to peer over the top edge.

And stared in shock!

A dozen little goats jumped and cavorted around my neighbor's backyard. A woman was carrying a bucket of something toward a wooden trough set low in the center of the yard.

"Hi!" I called out to get her attention.

Her yard was double the size of mine, extending well beyond her house. The rest of her yard was contained by chain-link fencing, much harder to break through than wood.

The older woman whose gray hair was pinned in a twist on top of her head looked over at me. "Hello, there."

She dumped the seed or oats, or whatever the hell goats ate, into the trough, and all dozen came hopping and jumping and head-butting their way over. One actually got knocked by another and went totally stiff, then fell over.

"Oh!" I pointed frantically. "One of them got knocked down."

She looked over her shoulder, continuing toward me, and laughed. "Nah. That's Zuzu. She gets excited about feeding time and has a little fit."

"She passes out? Over food?"

Couldn't blame her, really.

The white-and-brown-patched Zuzu sprang up, shook her head, then trotted to the trough with the others.

"They're myotonic pygmy goats."

I must've still looked confused.

"Fainting goats," she explained. "Though they don't really faint. They just go all stiff-legged and roll over sometimes."

I laughed, watching the black one that had snuck into my house. Even my usual grumpy self got a little giddy at how cute they were.

"My name's Gretchen," she said, removing her garden glove and reaching up a hand.

"Betty Mouton," I said, shaking hers.

"Hope you don't mind the noise. Most of the time they're not too loud, but every once in a while they can get going and make some racket."

"To be honest, I didn't hear them at all. Of course, I haven't spent much time on the back porch yet." I pointed a thumb over my shoulder. "Still unpacking."

"Can't say I was sorry to see Vincent go."

"Mr. Randazzo?" That was the man who sold me the house. He'd moved to New Jersey to be closer to his son and family.

"Yeah." Gretchen chuckled. "He hated my goats. Complained a *lot*. Called the police for disturbing the peace a number of times."

I smiled. I could totally see it. Mr. Randazzo had seemed very no-nonsense the two times I'd met him.

"Well, I'm not calling the police, but you do have one who is breaking the law."

"Do I?" She raised her brows, blue-gray eyes sparkling.

"Breaking and entering. But I promise not to press charges."

"Dang it." She looked back to the trough. "That'll be Gilbert, most probably."

"Is the black one with the white socks Gilbert?"

"That's him."

"Then yeah. He came right into my kitchen. My back door was propped open."

She laughed and shook her head. "Every time I repair one fence panel, he breaks another one to get out. Mr. Randazzo used to have pots of herbs on his back patio. Gilbert was partial to the mint leaves."

I laughed. "Bet Mr. Randazzo wasn't a fan of Gilbert."

"Not at all."

"Well, I don't mind him coming around, but I don't want him to get hit by a car or anything if he wanders."

"I appreciate that. I'll get the new hole fixed soon as I can."

"It was nice meeting you."

"You too, sweetheart."

I waved and climbed down, smiling at meeting one of my neighbors. It was starting to feel official.

I was a homeowner.

Traipsing back across the yard and leaning the ladder against the side of the house, I headed back inside to get back to work. Before I could even sit down, my phone buzzed on the counter.

It was a text from a number I didn't recognize. When I opened and read the message, my stomach did a somersault.

Him: This is Bennett. I'm heading over now.

Me: Excuse me. Why are you heading over?

Bennett and I had agreed to meet and work on our roles since our characters were onstage the entire show. We had exchanged numbers and addresses at the last rehearsal since Peter had demanded that we rehearse together in between regular rehearsals. And as Peter said, the comedic timing was essential in getting right for a great performance.

Him: You said you were free most Thursdays and Fridays. I had to work late yesterday.

SHIT, I REMEMBER AGREEING TO GET TOGETHER, BUT I HADN'T meant this week. I wanted to memorize more of my lines first.

I also remembered his snarky smile when I'd said I was free most Fridays. Like I didn't have a dating life or something. Which I didn't. But it was more that I had a longstanding, weekly date with my sofa on Friday nights. I was always too tired to go out after the work week and wanted nothing more than Netflix and a glass of wine.

HIM: ARE YOU NOT FREE TONIGHT? BUSY?

I LOOKED DOWN AT MYSELF IN A RATHER SHORT PAIR OF CUT-offs and my old t-shirt, then glanced at the boxes.

ME: NOT REALLY.

BUT HELL, HE COULD GIVE A GIRL SOME WARNING. WHAT IF I *DID* have a hot date or something?

HIM: BE THERE IN FIVE.

"CRAP!"

I jumped up and sped to my living room, where I'd dropped my shoes and bag for work and let a small pile of junk build up over the week.

Quickly, I snatched the to-go box from Antonio's that was my dinner earlier, my nail clippers off the coffee table, the stack of mail and the essays I was grading. Right as I chunked the bulk of it on my bed, the mail on my nightstand and the clippers in the bathroom, the doorbell rang.

Rushing back to the small foyer entrance of my house, I glanced in the hall mirror, refusing to worry about the fact that I looked bedraggled and messy.

This wasn't a date, and I didn't care what Bennett Broussard thought of me. That's what I reminded myself anyway as I swung open the door.

Damn him.

Why did he look even hotter in faded jeans, a dark hoodie, and semi-wet hair? He must've just showered. His gaze dropped down my body, lingering on my legs as I stepped back.

"Come on in." I gestured to the living room right off the front entrance.

He walked past me, leaving a wake of that mint-and-masculine scent.

"Are you chewing gum again?" I blurted out without thinking.

"No." He frowned as he sat on the sofa, dropping his script in his lap and stretching an arm over the back of my sofa like he belonged there. "I spit it out before I got here, knowing your aversion to gum. Why'd you ask?"

Like I was about to admit that I was sniffing him. His observant eyes crinkled with amusement, that cocky persona in full swing.

"Let me go grab my script. Do you want a water or something?"

"Water is good."

I disappeared into the kitchen to grab some waters and catch my breath.

What the hell? Why was my heart pounding like I'd just run a mile?

Telling myself to calm the hell down, I grabbed two waters and my script from my bedroom and returned, expecting him to still be sprawled on my sofa like he owned the place. But he wasn't. He was standing at my wooden mantle, looking at my family photos. He held my favorite, observing closely.

It was a picture of me, Mom, and Emma three Halloweens ago at a friend's party. We were dressed as the Sanderson witch sisters from Hocus Pocus. I'd had to tease my hair for an hour, but I'd done an awesome job getting that Winifred-witch height. Finn was taking the picture, and he'd caught us mid-laugh.

I noticed that Bennett was smiling as he stared at the photo, sending a bloom of warmth in my chest. Uncomfortable, I cleared my throat.

"Ready?"

He set the photo down. "That your mom and sister?"

"Yeah."

"You look good as the witch in charge." He settled next to me, smirk tilting his mouth in a way that made him even more handsome.

I wasn't sure if he was actually complimenting me or sneakily insulting me by calling me a witch. Maybe both, and I didn't know what to do with that.

He opened his water bottle and took a few gulps, dragging my gaze to the sexy cords of his throat. *Why* did this arrogant ass have to be so fine?

Turning away, I took a sip of my own before sitting sideways with my script in hand.

"Did you drink that wine yet?" he asked, pulling his phone from his pocket and setting it on the sofa between us.

"Haven't had the chocolate or bloody meat to pair with it as the wine-giver recommended," I answered, flipping to Act One.

"I can remedy that."

"Don't sweat it, Broussard. I live pretty close to this bougie supermarket some local dude just opened up. I can get what I need there."

A rough chuckle pulled my gaze to him.

"I happen to know they have the best chocolate desserts and red meat a girl could possibly want."

"I'll be the judge of that." Wiping my smile off, I said, "Let's start in Act One when Paul first gets home. Are we just going to do a read-through, or do you want to stop and discuss character motivation and inflection and stuff?"

"Let's do a straight read-through first, if you don't mind." He opened a recording app on his phone and started recording.

"Why are you doing that?"

"It helps me memorize when I listen to the lines while driving around or working out."

"Hmph. I never tried that before."

"Really? Most BPAL friends I know use this memorization method. You can plug in your earbuds while doing other stuff and memorize at the same time."

"This is my first big role."

"Oh, yeah. Right. Well, take it from an expert. You'll want to try this."

"I don't need advice from you, Broussard."

"No need to get snappy at me. Just trying to help."

And I know that he was and that I was, in fact, being snappy, but I couldn't help it. His advice was good, but for some reason, I didn't want it from him.

He watched me closely, a line pinching his brow, obviously irked. "Do you mind if I record?" he asked with a little aggression.

Realizing I was being overly defensive, I sat up straighter. "No." I waved a hand nonchalantly to his phone. "Of course not. Let's get going."

So we settled in and did just that. Falling into our characters kept us from going at each other's throats, thankfully. We read all of Act One and Two in character. I managed to wade through the romantic scenes without too much embarrassment though I caught his smirky smile when my face heated.

I'd read all of the stage directions in parentheses and was well aware there were a few kissing scenes. I was grateful Bennett hadn't stopped to discuss that because I wasn't quite ready for it. Especially not right here on my living room sofa.

We stopped for a bathroom break, and I brought out some chips and salsa, then launched immediately into Act Three. We were toward the end when his character Paul was wildly drunk. The scene was freaking hilarious and the way Bennett was acting out the lines with a drunken slur had me breaking character and laughing.

I leaned over the coffee table, still giggling, scooped some salsa and brought it to my mouth. A dollop of salsa dropped off the chip and landed on my boob.

"Shit," I muttered.

Abruptly, Bennett stopped talking as we both looked at my chest.

Bennett put both hands up, one holding the script. "It wasn't my fault this time. You can't blame me."

I grinned because he honestly looked scared like I'd somehow say this was his fault. I suppose I couldn't blame him for being skittish. I'd been pretty hard on him since the callbacks.

"I know it's not." Shaking my head, still giggling, I took a napkin and wiped it off.

When I glanced up, Bennett's smile had slipped, but he was still staring. Not at my boobs, but at my face. An awkward silence filled the room, both of us looking a little too long. His gaze dropped to my bare legs then he tapped the recording app off on his phone and stood up.

"Well, I think that's enough for tonight." He tucked his script into the front pocket of his hoodie.

I stood with him, a little off balance by his abrupt change in mood and wanting to leave. "Thanks for coming."

"Sure. Thanks for letting me."

I snorted as I held the front door open. "I'm not that much of a wicked witch."

He turned and arched a brow at me without responding.

"Am I?"

"I'm not answering that. I don't want to get beat up by a little redhead on her front porch."

"I am *not* violent!"

He reared back, palms up. "Whatever you say, Miss Mouton." He backed down the porch steps. "Anything you say, Miss Mouton."

Planting a hand on my hip, I said more calmly, "I'm not."

"I never disagreed with you."

"You're just saying that to appease me."

"Yep. And keeping my balls attached to my body. I like them right where they are."

"At least you know exactly what I would've gone for if I was actually violent."

Still walking slowly backwards, he cupped his hands protectively over his crotch, pulling my eyes south. For some reason, the playful move was sexy as fuck.

"Message received. I'll try not to piss you off anymore."

Shaking my head, I waved as he opened his truck door. "Goodnight."

"Goodnight, Betty."

I closed the door on a shiver, liking how his voice dropped deeper when he said my name. Liking it a little too much. I don't know why I was having these tingly feelings about a man I didn't like.

Bennett Broussard wasn't even my type. Too arrogant and perfect in every way. Annoying. I'd bet Mr. Business Bennett was all precise and robotic. Vanilla.

We shall assume missionary position, now, Betty, I imagined him saying.

Then I imagined him hovering over me and spreading my legs with his hips.

A flare of heat spiked right between my thighs.

Whoa, there! That's enough of that.

Wandering back to the living room, I picked up my script, the pages falling open to a scene where Corie was loving all over her husband Paul. The stage direction in parentheses read, *they embrace and kiss passionately*. Sweat broke out on the back of my neck.

I'd never been in a play where I had to kiss my scene partner or anything. In high school, I had to fake slap Tiffany Poirier in our production of *Legally Blonde*.

But this. Stage kissing. Bennett Broussard.

The thought made me both aroused and annoyed.

What would it be like to fake kiss a guy who I was attracted to but also firmly disliked?

Ignoring the sudden acceleration of my pulse, I picked up the chips and salsa, determined to deal with those thoughts later when I couldn't avoid them anymore. Fake kissing or not, I couldn't wait till rehearsal next week.

Chapter Five

~BETTY~

"GUESS WHO WON A TEACHER LOTTO GIFT FOR HOMECOMING?" Finn waved a piece of paper in the air as he met me halfway to the back exit of BHS as I was leaving school.

Our PTA always did a lottery drawing of gifts donated by local businesses for Homecoming.

"Awesome. What did you win? A car wash from Fred's or dinner for two at El Mariachi."

I might've been a bit snarky, but El Mariachi was legit the best Mexican restaurant for a hundred miles, and I'd kill for a free dinner there. If that's what he won, he was taking me.

"Just guess." He smiled with more than the normal amount of glee.

"No idea, Finley. Stop rubbing it in and just tell me." He handed over the gift certificate for two to a couples culinary lesson, "Italian Night" at Broussard's Fresh Market. I did a double-take and looked closer.

"What is that exactly?"

"They teach you to cook a meal, then let you eat it and drink a bottle of wine."

Not bad, Broussard. That was pretty creative. Something I was sure some locals would get into. Especially those who didn't want to drive a half an hour to Lafayette for a similar culinary date night.

"Very cool, I have to admit."

"Yes, I know it hurts to actually compliment the devastatingly handsome Mr. Broussard."

"I never said he was *devastatingly* handsome."

"No need. It's a fact, princess." He flicked my hair then turned toward the auditorium. "I'm hoping Michael will be up for Italian Night. Maybe he can fit me into his plans with a two-week warning."

"You're still going out with him?"

Michael was an orthopedic surgeon in Lafayette, and I had doubts that he was anything close to a good match for Finn. He was too cerebral and orderly. Finn needed someone a little disorganized and spontaneous and fun. Like me. But with a penis.

Although lately, I hadn't been much fun at all. I'd been more of a Negative Nelly. And I wasn't quite sure why. It's like I was stuck in a permanent PMS mood.

Finn turned, walking backward to say with dramatic effect, "He's *so* hot, Beatrice. I can't help it."

"Ugh. You need more than a pretty face, but I'll let you crash and burn again since you're dead set on it."

"Love you, too," he called before disappearing into the auditorium. Then he popped his head back out. "Oh, and have fun at rehearsal," he crooned before ducking back inside, laughing. Cackling, really, like the witch he was.

"Suck it," I called back.

Because he was my best friend, I couldn't help confessing that I was nervous about the kissing scenes at lunch today.

Finn had his own ideas about why I was nervous. Not because I would be putting my mouth on the mouth of someone I swore to myself to detest, but because I actually had the secret hots for Bennett.

Ignoring that possible and loathsome idea, I drove out of the back parking lot. At the school's side entrance, my student Trace was sitting on the curb, playing a game or something on his phone.

Frowning, I pulled up and rolled down the passenger side window. He looked up.

"Hey!" I said cheerily, not wanting my stress about him being stuck after school again with no way home to show in my voice. "Need a ride?"

Trace didn't live even remotely on my way home. He lived well outside city limits in the rural part of the parish with his single mom and three younger brothers.

I'd also taught Trace his freshman year and assisted with several of Finn's school plays, where Trace played many roles. I knew he had a hard home life, a mom who worked multiple low-paying jobs that never made ends meet. And I knew that Trace often came to school hungry.

He could've eaten breakfast and lunch for free, but it seemed his pride prevented him from eating breakfast. His friends never did since they came from homes where there was always enough food on the table, so he went hungry and pretended he didn't need the free breakfast.

I recognized this in Trace because I was him once upon a time. When my father first left us, Mom had been a stay-at-home mother. Suddenly, she had to find a job to raise two young girls on a minimum-wage salary by herself. That cold feeling of helplessness and occasional hunger permanently stained my heart permanently. It never leaves, even when you grow up, get a college degree, and earn a stable income.

So obviously, it wasn't in the curriculum that I offer snacks

—muffins, donuts, ham-n-cheese croissants—to those who correctly answered questions to my literature trivia game a couple days a week. It was a way for me to feed students like Trace that wouldn't bruise their pride.

And yeah, I'd given him a ride home a time or two since his mother couldn't afford a car or insurance for him yet.

"Nah," smiled Trace. "Mom said she'd be here in a minute." His gaze moved to the driveway leading into the school parking lot. "There she is." He stood and smiled as his mom wheeled the fifteen-year-old Nissan around beside my car.

She rolled the window down and waved at me. "I am so sorry! The teller who was supposed to take my place was late, and my boss wouldn't let me leave."

She looked frantic, and my heart squeezed at the obvious stress and guilt weighing this woman down at not being able to be everywhere at once.

So I put my acting skills to good use. "No worries at all." I waved it off. "You know Trace is my favorite student." Then I turned a sharp look at him as he rounded the car and waited outside while I talked to his mom. I pointed a finger at him. "Don't you dare repeat that in class. I'll deny it."

He chuckled, his cute face lighting up. "I won't, Ms. B."

I loved it when he called me that above all my students. An affectionate nickname they gave me freshman year.

"All right then. Y'all have a good night. Don't forget your chapters to read for homework, Trace."

He smiled as he folded his tall frame into the passenger seat, then I headed out.

I loved teaching for two reasons. One, I loved literature. But two, I loved kids more. Especially kids like Trace. If I could inspire him in any way and give him the skills and confidence to go out and achieve those goals, then I've done something good and worthy with my time and talent.

My mind was still buzzing with what I could pick up for

tomorrow morning's trivia game as I rolled into the parking lot behind the BPAL building. I always got enough treats for three winners in each class. I hadn't been to Broussard's Fresh Market yet, but maybe I needed to head over and see what I could get for my kiddos.

Pretending my pulse didn't lurch at the sight of Bennett on stage like it had every rehearsal this week, I sashayed down the aisle and dropped my purse onto a chair in the front row. Taking my script, I stepped onto the stage where Peter talked animatedly with Meredith and Frank.

Because I was forcing myself not to stare at Bennett, I missed the fact that the stage manager Brittany was close-talking with him at first. Bennett wore a polite smile, nodding as she was going on about costumes.

"I'm a really good seamstress, so even if I have to make something special to fit your shoulders—" She put her hand on his bicep.

Bennett immediately noticed and stepped backward to break contact. "That's fine, Brittany. I'm sure we'll work out what everyone needs later. Right now, we need to focus on the play itself."

"Oh, of course, of course," she crooned.

Was she batting her eyelashes?

I almost snorted, but I was also burning mad at her getting all handsy. Was he flirting with her back?

Then he marched toward me, a tightness around his eyes I hadn't seen before. Nope. Definitely wasn't flirting back with her.

I cleared my throat. "Hey."

His head jerked up and he smiled, much brighter than the one he'd given Brittany. "Hey, yourself."

"Soooo." I nodded toward Brittany walking down the stage steps. "Getting some special treatment already, Mr. Lead Role?"

He shook his head with a chuckle. "Uh, not the kind I was looking for, Ms. Lead Role."

"Is there a particular kind of special treatment you're used to as big man on stage?"

"No." His hazel eyes looked greener tonight, glinting with mischief. "Not something I'm used to. But there is something I want."

"What's that?"

"To take you on a date."

I swear to everything holy, my heart stopped for a solid two seconds. I was just playing around, but the grave expression on his face told me he most definitely wasn't teasing.

"Come again?"

That knee-buckling smile spread across his face—the kind that harnessed power to weaken females into silly, giddy states. And yes, even though I was currently falling under its spell, I kept my snarky visage in place.

"Peter's idea." He nodded toward the director. "That old theater Golden Oldies is playing *Barefoot in the Park,* if you can believe it. I thought we could go see it and talk about the characters."

Not a real date.

"Oh." I heard the disappointment in my own voice.

His smile slipped. "I mean, I could just buy it off Amazon, but I thought it would be fun to see it on the big screen since it was playing locally."

"Yeah. Of course."

He inched closer, and for some reason, my body decided she was good right where she was, wallowing in his delicious man-scent.

"We could catch some dinner beforehand."

"No."

"Why not? Don't you eat?"

"Pfft. I love food." But I was afraid of these mixed signals my brain and body were giving me.

"My treat. It'd be good if we got to know each other better."

"Why?"

He smiled, that merry mischief glint in his eyes. "It would help us onstage."

He was right, but…

"That would just feel a lot like an actual date."

"Betty." Every nerve in my body stood to attention when he said my name in that deep baritone. "Just a business date." He paused, raising his brow. "What? Are you afraid or something?"

Snorting, I was about to say something smart back, but he held up a finger to stop me. And strangely, I held my tongue. That was new.

"If we get to know each other and are more comfortable together, it will only make our performance improve onstage."

"Not if we get to know each other and decide we hate each other."

"I could never hate you." His smile was boyish and sincere. When I didn't say the same back, his brow lifted almost to his hairline. "You think you could hate me?"

I couldn't help but laugh because he was genuinely concerned at the very idea.

"Jury is still out."

He clasped a hand over his heart. "Ouch."

My gaze strayed to his firm pectorals stretching against his dress shirt. Then my mind wandered to visions of his luscious chest pressing me down to his bed.

Damn, I really needed to go on a real date soon.

"I'm not saying I'd hate you." I finally answered his question, snapping my gaze back to his face where it belonged.

"So it's a date?"

"A *business* date. Yes."

The smile that filled his face made my pulse jump. He truly was devastatingly handsome.

"I've got inventory to deal with all this weekend, so how about next Saturday?"

"Sure."

"Okay, everyone!" Peter yelled from the floor beside the front row. "Let's get ready to block Act One. I need everyone offstage, entering downstage left."

Thankful to be pulled out of Bennett's hypnotic orbit, I turned away from him, ready to focus on blocking. To focus on anything that wasn't the way Broussard fucked with my head—and my body.

Blocking was when the director instructed the actors' every placement in a scene—where to stand, when to cross to another part of the stage, when to grab a prop or put one down—basically every move we make. Granted, good directors allowed for some improvisation and suggestions on the actors' parts, but detailed blocking was essential for a good stage production.

Trish hurried to her spot and picked up her clipboard. Frank joined her in the audience since he didn't come on stage for a while. Brittany headed toward the balcony stairs, presumably to start collecting props for the stage since that was the stage manager's job, among other things, once the performances started. Refusing to admit to myself why, I was glad to see the back of her for a while.

"Just come in and begin," Peter told me as I was crossing the stage. "We'll stop and start as necessary for blocking."

Meredith was running over her lines, staring at the script when we exited.

"Do you need a pencil?" asked Bennett, handing over an extra one he was holding.

"Yeah. Thanks. Were you a boy scout?"

"Eagle Scout," he beamed, arching an eyebrow with his typical show of arrogance.

"Of course you were. Maybe you can show me how to build a birdhouse or tie a clinch knot or something when we get bored backstage."

I was standing right in front of him, facing the audience, waiting for Peter to signal me. A wall of heat pressed against my neck and shoulder blades. When he leaned forward close to my ear, the hairs on the back of my neck stood straight up at the whisper of his breath.

"I know several knots I'd be happy to teach you."

Nothing he'd said was particularly naughty, but the rolling timbre of his voice and the intimacy of his nearness sent an avalanche of dirty thoughts through my head.

Me, naked, tied to his bed. Him, in his business best, crawling over me, then taunting wickedly, "*You thought I was vanilla? Spread your legs and let me show you how wrong you are, Ms. Mouton.*"

"Ready, Betty! Action!"

I jumped and practically leaped onto stage, totally forgetting what I was supposed to be doing.

Oh, yeah. Looking at my new apartment in wonder.

Not a stretch because my brain was still frazzled enough to make me look dopey and lost after that little fantasy.

Focusing again, I started reading and acting the scene with my script in hand. As expected, Peter stopped and started us occasionally, telling us where we'd be on the stage at each point in the scene.

"Go upstage, right when on that part," said Peter at one point. "The bathroom door will be over there."

We diligently took notes in our scripts.

It was when we got to the first kissing scene that I shifted nervously. There was a sofa on stage for our use, a placeholder for the seventies-style couch we'd use for the performance.

"Stop," said Peter. "Okay, Betty, I'm going to need you to sort of sexy this up."

Bennett was sitting on the sofa, knees wide apart, hands casually on his thighs. I could imagine a number of ways to sexy this up, but I needed more direction. And a kick in the ass to remember that this was *acting*.

"Can you be more specific?" I focused on Peter, trying to ignore the flame of heat crawling up my neck where I could feel Bennett's stare.

"Sure, sure. So remember, you're newlyweds. Corie is a wild, passionate person."

I knew this already. I'd added my own touch to her personality in my mind, but I suppose I needed permission or specific instructions before I went wild on my *husband*.

"Your new husband is a stuffy lawyer who isn't keen on the apartment you found. So you need to butter him up a bit. Remind him that a small apartment means you can cozy up and keep each other warm. So, sit on his lap, tug on his tie, pet him."

I nodded as Peter went on, but when I glanced at Bennett, he seemed to be trying his damnedest to keep a straight face.

"Enjoying yourself?" I asked.

"You have no idea." Then he let a fiendish grin slip and patted his thighs. "Come here. I won't bite."

That was a lie. He was absolutely a biter. I could pretend that even in his business best, he was a stuffed shirt like his character Paul, but the truth was in those wicked eyes and teasing smile. One truth I knew for sure, Bennett was a devil in bed.

Ignoring the pleasant shiver running down my spine, I noted he was wearing a tie since he'd come from work.

"I didn't realize grocery store owners wore ties," I told him, trying to change topics as I crossed the stage to start the scene over.

"You know a lot of grocery store owners?"

"Just the one. But doesn't it get in the way of, like, checking stock or the deli and whatnot?"

"How so?" He kept his casual pose, lounging back like a lion at rest, watching over his pride. Or perhaps, waiting for his female to deliver a tasty carcass so he could pounce on her instead.

"What if your tie gets caught in a cheese slicer or something? From all of those cheese and charcuterie trays you're making."

He laughed because we both knew he wasn't the one working the deli.

But I needed levity, for Christ's sake!

I couldn't just go waltzing up and spreading my body on top of Bennett without loosening up a bit.

"Let's go, Betty!" Peter hurried me up.

Glancing down at my script, I said the opening lines where Corie was trying to defend the small, drafty apartment as I sauntered over to my exhausted, grouchy husband.

Bennett had even donned his Paul Bratter scowl as he delivered his snarky lines, which nearly made me break character and laugh. He was really good.

Then I stood in front of him and those hazel eyes came up to me, watching as I eased down onto his lap, my ass on his right thigh, my legs draping over his left. Bennett placed a hand on my waist and the other on my knee to keep me in place.

I teased and taunted, leaning my chest sideways onto his so as not to give the audience my back. I plucked at his tie and gesticulated to our apartment, keeping my face in profile, feeling the intensity of his gaze on my face.

Then I glanced down at the scene, having highlighted the stage direction of kissing in pink instead of yellow to give myself a warning when it was coming up. I froze after delivering the lines that preceded the apparent stage make-out session, just staring at the script.

"Can we stop a minute?" Bennett called out to Peter.

"Is there a problem?" he asked.

"No. I need to talk to Betty about something." He tapped my thigh, gesturing for me to get up.

So I did, watching him and wondering what was going on.

"Come see," he said, pointing offstage.

He didn't want everyone overhearing this convo? Now, I was nervous. Did I do something wrong?

When he turned to me backstage, concern etched his crinkled brow.

"Listen, I realize there are quite a few intimate kissing scenes in this play, but if it makes you uncomfortable, we can fake all that till the actual dress rehearsals."

Wow. That was not what I was expecting.

He'd obviously picked up on my stress without me saying a word. Rather than tease me and watch me unravel with discomfort, he was being courteous and careful of my feelings.

"So, what do you mean?" I finally asked, my heart squeezing at the fact he was genuinely concerned about my comfort level.

"It's easy," he said lightly. "We can just do the cheek-to-cheek thing until later on."

"Like that cheek mash thing they do in those old Humphrey Bogart and Lauren Bacall movies?"

He laughed. "Just like that."

"Yeah." I exhaled a relieved breath. "I'd rather do that."

"This is why our business date will help." He brushed the pads of his fingers up my bare arm, a light caress. "So you can be more comfortable with the intimate scenes."

Our gazes held for two heartbeats, then his winning smile was back, and my lady parts were shouting at me to shut the fuck up and do all of the kissing that was required. I blocked the voices out and followed him back on stage.

He resumed his position on the couch.

Peter stood at the edge, on the floor, worry furrowing his brow. "Is everything alright?"

"Oh, yeah," Bennett answered for us confidently. "We decided we're just going to fake the kissing till we get to performances."

"Ahh! Gotcha, gotcha." He clapped his hands. "Great! Let's get back to blocking. Resume your position, Betty. Get back on his lap, and we'll go from there."

My imagination immediately conjured another image of me naked—again—with Bennett standing directly behind me, whispering, *"Assume the position. Bend over my bed and spread your legs."*

Please let me make it through this rehearsal so I can get home to my battery-powered arsenal in my dresser. That's all I needed. That's all this heady attraction was. It had been a while since I'd tended to some self-care. Bennett was the first good-looking man I'd had close contact with in a long time, and my body was screaming for a little attention.

Once I scratched that itch, I wouldn't have this insanely horny reaction to Mr. Perfect anymore. I was sure of it.

Chapter Six

~BENNETT~

I'd spent thirty minutes going back over today's accounts along with an avalanche of sticky notes my bookkeeper had left for me. It was apparent that one bookkeeper handling inventory wasn't enough.

I had two employees handling Accounting and Payroll and had assumed one would suffice to manage ingoing/outgoing inventory. My father had no issues at the appliance stores, and my grandfather had one for all three of his specialty meat stores, which he still owned but didn't manage anymore.

Apparently, my new store had much more daily business, and I had miscalculated.

I plugged in my earbuds and hit play on the recording of Betty and I running lines from the other night as I did a quick round to each department. After reading the horror stories about the kinds of bacteria that can taint food from unsanitary industrial kitchens, I'd made it part of my routine to do a quick check before I went home.

But of course, as soon as Betty's voice filled my head, I lost track of what I was doing. She was a good actress. Great actually. But it wasn't her acting skills that had my brain misfiring at the sound of her husky voice.

I exhaled a deep breath, trying not to get an erection as I walked past the deli, waving to Miles who was closing up. I looked at the ready-to-go homecooked meals and high-end deli selections—seafood stuffed bell peppers, crawfish topped chicken breasts and slow-cooked brisket—trying like hell to distract my body from what Betty's voice did to me.

Not to mention the memory of our first run-through of the romantic scene on the sofa.

Fucking hell.

I'd offered that we forego the kissing until dress rehearsals, thinking it might be easier on both of us. She was still so tense around me, and I was entirely too fucking turned on every time she entered a room.

My solution? The cheek-to-cheek, fake kissing. Whatever moronic brain cell in my head said that would be a good idea should be removed permanently. The second she brushed her soft cheek against mine, saying, "Ohhh, Paul," in that throaty voice, my entire body went hard as stone.

I tried to finish rehearsal, hoping she didn't notice, but I'm pretty sure she did.

Her sultry laughter suddenly filled my ears, bringing me back to the fact that I was standing in my deli, staring at a honey-baked ham in the glass case, hypnotized by her voice. This was during my drunk Paul scene. Her unrestrained laughter when she broke character had me chuckling again.

Then Miles was standing there on the other side of the counter, asking me something. I plucked out the earbuds and shoved them in my pocket.

"Need something, Mr. Broussard?" His brow puckered with worry.

"No, Miles. Everything's fine."

I moved on, trying to forget about Betty for one damn minute. I glanced around our specialty deli and bakery sections, proud of what I'd accomplished so far.

When I'd decided to open this store two years ago, I watched and read about the upward trends of supermarkets that catered to the health-conscious customer as well as the busy parents in need of healthy, home-cooked meals.

Other supermarkets I'd tracked had seen a more profitable return by offering high-end, fresh products in more rural, secluded locations. Hence, Beauville was ideal. It was surrounded by dozens of smaller towns that didn't have more than a Dollar General, a mom-n-pop grocery, and two gas stations. But these towns supported a lot of country-living families who wanted better food options than what was currently offered.

I realized my store could fill that need. My bakery and deli could offer home-cooked meals for the soccer moms on the go and the organic, gluten-free, and keto-friendly foods. It was a highly popular trend that was climbing, unbeknownst to my father, who didn't believe in my approach to the store. Fortunately, I'd trusted myself even if I had all these niggling doubts put in my head, mostly by dear old Dad.

My Dad's version of fatherly guidance doubled the pressure I already put on myself. I know this type of grocery here in Beauville was a risk. But it was one I was willing to take. I'd been saving my salary I'd made managing Dad's appliance stores since college. As well as the loan Pop gave me. When I'd tried to refuse it, he said it was my inheritance money anyway.

"I wanna see you use it before I croak," he'd told me. "So spend it well."

I loved my grandfather. He knew about my plans, of course; he was basically my biggest investor and cheerleader without expecting anything in return.

Fortunately, business had been going well. My weekday rehearsals weren't interfering with my ability to keep on top of operations. Having that escape soothed some of my stress about starting a new business. It didn't hurt that my stage partner happened to be the most endearingly grumpy and enticing woman I'd met in ages. Perhaps ever.

The fact that she wasn't easily charmed was a turn-on. Her don't-give-a-damn attitude and snarky personality sucked me in like Netflix on Sundays.

Strolling toward the bakery, I looked up and suddenly stopped when I saw *her*.

Standing next to the gluten-free section in the bakery was Betty, a basket on her arm, while she stared at two women in yoga pants and workout tanks.

Correction. She was glaring at them with a mixture of murder and disgust blatantly screaming in her expression.

I couldn't help but chuckle because, at any moment, one of those women was going to turn and instantly jump out of her skin at the psychotic look Betty was giving them. I knew, without a doubt, she wouldn't look away politely and pretend she wasn't having murderous thoughts about the skinny workout wives chatting it up in the healthy section of the deli.

The question was, *why* was she trying to kill them with the venomous thoughts in her head?

One of the women I recognized was the wife of my dad's friend. She was nice—to your face—and as long as you socialized in her circle. I suppose that meant she wasn't very nice.

Hands in my pockets, I strolled over, immediately catching all three women's attention.

"Hey, Bennett," crooned the woman I recognized.

"Hi, Brenda. Getting some late-night shopping done?"

Betty blinked in surprise, her expression now a little sheepish, though she still remained in place three feet away from the other ladies.

"I just love your new store. I was just telling Michelle how *amazing* it is to *finally* have some quality fresh produce in town and the kinds of organic groceries I need to keep fit."

She gave me a seductive smile and splayed a hand on her hip, her fingers spreading wide, red nails contrasting on her white yoga pants. Yes. White.

"Thank you. Glad to hear it."

"So impressive for such a young man." She spread those red-nailed fingers on my bicep and gave me a *friendly* squeeze before letting go.

I wasn't shocked that she was blatantly flirting with me. She always did whenever I was forced to speak to her in social gatherings.

Betty rolled her eyes and wandered slowly away.

"Thanks again. Take care." I nodded to them both politely then quickly veered around them to catch Betty.

She'd stopped in front of the gourmet cheese section.

"Can I help you find a good cheese or charcuterie platter?" I asked in all seriousness.

"I was going to make my own, but the selection is shockingly stark."

I took in the array of Gouda, Brie, Camembert, Roquefort, Gruyere, white and yellow cheddar, gorgonzola, mozzarella, and so on. Not to mention variations of smoked, garlic-n-herb, habanero, cilantro, blueberry, cranberry, and even maple Bourbon-flavored cheeses.

When I blinked back at her, there was the tiniest curve to her mouth that jarred my senses before I could reply.

"You're right," I agreed before clearing my throat. "I'll take it up with the owner. I hear he's a total tool."

That got a real smile out of her. "He's not that bad. I was wondering if I was going to have to save you from the MILFs."

She glanced over at the bakery, as did I, but Brenda and her friend Michelle were gone.

"Does that happen a lot?" she asked.

I shrugged, not really wanting to answer that question. "Her husband plays golf with my dad."

She snorted. "You did not just say that. *Her husband plays golf with my dad,*" she imitated me with a deep voice, sounding so adorable I wanted to grab her and kiss the hell out of her.

Who was I kidding? I had the overwhelming need to kiss her no matter what she was doing. Even making fun of me. "Did that just put me firmly in the too-bougie-for-Betty category?"

She laughed, the sound loosening a tightness in my chest. Rather than answer, she picked up a pack of smoked Gouda, plopped it in her basket, and walked on. Hands in my pockets, I helplessly followed like a dog hoping for scraps of attention.

"No."

"So, why were you really so pissed about the MILFs?"

She raised her eyebrows at me.

"That's what you called them, not me," I argued, noticing a dozen glazed donuts and another dozen croissants in her basket. "You don't approve of the gluten-free, organic, Keto, kale lifestyle or something?"

"I don't care what kind of diet people are on. You can live on a cantaloupe juice diet for all I care. But don't carry on and on, complaining about how so many people eat red meat, destroying their bodies with high cholesterol." She waved a baguette at me before throwing it in her basket. "I mean, some people can't even afford to buy red meat."

There was a thread of true anger underlying her irritation.

"What happened?" I asked softly. "Why are you really angry?"

She heaved a sigh, turning her head away as she shifted the basket to her other arm. "It's my student, Trace. He's a good kid. Works hard. Straight A's. Funny as hell." Her mouth quirked with amusement as if remembering something about him. "I just saw him waiting for his mom again before I headed to rehearsal today. She works, like, two or three jobs to keep a roof over their heads and food on the table."

I nodded with understanding, glancing at her basket, knowing full well she wasn't planning to eat all of that herself. "And Trace doesn't always eat as well as most, I take it."

When she shook her head, I took a stab in the dark. "Then you hear uppity women complaining about high cholesterol when your boy Trace could use a little high-fat and extra cholesterol in his diet."

Her gaze came back to mine, a look of sweet understanding on her pretty face. "Yeah."

She shifted her basket again.

I wanted to take the basket and carry it for her. I wanted to carry all of her weight, including what she carried for her student, Trace. But somehow, I knew I had to tread lightly with her.

There was a reason she had a chip on her shoulder and a shield up against the world. I wasn't quite sure why I set her off, but I was determined to find a way inside her inner sanctum.

I didn't want Betty because she'd turned me down or because I liked a challenge. Though that was also true. I wanted her because she was singular. A jagged edge among smooth surfaces. A brighter star among so many dim, distant ones.

She was beautiful, brilliant on stage, and refreshingly different from any woman I'd met. She had zero fucks to give about most things.

Except for the stage. And her students. It made me want her even more.

She was an artwork of contrasts. Her flaming red hair and

hard exterior against silky, ivory skin and a sweep of freckles across her nose softened her. She rattled me. And attracted me. Unnervingly so.

I waited for her to check out near the exit. As she carried her bag in one hand, I itched to take it from her again. But I was a little lost on how best to approach a wild thing like Betty Mouton.

Most women would accept the help gratefully, but she wasn't most women. What if she got offended and accused me of thinking she was incapable of carrying a fucking bag of baked goods and cheese to the car?

See what I mean? Rattled!

"You okay?" Her mouth quirked into a crooked smile when she met me at the door.

"Sure, yeah. Long day."

She nodded, not seeming to mind that I walked out with her. "I didn't realize you still had to work after rehearsal. You must be tired."

Her expression was more tender than usual.

Hands still in my pockets, I slowed my fast pace to match hers as we headed to her car. "I'm used to it."

She stopped in front of her door, pressing the fob to unlock her silver sedan. After setting the grocery bag in the backseat, she frowned up at me. "That's not good for you, Bennett."

Peering at the lit sign of my store behind her, I shrugged. "Like I said, I'm used to it. Anyway, how are the lines coming for Acts Two and Three?"

We'd only rehearsed Act One tonight, but she seemed to have memorized almost the entire first half without looking at the script much. Her dedication pushed me to want to learn my lines even faster.

"Not great, really," she said. "I'll study this weekend." Peter had scheduled weekday-only rehearsals for now, and tomorrow was Friday. "I would work on it tonight," she added, "but I've got some Jane Eyre essays I still haven't graded and a cheap bottle of wine waiting for me at home."

"You also have a pretty *good* bottle of wine unless you drank it already."

She scoffed, one arm propped on her open door. "That's fancy wine, Broussard. No matter how much I love and adore Edward Rochester, I'm not wasting it on him."

I had the strangest desire to punch out a fictional Victorian lord.

"Well"—she flashed a small smile and slid into the front seat —"thank you for walking me to my car and protecting me from the vast number of criminals in Beauville."

Again, the need to stop her snarky mouth with my own beat wildly inside my chest. I kept my hands in my pockets and my body parts to myself. For now. "Goodnight, Ms. Mouton. Pleasure to be of service."

With another flashing smile, she closed the door and started her car. I strolled back toward the store, not done with my close-out checklist for the night, but my gaze followed the little silver car as it took a right onto Evangeline and then another right onto Acadian Trail Road that led out onto into the country where her house was.

The memory of rehearsal hardened my body all over again. When she'd pressed her soft face to mine, sweet scent surrounding me, I'd nearly come undone. She drove me fucking insane with desire. Having to hide my feelings was the hardest acting I'd ever done.

But I was following my instincts with Betty, which told me she was easily spooked when it came to dating and relationships. Or maybe, it was just me who spooked her. Either way, I was going to play it cool till I knew she was ready for me.

Still, I didn't think I could wait till next week to see her again. I had inventory to handle all day Saturday and part of Sunday, but I could go home a little early tomorrow.

Pulling my earbuds from my pocket, I popped them back in and pressed play on my phone, smiling as I returned to work.

Chapter Seven

~BETTY~

"How in the hell did you get up there?"

Gilbert bleated at me, then did a little circle dance on top of my roof, utterly proud of himself.

Yes, my roof!

I suppose the shed was within leaping distance of the covered patio, but how did he get up on top of the shed? This goat was some kind of Houdini or something.

"Hang on!"

He bleated back as if answering me. It sounded like a sassy bleat, to be truthful.

Hauling my ladder around to the side of the house where the slant of the roof wasn't quite as steep. I could get up there and get him pretty easily from this side.

So I thought.

Once I'd reached the ladder's top step, I rested my arms on the roof's edge. I'd have to hoist myself up. Peering down, my tummy did a flip. I wasn't afraid of heights. But I sure as hell was afraid of breaking my damn neck.

Maybe Gretchen had a taller ladder.

"Baaaa!"

"Alright! You little devil. I'm coming."

Gilbert danced again, his back leg skidding on a shingle. I screamed. But he caught himself. It looked like he could totter right off if he wasn't careful. My stomach squeezed into a knot. What if he had one of those fainting fits and rolled right off?

"Be still, boy," I told him as gently as possible. "I'm coming to get you. Just don't move, Gilbert."

Planting my palms firmly, I hoisted myself up, pushing with my legs. One foot caught the top lip of the ladder, and then I felt nothing but air beneath my feet but heard a clatter in the grass below.

"Fuck!" I yelled.

One cheek pressed to the roof, I had my entire upper body laid out on the roof, my arms spread wide to balance myself because my legs were dangling freely in space.

Don't panic.

"Shit!"

I was panicking.

Gilbert agilely stepped right up to me and licked my cheek.

I would've laughed if I wasn't afraid it might make me lose my balance and fall right off the roof.

A car door slammed in my driveway.

Oh, please be Finn dropping a Friday night daiquiri off. He'd asked me to go out for dinner and drinks in Lafayette, but I'd really wanted to work on my lines. The sooner I got them memorized, the sooner I could really internalize Corie Bratter and better become her on stage.

Besides, I wouldn't admit it to Finn, and barely even to myself; I didn't want to disappoint Bennett.

Okay, if I were being totally honest, I wanted to do more

than that. I wanted to impress him. To prove that I deserved that lead female role. He hadn't given me any inclination that I wasn't suited to it, but Mandy's backhanded comment at the call-back and my own insecurity at gaining my *first* lead role had me pushing myself even harder.

"Finn!" I screamed, knowing he must be coming up the walkway by now. "Around the side of the house! Help!"

I heard the distinct long strides of someone rounding the side where I was dangling.

"Hold on," came the deep, rolling timbre of Bennett Broussard.

"Shit," I muttered. "Bennett?" Though I knew it was him.

"I've got you." Then he had his hands wrapped around the backs of my thighs near my ass.

I didn't get embarrassed often, but flames of heat flushed my face. All I could think was, thank God I was wearing jeans since the weather had finally turned cool. Otherwise, he'd be getting a nice peek at my ass cheeks hanging out of the tiny shorts I was wearing last time he was here.

"Just let go, Betty. I've got you."

His long fingers and big hands spanned a good bit of my thighs. Suddenly, I wished I had on the short shorts so I could feel those big hands on my naked skin.

"But Gilbert," I whined, "he's stuck up here."

A masculine chuckle came from down below. "I think you're the one who's stuck. Just let go, and I'll catch you. I'll get Gilbert after."

"It sounds easier than it is."

With zero amusement in his voice, his tone having dropped even deeper, softer. "I won't let you fall, Betty. Trust me. Just let go. I'll catch you."

Now not only was my face in flames from humiliation, but my tummy was doing backflips at the tenor of Bennett's confident promises.

"Okay," I muttered. "On the count of three."

"One, two—" His steady voice made me feel sure and safe, so I dropped when he said, "three."

Strong arms caught me around the thighs and waist, holding my body tight, my back to his front. Air left my lungs, and I gripped his forearms as he let me slide down his body, his breath warm against my ear.

"Thank you," I whispered, not about to turn my head and look at him this close.

It was already getting too uncomfortable in rehearsal to be near him and maintain my nonchalance. Those husband-and-wife scenes where I had to cuddle and press my cheek to his haunted me already. The roughness of his scruff and the smell of his manly soap or cologne was still on me when I'd gotten home last night. I'd had to pull out my BOB to take care of myself, so I could settle down and sleep.

There, on stage, I had the setting of the play to back up my reaction to him, that it was all an act for the audience.

Here, in my backyard—or side yard, rather—it was more difficult to lie even to myself that my body had a very distinct reaction to this man. The kind that had me conjuring more fantasies, like Bennett and I doing this exact pose…in my bedroom, naked, in front of a mirror.

In front of a mirror?

Dammit. I really needed to get laid. Unfortunately, this was Beauville. The one thing I didn't like about my hometown was that it was difficult to have casual relationships without every busybody knowing about it. In particular, my mother, who was already hounding me about grandchildren. I was twenty-six, for Pete's sake.

"Baaa!"

Gilbert peered down at us over the top edge of the roof. That seemed to break the spell. Bennett released me, finally allowing my feet to touch the ground. I hadn't even realized he'd been holding me aloft in a vise grip against his body. Like I said, I wasn't complaining. It was the most action I'd gotten in a year. But I did feel awkward all of a sudden.

Bennett grabbed the ladder and righted it, headed up a few steps, grabbed Gilbert with ridiculous ease, and hauled him down like he plucked goats off roofs every day of his life. He made everything look easy. Because he did everything with extreme confidence.

"Your goat, my lady." He stood right in front of me and set him down.

"Bad Gilbert," I fussed down at him.

He toddled a step, went stiff-legged, then keeled right over on his side.

"Oh, shit!" Bennett blurted, taking a step toward him. "He's hurt."

"No, he's not." I grabbed Bennett's forearm to stop him. He was wearing a T-shirt, exposing those nice, veiny forearms. I couldn't help but think how lovely it was to feel those arms around me. I let my fingers linger on the tight muscle for a few seconds. "He's faking it." Then I called down to the goat, barely twitching. "You're not a 'possum, Gilbert!"

The goat suddenly righted himself but was still unsteady. When I corralled him to keep him from heading to the front of the house, he turned and took off running into the backyard. I followed, and Bennett followed me.

"I don't think Gretchen fixed the fence well enough," I commented more to myself.

Gilbert darted right under the hole he'd come through last time, wiggling his tail as he went.

"So," he said casually next to me, "your neighbor has goats."

"You noticed?"

We were standing near my patio now.

"And they…faint?"

"Yeah. It shocked me, too, the first time. Gilbert is some

sort of magician. He gets out of the yard and manages to break into my house. Or apparently, climb on top of it now."

"Gilbert's got a crush." His smile and the flicker of his hazel eyes sent a tingling shiver along my skin. "I don't blame him," he added softly.

"Anyway," I said brightly, ignoring his comment because I didn't know what to do with that. "Thanks for the help." A fresh wave of embarrassment filled my cheeks with heat.

His smile widened, and now that I didn't hate him quite as much as I did on that first day, I had to admit it was...devastating. If he could melt my lady bits with a smile, imagine what he could do with his other parts.

"You want a cup of coffee?"

He blinked, looking back toward the side of the house. "Actually, I brought something for you. Let me go grab it." He stalked off around the side.

"I'll open the front door."

I rushed inside through the kitchen and living room, stopping at the mirror in the foyer to see what sort of mess I looked like. My jeans were nice and tight, highlighting my assets, but I had on a baggy long-sleeved T-shirt, my hair in a messy bun. I'd decided to do a little more unpacking then work on lines tonight.

Wild Friday night, I know.

When I swung open the door, he had a bakery box in his hands. "I brought you something to go great with the wine."

"That doesn't look like a steak."

"Dark chocolate cake with Bavarian cream. Trust me. It pairs perfectly."

Trust me.

He'd said the same earlier when he had his hands right below my ass and before he caught me in his arms. That was really the crux of my initial animosity toward him. I didn't trust him. But why? What was it about Bennett that had my shields up so high?

I had sincerely gotten over the booby glitter bomb incident. Was it that he was rich? Was I such a snob like Elizabeth Bennett against Darcy because he had money?

I'd witnessed for myself how much and how hard he worked. He didn't depend on his name to carry his new store. He put in all the late hours, even after rehearsals at BPAL. The confidence I'd mistaken for arrogance from afar was lined with a vulnerability I hadn't expected. He was hard on himself. Very much so.

"If you're busy," he said, smile slipping, "I'll just leave it with you and go."

"Oh." I stepped aside and opened the door wider. "No, come on in."

When he stepped into my tiny foyer, it felt even tinier. Why I tended to forget how big he was up close, I had no idea.

I led the way back to the kitchen and pulled his bottle of wine off my eight-bottle wine rack on the counter.

"Did you just move in?"

"How could you tell?" Littering the kitchen table was a stack of boxes and an unopened microwave I still had to install.

He chuckled. "I didn't see any the other night."

I uncorked the wine. "Well, I wanted at least one room that was finished, and that was the living room."

"It's a nice house," he said from the arched doorway leading to the living room.

"Thanks." I pulled two wine glasses from the cabinet, assuming he was joining me. "It's coming along."

I might play like I didn't care, but I appreciated his praise. This was my first house, and though it could probably fit inside his own house or in his yard as a man-cave, it was mine. She was pretty and charming, good bones and airy with plenty of windows, and let in lots of natural light. And I'd gotten her through my own sweat, tears, and hefty college loans.

I served us both a piece of cake then handed him a glass and plate. "Let's go sit in the living room. It's still a mess in here. If you couldn't tell."

As soon as we sat on my sofa, he caught sight of my script on the coffee table. "Memorizing tonight?"

"Yep. Some girls like to go out and party on a Friday night. Not me. Give me Neil Simon and hours of studying lines. That's what gets me excited." I took a bite of my cake at that.

Bennett's playful gaze darkened, zoning in on my mouth again. I wasn't doing anything sexy, just taking a bite of the cake.

And, holy hell, it was good.

I must've made the tiniest sound of pleasure because I wasn't the type to moan over food. But this cake was fucking ridiculous.

"Good?" He blinked away as he took a sip of wine.

"Amazing. Now I see why you're here."

"Why?" He looked panicked for a second.

"You're forcing me to eat this damn cake, so I get addicted and spend a ton of money at your store."

"You got me." He laughed lightly. "I came here to lure you into being a repeat customer. That was my sole aim."

Before I could make a smart comment back, he pulled his script from the back pocket of his jeans. It was already wearing at the edges as if he'd been spending a lot of time with it. It looked just like mine.

"Want to rehearse?"

Setting my half-eaten cake down, I said, "So that's why you came over. To sneak in here and force me to practice lines with you."

"I don't want to force you to do anything," he said rather thoughtfully. He sat at an angle, facing me, one ankle casually crossing his other knee, his wine balanced on his right thigh. However, there was nothing casual in his expression or his gaze—all grave and watchful. "But I'll admit I want to spend more time with you."

Okay. This was more than his teasing, flirty charm. He was being serious.

"Let's go over Act Two," I finally said, unsure what to say. Not the norm for me.

Breaking his intense hold on me, he blinked with a half-smile and set his wine down to open his script.

This, I could handle. Working in a professional capacity where the lines were clear and resolute.

His predatory gaze lingered at my mouth, dipping over my body—that I could not handle. For one, my vagina was one hundred percent in compliance with Operation Clean Out The Cobwebs in the hands of General Broussard. And I was slowly starting to think that my vagina had more sense than I did.

I was totally wrong about him being a stuck-up snob like I'd assumed he would be. So why was I still holding out? I honestly had no idea.

I was nervous. *He* made me nervous. And that was new. Guys rarely knocked me off of my game, but Bennett, with his broad chest and hazel eyes, and hypnotic charisma, actually made me all aflutter.

Like right now.

Bennett took a deep sip of wine and set his glass on the coffee table. "Let's start with Act Three since we haven't done that one much."

"Sounds good."

So we dove in. Just like on stage, Bennett's performance inspired me to be even better at my role. When he pushed, I pulled. When he went down in tempo, I went up. When his character threw a fit about the eccentric neighbor Mr. Velasco, I soothed him as only a good wife could.

The balance we'd found together would be magical on stage, especially with an audience. There was an intangible energy you couldn't define or explain when performing for a live audience. I couldn't wait to experience that with a superior actor like Bennett.

We'd wound down Act Three, and Bennett had gone silent. I was still waiting for his final lines. When I glanced up, I realized that I'd reached out and touched him as I would on stage, my hand cupping the muscular ball of his shoulder.

Bennett wasn't looking at his script. He was focused entirely on me. His chest rose and fell quicker than normal, his lips parted, his gaze on my mouth.

"What?" I asked in a whisper, dropping my hand to my lap.

Clearing his throat, he rumbled, "You have some chocolate right here."

He touched the corner of his mouth, dragging my attention to his sensuous lips.

"Oh." I wiped frantically and glanced back up. "Is it gone?"

Shaking his head, he leaned forward and reached up with his hand. I froze, mesmerized at his slow movement.

He cupped my jaw gently and swiped his thumb along the opposite corner of my mouth. "Other side."

That woodsy masculine scent of his filled my space, mixed with red wine and lustful thoughts. His thumb dragged slowly from the corner of my mouth and along my lower lip, his pupils blown full-black.

I barely breathed when he finally blinked and dropped his hand, his expression shifting to one of surprise and...pain?

"I should go." He stood with his script in hand, clearing his throat. "I need to be at the store early tomorrow."

"Oh." I stood with him, feeling awkward. "Okay," I murmured, my voice rusty.

He nodded and swallowed hard, his throat working as he stared at me with feral intensity. Then he turned abruptly and strode for the door, strangling his script in both hands as he went.

"Thank you for the cake," I said as he walked out onto my doorstep and turned. "And the wine," I added with a nervous smile.

The tension was still there in the stiffness of his stance and the wildness of his eyes. "My pleasure," his voice rumbled, gaze flicking to my mouth one more time. "See you at rehearsal, Betty."

Then he was striding away like his house was on fire.

I wasn't stupid. I'd felt the magnetic pull between us too. I thought he was going to kiss me. Was pretty damn sure of it. Then he didn't.

I pondered what had just happened as I shut and locked the door.

He'd invited himself over with cake and the intent to rehearse lines. I wasn't mad about it. But maybe he thought I was annoyed or something?

Then came that sizzling moment where I wanted to know what his mouth tasted like, what his tongue felt like. I was imagining it quite clearly when he jumped off the sofa and fled my house.

He obviously wanted to kiss me, but I hadn't moved. Hadn't given him any signals. I'd wanted it too. So he'd backed off quickly like the gentleman I was beginning to understand that he was before doing something impulsive like rip off my clothes and have his wicked way with me.

Sighing to the ceiling, I realized I needed to screw my head on straight and focus on the play, not all the reasons I wanted to lick Bennett from head to toe.

Chapter Eight

~BENNETT~

TRISH AND PETER WERE ARGUING OVER SOME PART OF THE staging in the "shama, shama" scene, as Betty was calling it. This was the part of the play where Paul, Corie, Ethyl, and Mr. Velasco come back after drinking lots of ouzo at a Greek restaurant, and Corie is tipsy, dancing seductively around and on top of her husband, Paul.

Today was a rehearsal just for Betty and me. Peter scheduled some rehearsal days where we worked on just our scenes since we had so many.

I was still stifling my laughter at Betty's first attempt. Peter had me sitting in the club chair. Betty's character was supposed to parade around me, singing the "Shama, Shama" song while doing a sexy dance in a drunken state.

The problem was, Betty looked more clumsy than drunk, and she was stiff as a board, doing an awkward, not-so-sexy jig around me in the chair.

"Okay, okay!" whisper-yelled Trish. She walked up to the

edge of the stage and crooked her finger toward Betty.

She heaved an irritated sigh and met Trish downstage.

"So, maybe you could try using the scarf."

"The scarf?" Betty had both hands on her curvy hips, drawing my eyes there.

"Yeah, Paul's scarf. You come in with it around your neck and when you strip your coat, you shimmy around. Go around the chair once, then fall into his lap, singing the song. Let's try that. Less dancing, more touchy-feely with Paul."

I gulped hard, preparing myself.

The fact that Betty needed guidance on how to play out this part of the scene had only pissed her off even more.

When she spun around to go back to start the scene again, she glared at me. "I don't want to hear it, Broussard."

"I didn't say a word."

"I can hear your thoughts," she snapped.

Oh, she definitely could *not* hear my thoughts. If she had, she'd have slapped me ten times already. Biting my lip so I wouldn't laugh, I cleared my throat and tried to focus so I wouldn't break her concentration. I was entirely on board for more touchy-feely with my character.

"You just worry about maintaining your *stuffed shirt* personality as Paul. Shouldn't be too difficult."

I chuckled, knowing she was being prickly because she was so uptight about her failure at playing up the sexy side of Corie Bratter.

"Okay, let's go again!" called Peter. "Action!"

Betty had her back to me. She was wearing those same tight-ass jeans she wore last Friday night when I found her hanging off her roof.

I admit, my brain went in two directions when I first saw her on Friday. One, pure panic mode. She could've hurt herself if she fell. She wasn't very tall, and that drop would've damaged her ankle at the very least. The thought had flooded me with anxiety and, for some reason, anger. I didn't want to think about what would've happened if I hadn't dropped by last Friday night.

The second thing that ran through my mind—and had been doing so on loop all weekend—was that her ass looked fucking fantastic in those jeans.

And here she was, wearing them again, along with a fitted red V-neck that kept riding up to reveal a sliver of pale skin on her stomach when she moved. Was she torturing me on purpose?

She pulled her hair out of the messy bun on top of her head and shook out all that gorgeous red hair. Then she picked up the scarf hanging on the back of the sofa and started the scene, singing "Shama, shama."

This time, I wasn't laughing. There was a seductive tilt to her head, her fiery hair cascading over one shoulder. She moved her upper body and hips in tandem, that red shirt riding higher and higher, showing me the clear indentation of her waist and a wide swathe of creamy soft skin.

Hoping like hell she didn't notice how hard my dick was when she sat on my lap, I shifted as she wrapped the scarf around my neck and shimmied in front of me. My hands were on autopilot, reaching out to span her waist, fingers barely slipping under her shirt as she plopped her ass down on my thigh.

Her eyes widened, but she kept singing and playing the flirty wife, wrapping her arms around my neck. Then—fuck me—she pressed her breasts to my chest, leaning to the side, so she wasn't blocking me from the audience, which was only Peter and Trish tonight.

At least, that was vaguely noted by my sizzling brain. The rest of my body was highly attentive and focused on how fucking amazing she felt in my arms. Her petite, curvy body would fit me so good if she straddled me—naked. My mind completely fizzled out, conjuring every hot, carnal way I could possess this woman on my lap, my hands tightening on the bare skin of her waist.

"Bennett," she whispered in my ear.

Her warm breath and soft voice sent a shiver down my body that jolted my dick to full attention. As if he wasn't on full alert already.

"Hmm," I managed.

"Your next lines."

Fuck. I'd completely forgotten where I was, my libido making me mindless.

No, it was her. This wild vixen sitting in my lap, giving me a knowing smile. She knew exactly what she was doing.

I scoffed, then said low, "You proud of yourself?"

Her brow rose in innocence. "I don't know what you're talking about."

"The hell you don't."

She blinked sweetly again as if she had no idea, then burst out laughing. She leaned back to stand up. Having minds of their own, my hands tightened on her. They wanted to hold on forever and keep exploring.

If only.

"The scene isn't over."

Her laughter died at the low rumble of my voice and the warning in it.

"Do you need a line?" Trisha shouted, obviously to me, since I was still frozen and staring. So was Betty.

"No, I got it." I fell back into my character of Paul, scowling and put out that my drunk wife had so much fun at my expense.

I picked up my script again since I didn't have all of the lines yet in this Act. Then we finished the scene, stopping before the final part where I crawled on the roof and Betty comes after me. The rooftop of the set wasn't finished.

"That was perfect!" shouted Peter.

"Looks good, guys," said Trish, glancing at her watch.

"Do you guys mind if we run through Act One before we go?" I asked, my gaze on Betty.

Her eyes rounded as if she sensed I had an ulterior motive.

"Of course, we don't mind," Peter responded cheerfully. "Trish will call lines if you need them."

"I think I've got these lines," I told Peter, putting my script. "I'm going to try without the script."

Plus, I wanted my hands free to *act* this scene out to the best of my ability.

"Terrific! Let's get going from the moment Paul comes home."

I noted Betty's quizzical frown as I sauntered across stage to make my entrance. She knew something was up. I didn't have anything devious planned. Not really.

She'd agreed to the cheek-to-cheek stage kissing, and we'd done one rehearsal where I'd been more standoffish in these scenes. I didn't want to make her uncomfortable. Still didn't. But her teasing—and she knew full well how hard she'd made me—could go both ways.

I entered the scene, carrying a briefcase, pretending to be exhausted by the flight up the stairwell as always, and she threw her arms around my neck to greet me. Rather than let her cling to me without any reaction, I wrapped my free arm around her waist and pulled her tight against me.

Damn, did she feel good.

Her breathy gasp in my ear made my whole body go hard, imagining that sound if we were alone in the dark. Then she pushed out of my arms and went through the motions of the scene, helping me get comfortable and flitting around the apartment, telling me about her day.

When she got to the part where she sat on my lap, and we were supposed to do our stage kissing, I kept to our bargain. But this time, I scooped my hand under her fall of silky hair and wrapped her nape, giving her a firm squeeze while I scraped my jaw—a little scruffy at the end of the day—along hers till my breath coasted against her ear. I didn't kiss, lick, or bite like I so desperately fucking wanted to, but I let my lips graze the delicate shell.

Her responding shiver and tightening of her nails in my shoulders where she held onto me told me I wasn't alone in this attraction. No matter how hard she seemed to be fighting it.

She quickly stood and separated us to go through the scene, shooting me a glare over her shoulder as she flounced over to the kitchen area.

"Stop, stop," called Peter. "I'm not sure if I want you crossing behind him like that. It puts more of your back to the audience."

"Well, she can't walk backwards," added Trish. "We decided we wanted more domestic interaction in this part, so she has to retrieve the drinks from the kitchen."

"I think we should add a bar on the sidewall and have her go over there and fix the drinks."

"I don't know," said Trish.

"Just trust me for once, Trish." Peter gave her a look.

Those two sometimes fought more than they agreed. Trish rolled her eyes. "Fine. Betty, can you go back to the beginning, and let's try it again?"

Betty's eyes widened, which had me grinning as I picked up the briefcase and crossed to the door.

"Yes, I want to do that again," I agreed with a laugh.

I'd expected a smart comeback, but she didn't say a word.

"Okay, ready when you are," called Peter.

I entered the scene as before. Betty hugged and welcomed her husband home. As before, I hauled her close, this time brushing my lips along the side of her slender throat when I embraced her. Her body stiffened, but she didn't push away.

I released her quickly enough and stumbled to the sofa as before, doing my exhausted husband routine. Betty came to me and draped herself on my lap, more tentatively than before, those sapphire eyes assessing me. More than assessing. Her gaze roamed my mouth as she settled into the flirty wife position atop my lap.

I repeated my movements as before, basking in the way she arched her spine, pressing closer, and then her neck ever-so-slightly, offering me access.

Fucking hell.

My hand wrapped around her nape again. I coasted my thumb across the pulse-point at the base of her throat, holding her in our fake cheek-to-cheek position.

But there was nothing fake about the fire burning through my veins or the steel grip my arms had around her body, wanting to keep her close, get her closer.

She drew back, those blue eyes dilated with desire. I clenched my jaw against the impulse to haul her against me and show her I wasn't faking a goddamn thing.

Then something shocking happened. She swayed closer, her gaze on my mouth, our lips inches apart. She stiffened, clenching the hair at my nape, her breath coming faster.

I couldn't believe it, but Betty was fighting the same desire I was. Without even thinking, I slid my hand into her hair, sculpting the back of her head, and crushed my mouth to hers. She made a little sound in the back of her throat then opened her mouth to me, letting me slide my tongue inside. I groaned, nipping her bottom lip before I kissed her deeper, my entire body going hard with need. My blood racing, I was lost, wanting more—

"Cut!" shouted Peter, breaking the spell but not the trance she'd put me under.

I abruptly stopped and pulled away, realizing too late what I'd done. I was caught in the moment, my brain shutting off while my body reacted.

"I thought y'all were going to wait for dress rehearsals to do the stage kissing," interrupted Peter, sounding completely confused.

"Uh, sorry," I said, still looking at Betty, who wasn't saying a word as she panted lightly through parted lips.

"It's fine if you want to add it in now," continued Peter, totally oblivious, "but that's a little too intense, Bennett. It should be more of a welcome-home-honey kiss, not an I-want-to-rip-your-clothes-off kiss. Right, Trish?"

"Yeah, yeah. Right."

I finally glanced away from Betty and picked her up by the waist so we could both stand. I took a decided step away.

"Got it," I said, tightening my fists, wanting the sensation of her hair and skin beneath my fingertips again. The softness of her mouth against mine. "Not a rip-your-clothes-off kiss."

I dared to glance at Betty, but she wasn't looking at me, purposefully avoiding eye contact.

"I'm sorry," I murmured. When she didn't respond, I stepped closer and said lower, "Really. I shouldn't have done that."

Finally, her bright eyes came back to me. "It's okay." She laughed and waved a hand. "It's just fake kissing. All for the play, right?"

Rubbing a palm over my chest at the sudden tightness, I added, "Yeah. Fake kissing."

"Just remember what Peter said. Ease up, tiger. Not so intense." She was all lightness and ease, which somehow formed a weighted lump in my stomach.

I couldn't even respond because my heart was still hammering like mad, not understanding that this was *fake*.

"Let's finish this scene, then stop there," called Peter.

So we did. My acting skills were put to the test because all I wanted was to be far away from this stage and from Betty. She continued on like nothing had happened, easily performing, not missing one line. I'd called Trish for three before the scene was done.

Then I hightailed it out of there. Betty had obviously accepted my apology for overstepping on stage. I should be grateful. Happy. Not surly as fuck because that fake kiss had obliterated my soul.

And it had meant absolutely nothing to her.

Chapter Nine

~BETTY~

"BUT ROCHESTER SHOULD'VE TRUSTED HER ENOUGH TO TELL HER the truth." Caroline bent one leg underneath her and sat on her foot, leaning forward on her desktop. "It's his fault that it blew up like that, so Jane had no choice but to leave him."

Trace, sitting sideways in his chair, facing Caroline, stopped tapping his pen on the desk and frowned at her. "You actually believe that if he'd told Jane that he had locked his psycho wife in the attic, she would've just been like, 'Oh, no problem. Let's get hitched.'"

Caroline angled her body in his direction. "If she truly loved him. Yeah, I do."

"You're delusional. No chick is gonna accept that. She'd freak the hell out and run for the hills. Just like she did in the book when she found out."

"Oh, so you think it would've been okay for him to marry her, making himself a bigamist and basically taking her virtue under false pretenses so she'd be forced to stay with him?"

"Exactly." Trace shrugged. "Like you said, if she loved him, she'd forgive him. If she had to stay for the marriage, then he could've explained himself without her tearing across the country and abandoning him, breaking both their hearts."

This was the exact kind of heated debate I longed to spark between my students in my literature classes. But I wasn't prepared for the passion crackling between these two as they battled it out. I couldn't tell if Caroline wanted to slap him or kiss him. I think maybe both.

"You are morally ambiguous," declared Caroline haughtily.

Okay, slap him.

"Why would he be ambitious?" asked Emmitt, Trace's friend, who wasn't the brightest lightbulb in the box, bless his heart.

"Ambiguous, idiot," said Sarah on the other side of Caroline. "Not ambitious."

Trace ignored them, his focus still on Caroline. "Never said I wasn't. I know right from wrong. And I know some things are worth fighting for, even lying for. Rochester looked at Jane and knew he'd found his soulmate, not that crazy woman his father saddled him with. He wasn't going to let his past mistakes or the cruelty of fate or his asshat father take away what was rightfully his."

Caroline and the rest of the class sat in silence. Trace's face was flushed pink with emotion. Even though he'd kept his voice even and steady, there was an intensity in his words. I was sure he harbored some ill will toward his father, who'd abandoned them, and perhaps his feelings were tied up in the debate.

I could certainly empathize with those feelings. Though my father hadn't abandoned us all at once, it felt the same. He slowly disappeared until I didn't want or need him anymore.

He sent Mom a few checks that first year after the divorce, none of them enough to cover his child support payments.

Then they dwindled to half that the second year then nothing at all. Not even a card on my birthday or Emma's. He remarried and forgot about us.

I'd tried to reach out once or twice with half-hearted reception, then realized he was emotionally bankrupt, and I didn't need that kind of man in my life. After I'd cried my eyes out and smashed my favorite picture of me sitting on his knee when I was five, that is.

When Mom found me sobbing in my closet that day, she hugged me close and whispered to me over and over how beautiful, amazing, and brilliant I was. That my father was an asshole who wouldn't know a pot of gold from a bucket of shit if he saw it.

"After today, Beatrice, you will never cry over him again. He doesn't deserve one more of your tears," she'd said.

Heartsick but comforted, I'd told her, "I'm just sorry you have to live with the mistake of marrying him."

"Oh, sweetheart, it wasn't a mistake," she'd said, cupping my cheeks and wiping my tears with love in her eyes. "I wouldn't have you or Emma otherwise."

One thing I learned from my father and strong-as-hell mother was that I didn't need a man to take care of me. I'd gotten a job as soon as I turned sixteen and hadn't stopped working since. I'd been doing just fine taking care of myself. Maybe that's why I'd bristled so much at Bennett's wealth.

Was it fair that it bothered me that he'd been born wealthy and with more advantages than me? No, of course not. But I was a human being with ocean-deep feelings about abandonment, independence, and self-worth. I couldn't help that the privileged rubbed me wrong sometimes, simply because they were born. No matter how irrational I knew my feelings were.

Bennett...

No. I wasn't going to think about him right now. Or that insane stage kiss that had fried my brain. It had taken everything in me to finish that scene like he hadn't just rocked my world.

"Wow," said Sarah on the front row, snapping me back to the present.

Caroline's face blushed pink as Trace stared at her, waiting for another comeback.

I was about to end the discussion and bring us back to something more docile when the bell rang. On autopilot, the students shoved notebooks in their backpacks, hauled them over their shoulders, and made their way out the door. Caroline moved more slowly, her head down as she packed. Trace stood at his desk.

"Great debate, guys." I crossed my arms over my chest. "One of the things I want you to gain from my class is how to think for yourselves. You two have proven that more than once."

"But who would be *more* right?" asked Trace, his tilted smile returning as he stood and hauled his backpack over one shoulder.

"It would be *righter,* not *more right,*" I corrected, but his eyes were on Caroline, totally uninterested in correct grammar.

"Please, Trace," she said haughtily. "There isn't one correct answer. Right, Ms. B?"

"Correct, Caroline. Sorry, Trace. Your charming smile can't help you win this one."

He chuckled as they both headed out the door. I followed to stand and watch the hall as Mr. Burke liked us to do. I couldn't help smiling at Trace and Caroline walking side by side, chatting together. Trace's head bent down to hear her as they headed to their next class.

"Don't forget to buy your Homecoming tickets!" Lily called out to her kids as they left.

"Keep us updated with that pig sighting, Ms. Breaux," said a hefty freshman walking out the door.

Lily appeared at her door a second later.

"What pig sighting?" I asked.

Lily's entire face lit up as she practically leaped across the hall to me. "You haven't seen it on Facebook?"

"No."

She pulled her phone from the pocket of her dress. Lily mostly wore casual but pretty dresses to school. I could never manage that sort of effort. I'd have to regularly shave my legs, and yeah, that wasn't going to happen. Unless I got a boyfriend.

Bennett's face and mouth, and hands popped to mind.

"It started about a week ago." Lily did a quick search on FB and pulled up a page. "Everyone's been posting updates on Beauville's town page. It's hilarious."

I was rarely on social media, let alone Beauville's FB page.

She scrolled to the bottom and pointed. "Look. So someone first spotted him trotting along the coulee on Broken Arrow Highway."

The picture showed a giant pink pig with black spots. Definitely belonged to a farmer. "Do they know who owns it?"

"Yeah. Mr. Guillory posted here." She scrolled up, laughing a little as she said, "He posted a one-hundred-dollar reward for anyone who can trap her long enough for him to get there with a trailer."

"How the hell is anyone going to keep that beast in one place? He's got to be five hundred pounds."

"Seven-hundred thirty-two. Mr. Guillory posted her stats."

"Her?"

"Marigold. And she's a wily girl. Every time someone spots her and calls the police, she's disappeared by the time they get there."

Lily showed me three more pics of Marigold walking across the parking lot of the Tractor Supply store, which was on Acadian Trail Road, then near a dumpster of McDonald's in town, and finally walking across the parking lot of Broussard's Fresh Market.

I instantly smiled, imagining Bennett trying to corral that giant pig long enough for authorities to get there.

"Hey. What are you two looking at?" Finn popped up next to me.

"The pig sighting around town," Lily answered, showing him her screen.

"Oh, Marigold. Yeah. They'll never catch her."

I rolled my eyes. Of course, Finn—Mr. Socialmedialite—would know about the elusive, behemoth pig wandering around town.

Finn pulled his phone from his back pocket and checked a text then shot one back to whoever was messaging him.

"Who's that? The *surgeon?*"

"A friend in the Navy," he answered, one corner of his lip lifting into a crooked smile.

"*Just* a friend?" I asked with loads of innuendo.

He tapped one last message and shoved it in his back pocket on a wistful sigh. "No, seriously. Just a friend. He's straight. Unfortunately."

"Who, Liam? You're still keeping up with him?"

Liam was a friend from high school but had mingled on the perimeter of our group. Nice, quiet guy, running back on the football team. But he and Finn had been on student council together and were sort of buddies.

"Kind of," he said noncommittally.

"So, what are you doing? Don't you have a class?" The tardy bell was going to ring any second.

"Yes." He grinned, his green eyes brightening with mischief. "You're coming with me to Italian Night tonight at Broussard's."

The mere mention of his name caused an explosion of

sweet burning that started in my chest and ended right between my legs.

"What are you talking about?"

"Michael can't go, so I need a date. And I'm not losing out on free wine and a meal. So be ready at five." He started backing away. "I'll swing by and pick you up."

The tardy bell rang. Lily hurried back to her class and shut the door.

I did the same, but I moved in slow motion. I'd been purposefully banning Bennett from my thoughts after the incident at the last rehearsal, which had sent me home and straight into a hot bath where I masturbated to the memory of his mouth and hands on me.

Good Lord! That man could kiss. I mean, I was no novice. I'd dated plenty of guys, even phenomenal kissers. But damn. Not one compared to Bennett Broussard. And that was a problem.

If he was that good at kissing and touching, I couldn't stop thinking how good he would be in bed.

Even though part of me hesitated going out with Bennett for some reason that I still couldn't pinpoint, the other part of me was doing a strip tease and buying condoms.

Not that he'd asked me out on a real date yet. Only the fake date we had on Saturday to the Golden Oldies theater. He'd texted me last night, sending my heart rate into the stratosphere. But there was no Bennett teasing and flirtation. All business.

Him: Peter still wants us to go and see the Barefoot movie. Are you free Saturday?

Me: Yes, that sounds great. Do I still get a free meal out of this business date? ;)

. . .

Lengthy pause that made me uncomfortable.

Him: Sure. Pick you up at 6:00.

And then absolutely nothing. He'd bowed out of rehearsal yesterday, telling Peter that he had to handle something at work and couldn't get free. It was the first time he'd ever canceled rehearsal. It was also the first rehearsal following our fake kiss fiasco.

I'd told him it was okay after he'd apologized. I hoped he wasn't beating himself up over it. Surely, he wasn't avoiding me. He'd set up our business date for Saturday. If he acted all weird then, I'd confront him and we'd work it out. Like adults. Then we could go back to being friendly theater colleagues and that's all.

Chapter Ten

~BETTY~

"I THOUGHT YOU SAID YOU COULDN'T COOK," FINN OBSERVED over my shoulder as I stirred the Bolognese sauce.

"I said I couldn't bake. I'm a good cook. There's a complete difference."

"Enlighten me." He took a sip of his second glass of red wine.

"Baking requires precision and attention to detail. Something I'm not good at."

"True."

I hip-bumped him. "Cooking is more of an instinctual taste-as-you-go sort of thing. Here, try."

I dipped a fresh spoon into our sauce and held it up for him. The three other couples were almost finished as well, one already taking their bowls to the high dining table set up for us in the industrial kitchen of Broussard's.

"Oh, my God. Give me another," demanded Finn. "That's delicious."

Smiling, I ladled him another spoonful.

"Now I need to cut the pasta we rolled out earlier. And by we, I mean me." I'd never made my own pasta, but it was definitely something I'd be doing again. It was easier than I expected when I had the right tools.

Finn eased behind me, wrapping his arms around my waist as if to assist me.

"What are you doing?" I asked, laughing.

"Helping you cook. I haven't done much tonight."

"Finn, this is weird."

He was behaving as if he was flirting with me like I was an actual girlfriend candidate. Which I most certainly was not. I booty-bumped him backward to get some distance.

"Go drink your wine, weirdo." I continued slicing the pasta into fettuccine-sized noodles for the boiling water.

He kissed me on the cheek before taking up his post next to me, wine glass in hand.

Why was he acting affectionate all of a sudden?

"You guys have done a fabulous job," said Christina, the guest chef from a Lafayette restaurant who'd been hired for Italian Night. "Let's thank Mr. Broussard for putting this together."

I snapped my head to the chef. Sure enough, Bennett was standing right next to her, his gaze intensely focused on me. He was *not* smiling.

"Shit," I whispered, dropping the spoon to the counter. "Get our bowls," I told Finn as Bennett made his way to another couple, who he greeted warmly, no longer looking my way.

I quickly dropped the pasta into the boiling water and watched the time, glancing at Finn with bowls in hand and a wide, devilish grin.

Then it hit me.

"You asshat," I hissed, realizing what that display of affection was all about.

To get Bennett jealous. Which was ridiculous. Bennett didn't want to date me. Did he?

I fished the pasta out after two and a half minutes, dividing it into our bowls.

"Hi, Betty."

I jumped at Bennett's deep rumble right behind me. His voice was tight. Formal.

I spun around. "Hey. What are you doing here?"

Wow. Stupidest question ever. *He owns the store, dummy.*

His gaze darted to Finn, those lovely jaw muscles clenching. "Are you going to introduce me?"

Finn threw an arm around my shoulder and reached a hand out with the other to Bennett. "Finley Fontenot."

While Bennett politely shook his hand, his eyes had frosted with anger. No. It was *jealousy*, definitely jealousy. While that thought made me want to preen like a peacock and wiggle my feathery tail, I also had the urgent need to clarify this situation right here and now. Before Finn went too far. He totally could and would, just to get a reaction out of the guy I kept insisting I wasn't interested in every day at lunch.

"Finn is my best friend," I explained. "We work together."

Finn hugged me against his side, chuckling to himself. "Yeah. Had to take my girl out, or she'd spend another Friday night at home."

Oh, no. He was about to escalate this.

Then Finn smiled down at me adoringly. Like a lover.

Mouth dropping open, I shoved his arm off my shoulder and leaned closer to Bennett. "He's gay. He's very, *very* gay."

"What's the difference between gay and very gay?" asked Finn curiously.

"You're an idiot," I hissed.

"I'm the idiot? This from the girl I've had to strip down and put to bed every time she thinks she can drink Vodka."

"Shut *up*, Finley," I grit out.

"She's a slow learner," he whispered conspiratorially to Bennett. "But a cheap drunk. A definite keeper."

I elbowed him farther away while Bennett tried to hide his laugh, a wave of relief sweeping his expression.

"Seriously,"—I nodded my head toward Finn—"he's just messing around."

Bennett smiled, that mischievous one that made me think of gasping moans and sweaty sheets.

While I'd denied that I wanted to date the man for some time, I was well aware that if we did, he'd set my body on fire in the bedroom. The look he was giving me now had already sent a hot-flash licking down my body.

As if he knew what I was thinking, his gaze wandered to my mouth and down my neck, then back to my mouth. Suddenly, I couldn't give a shit about the Bolognese pasta. He hitched in a breath, his heated hazel eyes finally finding mine.

"Enjoy your dinner with your friend." His words were polite but also some kind of warning. Like Finn better only be my friend.

Scatterbrained once again by this man, I rejoined Finn, who was grinning like the cat who got the cream.

"Don't say a word."

"Not even a teeny tiny one," he assured me, still smiling as he dove into the bowl of pasta.

After a painfully long meal—nine minutes—with the other couples, I excused Finn and I. Finn didn't seem to mind, knowing full well my concentration had been on the door leading into the store the entire meal.

"Someone's in a hurry."

"It's been a long day," I bit back.

"Mmhmm."

Not caring what Finn thought, I hustled out to the store as he trailed me, not even pretending that I wasn't hunting down Bennett. I found him standing at customer service, talking to someone behind the counter. He immediately looked up when we approached the exit.

"I'll wait for you by the car," said Finn, carrying our leftovers out with him.

My gaze slid to the woman behind the counter. "Ms. Theriot?"

It was Trace's mother. I stared, confused.

"Hi, there, Ms. Mouton." She beamed and waved as I approached. "It's so good to see you."

"Uh, you too. When did you start working here?" I glanced at Bennett, whose expression was unreadable.

"Just this week, actually." She smiled, glancing at Bennett. "I met Mr. Broussard when he came into the bank, and he happened to mention in passing that he was looking for a bookkeeper. And since I have experience from working the accounts at the café Drunk Pelican, he offered me a job." A burst of laughter left her chest. "Can you believe the coincidence?"

"Wow, I sure can't." I smiled back, glancing at Bennett, knowing this wasn't a coincidence. At all. "Well, it was good to see you."

I turned for the door, Bennett beside me.

"Bye, now. Goodnight, Mr. Broussard," she called before returning to the computer.

"Goodnight, Mary."

Bennett stepped up beside me, and we walked out like this was an everyday occurrence. Of course, it was the second time he'd walked me to my car from his store. Well, this time, Finn's car.

"You gave her a job without knowing if she was qualified?"

"I gave her a job because she needed one and had some experience, and I needed a bookkeeper. If she doesn't work out, I can always find another."

I stared at this man who'd caught me off guard again. Doing

something extremely kind for someone who needed it. He'd done it out of kindness. My heart clenched at the truth of it. There were hidden layers to this man. Kind, compassionate ones that I'd ignored, holding on tight to my prejudice toward him.

"You won't find another," I predicted aloud. "And I'll bet she has a salaried wage complete with benefits so that she could quit her other jobs."

"I need a full-time bookkeeper, so yes, of course." His demeanor was formal and guarded, very different than his normal charming self.

He most certainly was not the stuck-up rich boy I'd judged him as back when I didn't know him. It shamed me now. "You're a good man, Broussard."

He didn't reply to that, but I saw a flicker of emotion I couldn't identify cross his face. Then he stopped halfway through the parking lot. "Are we still on for tomorrow night?"

"Of course," I replied instantly. "You thought I'd back out or something?"

Those hazel eyes—intelligent, knowing, watchful—held me captive. His expression was completely unreadable.

All the same, we stood there, staring at each other, the magnetic tension ratcheting higher. I'd thought if I spent more time with Bennett that my attraction for him would lessen. Make it wear off. But it had the opposite effect. The more time I spent with him, the more I wanted and craved him.

He gave me a stiff nod, his hands tucked in his pockets. "Guess I'll see you tomorrow night then."

"Yep. Six o'clock."

Another tight nod as he clenched his jaw. Then he turned quickly, hands still in pockets, and strode back toward the store.

"Goodnight," I said, enjoying the view of watching him go.

Heading to the car in a daze, I ignored Finn's ridiculous grin and wondered how much longer I could keep my hands off Bennett Broussard. First, I needed to get brave enough to ask if he wanted to move beyond frenemies. Tomorrow night.

Chapter Eleven

~BETTY~

WINDING PAST THE PARK WHERE TOWERING LIVE OAK TREES shaded the walking paths, I turned right onto Myrtle Oak. Signs dotted a few lawns, advertising the upcoming Gumbo Cookoff, where local businesses competed for the title of *Best Gumbo* in town. My mouth watered at the thought, and I hoped it would be cool for this year's event. Our weather was a moody bitch, constantly changing on a whim this time of year. October in Louisiana could either be pleasantly fall-like or still hot as hell.

Emma's car was in the driveway when I pulled up at Mom's house, the little home I'd been born and raised in.

"Dammit," I mumbled as I parked and headed inside.

I was hoping she'd be gallivanting around Lafayette so I could raid her closet in secrecy. And peace.

Now she'd hound me to death to find out why I wanted to dress up.

It served me right. Every time I needed to look better than

business casual, I shopped in Emma's closet rather than an actual department store.

I was just one of those people who hated shopping. For one, I hated spending money on what I considered frivolous things like clothes. And two, shopping was so annoying. It was aggravating when I couldn't find exactly what I wanted in less than ten minutes. My sister happened to be one of those people who spent every free moment scouring the shops in Lafayette to find a *good deal,* as she would say.

Since we were the exact same size, why should I bother to do all the manual labor when I could just steal—I mean borrow—from my beloved sister?

"Hey, Mom." I dropped my purse on the table. "Mmm, what are you cooking?"

"Hey, sweetie. Shrimp Creole. Dan is coming over tonight."

"His favorite." I grinned as I gave her a hug and kiss on the cheek.

She was wearing her loose-fitting linen pants and hippie shirt, her long, gray-streaked-auburn hair twisted up on her head. I loved being around my mom. Her relaxed demeanor and radiant love gave me instant comfort and eased my mind and spinning brain, no matter how stressed I was.

Dan was her boyfriend of two years and was a supervisor for Tractor Supply Company. I liked him, but more importantly, he made my mom happy.

"I'm making plenty. I didn't know you were coming, but you're welcome to eat with us. Emma is going out, of course."

"This is just a drive-by, Mom. I need a dress."

"What for? Finn taking you to the Heymann or something?"

The Heymann Theater in Lafayette often had musical performances that Finn and I went to together.

"Uh, no." I leaned my hip against the counter. Though I'd rather not get my mother's hopes up since it had been an eon or so since I'd gone on a date, I wanted to tell her. Even though this wasn't an *actual* date. "Not Finn."

She stopped stirring. "Where are you going? And with whom?"

Unable to stifle the stupid smile from creasing my face, I told her. "Bennett Broussard."

Mom had come with me to BPAL's performance of *Chicago* last year and had drooled while watching Bennett onstage. So had I. After the show, she wouldn't shut up about how *magnetic* and *handsome* and *fantastic* he was.

"You're lying," she accused, blue-gray eyes round.

Laughing at her disbelief, I snapped back, "That hurts. What? You don't think I could get a date with a guy like him?"

She narrowed her eyes and pointed her wooden spoon at me. "You told me he was an arrogant, entitled asshat who you would ignore even if you were the only two people on a deserted island together. I remember because you made such a big deal about how he was not your type, and you'd never go out with a guy like him in a million years."

"Go out with who?"

Emma stood in the doorway, wearing Mountain Dew yoga pants and a matching green tank top. My sister was loud and wild and daring in every way. Even though I was the oldest, I always felt that I was the watered-down version of her.

Not in a bad way, just that she was a five-alarm fire waiting to happen. I was more like a simmering four. Granted, I'd been much like her back in college. But growing up had mellowed me just a tad. I didn't pull all-nighters doing tequila body shots off strangers and waking up with the hot bartender in my bed anymore.

"You're going running in that?" I tried to deflect, knowing it was useless.

Emma ran like a hundred miles a day. It was disgusting. I

had to promise myself a high-carb meal afterward to get myself to the gym.

"Don't even try to change the subject. What guy?" she demanded while twisting her strawberry blond hair into a ponytail.

"Bennett Broussard," Mom said with an overdose of saccharine sweetness.

"You're dating *him*!"

"Would you stop yelling?" I strode past her, heading to her closet. "We're doing the play together. We're going on a business date. Or theater date. Or whatever."

I'd told my mom and Emma that I'd gotten the lead the night I heard the news, but I'd failed to mention who my leading male partner would be.

Emma was hot on my ass back to her bedroom. "Didn't you say he was an *overprivileged tool* once upon a time? The guy who maliciously glitter booby bombed you?"

"It wasn't malicious." I winced. "I might've been hasty in my judgment," I said as I stepped into her walk-in closet and flipped through her rack of dresses.

"Shocker."

"Ouch."

Another reason I loved shopping in Emma's closet was everything was nicely organized, so I could quickly find what I needed. While our lack of funds for frills growing up had made me a miser and penny-pincher, Emma had gone in the opposite direction, enjoying spending every available dime on little luxuries.

She leaned against the door jamb. "So if this isn't a real date, why are you looking for dresses in my closet?"

"Well, we're going to dinner first, and I don't want to look like a slob."

I skimmed past her more daring, strappy dresses in blood-red and animal print to the simple black ones. And by simple, I mean they were a solid color. I liked wearing black because it was a striking contrast against my fair skin and bright hair.

"Betty. If *you* are actually putting on a dress, this isn't a fake date."

Speaking of fake, my brain hazed a moment, remembering that kiss he laid on me at rehearsal. Could you call something like that just a kiss? It felt more like a glorious invasion. A catalyst for something far bigger than I was prepared for.

The thing was, it wasn't a fake kiss. Not at all. He'd let me have a small taste of the blazing wildfire burning between us. I was ready for him when his mouth melded to mine, but I just hadn't realized he was going to realign my thoughts about what kissing was.

I'd kissed lots of guys over the years, and it was always a favorite part of the pre/post-sex regimen. But what Bennett did with his mouth and his hands gave me great cause for alarm. I was playing with fire here and was completely willing to get burned to a cinder.

"Hellooo, Betty." She waved a hand in the air. "Come back to me."

Blinking away those thoughts, I lifted three black dresses off the hanger and bypassed her to toss them onto the bed.

"Okay, here's the deal, Em. At first, I really hated him. He's cocky."

"But you knew that."

"Yeah, and that hasn't really gone away. It's just that… there's more to him than I'd realized."

"Like what?"

I stripped out of my jeans. "I was overly harsh, thinking he was just a rich boy with everything handed to him. He's a really hard worker." I sighed as I pulled off my t-shirt. "Harder than me. He goes back to the store after rehearsals and works heaven knows how many hours."

"Doesn't sound like a spoiled rich boy to me."

"No," I admitted softly as I shimmied into one of the dresses. "And he's really kind. He gave my student's mom a job after I mentioned she needed something more stable with a better salary and benefits."

"Awesome. So Bennett's a nice guy with a good work ethic. He's not an arrogant asshole. On top of that, he's *super* hot."

I laughed as I zipped up the dress. "He so is. I'm insanely attracted to him. Still…"

"Still what?"

"I think he really likes me. And for some reason, that makes me really nervous. Like push-him-away nervous, and we aren't even dating."

I stared at my reflection. The dress had long sleeves and a deep-vee bodice that hit my sternum. I had small breasts anyway, smaller than Emma's, so I was always able to wear tighter, more revealing dresses without worrying about whether my boobs were going to fall out. I fiddled with the neckline, frowning at what I couldn't put into words.

Em stepped up behind me, holding my gaze in the mirror. "I know why you're nervous," she said softly.

"Good. Then please tell me." I dropped my arms to my sides in exasperation.

She cupped my upper arms and set her chin on my shoulder. "Because you really like him, too."

I scoffed. "So what. I've liked tons of guys."

She shook her head. "You've liked party guys and fun, fuckboys. You want to push Bennett away because you could have something real with him."

"That makes no sense at all."

"You've never had a boyfriend, Bea. Not a real one."

"Because I just wanted to have a good time in college. I didn't want to settle down or get serious then."

"No." She lifted her chin off my shoulder, still looking at me in the mirror. "You've never wanted to get serious because you don't trust men. You never have. You don't want to love someone who might let you down. Or disappear." She squeezed my arms and let them go. "Like Dad."

I flinched at the piercing pain of her words. Not because they were meant to hurt, but because they were real and true. I swallowed hard past the lump in my throat.

"We're not even dating, Em. We're just—"

Wildly lusting for and falling deeper into like with each other every time we're together. That stage kiss told me how he felt well enough.

"You want my advice?" she asked, brows raised.

"Yes."

"Go for it. Make tonight a real date." She stepped to the side of the mirror to get a better look at me. "And wear this dress."

Blowing a heavy breath and shaking out my nerves, I looked at myself in the mirror. "Too much?"

"Not if you want him to swallow his tongue when he first sees you." She smiled. "Wear your hair down. Put a little effort into it. Curl it in waves like I taught you with the flat iron."

I slouched with a heavy sigh, glaring at her.

"And don't fucking slouch like that. Shoulders back. Tits up."

She was back to teasing me, which helped me shake off the tension from the tough love she handed to me a minute before.

"I hate curling my hair," I muttered. What could I say? I was low-maintenance and lazy as fuck.

"Come on, Bea," she said affectionately, using my childhood nickname. "Just think of Bennett's face when you open the door for this—" she used air quotes— "theater business date."

I stared back at my reflection, taking in her words. Emma knew me better than anyone on the planet. She was right. She knew that only someone I deemed very worthy could jolt me out of my laziness and force me to put in the extra effort. To even agree to a date.

"Yeah," I replied, unable to prevent the smile that thinking of Bennett always conjured. "Now, what shoes have you got?"

~

HELL, YES. THE HOUR-AND-A-HALF PREP TIME TO WASH, SHAVE, primp, and pretty myself was worth every damn second.

Bennett stood on my doorstep utterly speechless. It was a beautiful thing. The man with an easy smile and charming words for everyone seemed to have been struck by lightning.

"Fuck," he muttered, shaking his head as his eyes roamed everywhere. "You look"—he cleared his throat nervously —"amazing."

"You look nice yourself."

And by nice, I meant GQ model, hotter-than-a-fucking-fireman, lick-a-licious. In black slacks and a tailored, gray button-down that fit him to perfection, highlighting his broad chest and tight ass, this man was *fine.*

"You ready?" he asked, still gawking, his eyes roaming all over me.

"Yep." I shut the door and enjoyed the way he escorted me to his vehicle with a light hand on my back. After opening my door, he climbed in and veered his truck toward the highway.

He didn't say anything, but I could feel him glancing at me. A lot.

"What?" I smirked. But I knew what. And my ego did a pirouette at the attention.

"You're so fucking beautiful," he murmured in that low voice that sent a tingle spiraling down my body.

Whoa. Swallowing hard against the sensation of being thrown off-track at that unexpected compliment, I resorted to my usual defense mode by switching subjects quickly.

"I have to say I'm surprised you're a truck guy."

Mind you, it was a nice truck. New and maxed out with all

the bells and whistles. The dashboard looked akin to a NASA console.

"Why's that?" he asked.

"I don't know. I expected you to drive a beamer or an Audi or something."

He laughed, taking the entrance ramp from Broken Arrow Highway that headed out of Beauville toward Lafayette.

"You make a lot of assumptions about me."

"Don't take it personally. I make assumptions about everybody. It's my fatal flaw."

His mouth quirked in the most adorable way. "I like that about you."

"That I'm a judgy bitch?"

"That you're honest and direct about what you think."

"And you're not?"

He tapped his forefinger on the top of the steering wheel where his hand rested. The other was on his thigh. My thoughts wandered to what those big, masculine hands would feel like on my skin.

"Not all the time," he admitted.

"Why not?" I asked.

It had always been easy for me to be upfront with people. My laissez-faire attitude stemmed from the fact that I gave two shits if people liked me. I'd always believed that if someone didn't, they weren't meant to be in my circle of friends.

Granted, my circle was small. But that was also perfectly fine with me. The friends I had were loyal and true, and I was the same. I'd burn the world down to help or protect those I loved. That was the only kind of friendship I wanted.

Bennett was contemplating my question for far too long.

"Bennett?"

"I was trying to figure out the answer to your question. To be honest, I don't know why. I've just always wanted people's approval. So if I had negative thoughts, I'd keep them to myself."

My chest squeezed at how open he was being with me.

"I get that. Even though you're arrogant sometimes, you're a nice guy deep down. Admit it."

His gaze slid to me again, trailing down my body. Slowly.

Oh, my. That was not a nice-guy look. That was an intensely naughty one.

"I think you confuse arrogance with confidence."

"You think so?"

"I know so. Arrogance implies I have an exaggerated belief in my own abilities. Confidence means I know what I'm doing. Trust me." His hand slid along the steering wheel, then tightened as he made a turn. His gaze left the road, flicking to me again with a flash of heat. "When I put my mind to something, I know what I'm doing."

A flush of heat swept up my chest and neck. The air in the cab felt suddenly thick and oppressive, my nipples coming to full attention at his growly declaration. My gaze strayed to his big hands tightening on the steering wheel once again, my thoughts wandering to what he could do with those hands.

"So, where are we going?" I noticed the thickness of my voice, like even my vocal cords decided to sex it up to join in the mood of the rest of me.

"Dinner first. Ever been to Ruffino's?"

I almost laughed, but I refrained. "No. Sure haven't."

Ruffino's wasn't crazy expensive, but it was a step or four up from The Outback, which was more my norm for a night out.

I was a teacher. In Louisiana. Enough said.

Unless there was a very special occasion, I didn't go to restaurants like that. And I hadn't been back home long enough to find such an occasion. But if Bennett wanted to spend some of his money—hard-earned, not handed-down now that I knew him better—I was completely okay with that.

"I thought since you liked Italian, you'd like this place."

"Something you should know about me, Broussard. I love all food. Especially the expensive kind cooked by fancy chefs."

He glanced at my body again. "Where does it all go?"

"My ass," I promptly replied.

Even though he couldn't see said ass, he glanced at my lap and then focused back on the road. "Don't remind me," he muttered, a flush of pink cresting his cheekbones as he shifted in his seat, unable to disguise the big bulge in those nicely tailored pants.

I *really* liked this new game. Tempting Bennett Broussard. Now that I'd decided I wanted more than fake kisses, I was ready to *go for it* as Em suggested. I just had to find the right moment to tell him. This was going to be an interesting night.

Chapter Twelve

~BENNETT~

I COULDN'T DECIDE IF I WAS FUCKING ECSTATIC OR TERRIFIED AT how hot Betty looked tonight.

No woman had ever made me *want* them like Betty did. Want to be with her, talk with her, or remove her dress…with my teeth, then fuck her senseless.

But this wasn't a real date, so I reined it in as we were seated at our table near the window overlooking the Vermilion River that wound behind the restaurant. Still, the fact that she'd put some obvious extra effort into her appearance for me was encouraging.

After ordering a bottle of red wine, a Pinot Noir since I noticed she liked that at Italian Night, we both settled in to look over the menu. Of course, I was literally looking *over* the menu to stare at her.

Fucking hell, she was gorgeous.

All that silky fair skin, her shiny red hair waving gently over her shoulders and breasts. There was no way she was wearing a bra in that dress, which wasn't what I should be wondering right now. Because my cock was painfully hard enough.

And that dress. It's not that she wore baggy clothes or hid her figure, but the way that material hugged her just right had me literally salivating. The deep vee pointed to all the places I wanted to taste.

I couldn't drag my eyes away from her.

"I would ask what's good here, but everything looks delicious."

"Sure does." My quick reply came out a low rumble.

Her eyes came up. Dark sapphire. My heart pumped harder. Every nerve came alive at a flicker of her attention. I couldn't even imagine what it would be like to be inside this woman. The only one who ever made me lose my cool, kept me awake at night, haunted every waking step of every single day.

One reddish-brown eyebrow arched haughtily. "You need to actually look at the menu to order your meal, Broussard."

"I'd rather look at you." It came out automatically. I couldn't help it.

I usually behaved more conservatively and more gentlemanly with women. Or even held a little of my interest back, just in case it wasn't reciprocated. I preferred not to come on too strong. But Betty cracked me wide open and made me want to tell her everything. To be her everything.

Her response was a sultry smile.

Very encouraging.

"Here we are," said the waiter, delivering the wine glasses and pouring each of us a glass. "Would you like a few more minutes? Or can I get you an appetizer?"

"Do you like oysters?" I asked her.

She nodded.

"We'll have the oven-roasted oysters," I told the waiter,

never letting my eyes leave her. "And a few more minutes on the main course."

He disappeared, saying something I didn't hear. It didn't matter. Nothing could take my attention away at this moment. We sipped our wine, both of us suddenly quiet. I knew why I'd gone silent.

Because I wanted to tell her how I felt, that I wanted this to be more than a getting-to-know-you date for stage chemistry. But I was terrified she'd reject me. Then it would get really awkward at rehearsal.

She'd blown off our stage kiss like it was nothing, but I'd come to terms with it, realizing I needed to keep this professional. Then she'd opened the door in this wicked, soul-damning dress and turned my world upside down. I couldn't even think straight.

"Tell me something about your childhood," she said, breaking into my downward spiral. "A memory you remember fondly."

Clearing my throat, I tapped a finger on the stem of my wineglass. "Anything in particular?"

"Nope. Anything at all you'd want to share."

My thoughts wandered to my brother. "Growing up, it was just me and my brother, Hale. Dad worked a lot. Still does." I tried not to sound bitter on the last part. "Hale's only two years younger than me, so we were close."

"I remember he was a couple years ahead of me in high school, but I didn't know him." She smiled. "What's he like?"

"The exact opposite of me."

"So, he's hideously ugly and a lazy ass?"

"No." I laughed, heat flaming my neck as I realized she was complimenting me. "He's more laid back. A lot more."

"Interesting. What does he do?"

"He owns a local construction company."

Her brow rose. "Residential houses?"

"That's right."

"Let me guess. His company is Hale Building, Inc."

"It is."

"Yeah, I actually looked at houses in a neighborhood near the park where there was some new construction. I saw the sign on a few lots."

Nodding, I added, "He buys the lots and builds, then sells the homes, rather than custom-builds for landowners."

"Why?" she asked, genuinely confused.

"If you knew my brother, you'd understand. He hates dealing with people and all their demands and hovering. He'd rather invest and build and hope he can sell quickly rather than deal with the headache of homeowners." I poured her another glass since she'd emptied hers. "It's risky. I could never do it. But that's Hale. He was always taking risks. I think he enjoys the thrill of it."

She took her refilled glass and swirled it in one hand, focusing intently on me. "So tell me about the childhood memory."

I tapped the wine glass again. "Christmases were always fun growing up. Mom always banned Dad from working. He couldn't even check his email the week of Christmas Eve and Day. Some kind of bargain she made with him."

"I like your mom already." She smiled.

"She'd like you, too."

The thought of her meeting my mom spread warmth in my chest. The fact that I knew they'd get along so well and that I definitely wanted them to meet sent my pulse racing. Not for the first or second time tonight.

Her smile wobbled, pink flushing her cheeks.

"But there was one Christmas when I was thirteen, Hale was eleven, that it snowed. Do you remember that?"

It only snowed this far south once a decade and never stuck to the ground very long, so it was a big deal when it happened.

Blue eyes widened. "Yes! I was eight at the time."

"At our house, it had frozen over the edges of the bayou in the shallows. We had a little dog back then. A terrier named Joey. We got the bright idea to take him skating on the ice that had built up along the icy edge."

She laughed. "Oh, no."

"You can see where this is going." Leaning back in the chair, remembering that day fondly, I said, "We fashioned a small cardboard box onto a swimming pool float with a little strap to hold him in there. It was ridiculous looking. But we were proud of our invention."

"Masterminds at work," she said with a wink.

"Exactly." I chuckled. "We took Joey down to the bayou, and he was happy as could be to play our game. Let us put him in the box, buckle his collar to the strap. Then Hale went a few yards down on the ice and I slid Joey to him. It worked. Hale caught him, no problem. It was awesome," I laughed as I drank down the rest of my wine. "Joey barked as we laughed about it. Then we got overconfident. I kept stepping farther and farther back. We wanted to see how long we could make him slide. It became a competition."

"Just like boys. Always comes back to competition. And idiocy."

"Pretty much," I agreed. "It was Hale's turn to shove off. He took a few steps back and the ice broke."

"I knew it."

"At first, I laughed, but then I realized it was a lot deeper there than I thought. Fortunately, Joey had jumped out of the box, his collar still attached to it, which was now sinking. But Hale started thrashing around, and I panicked. I ran to him and leaped into the bayou. The water was fucking freezing."

Betty's expression was one of sheer anguish as if she were witnessing the event firsthand.

"The water was up to my chin, and Hale was almost a foot

shorter at the time. The cold was turning my limbs numb within seconds. I could barely move my arms and legs. I managed to grab hold of Hale around the waist and haul him above water. Still, the thought of his wide eyes looking up at me makes me panic. Then I managed to grab the box and toss it onto the bank at the same time. Otherwise, it might've pulled Joey into the water as well."

"Oh, my God. How is this a good memory? You could've died, the both of you!"

I'd known it then, too. At thirteen, I'd come face to face with my own mortality. It had scared the hell out of me.

"Be patient," I told her. "So Joey was yapping like crazy, which had our mother racing into the yard. She saw us down by the bayou just as I was dragging Hale onto the bank. He was conscious, but his lips were already turning blue. And he couldn't say a thing."

I swallowed hard against the remembered fear I'd felt that day.

"My Aunt Mary was there, my mom's sister, and they helped us both back up to the house. Then into a warm shower. Of course, I didn't want my mom or aunt to see me naked, so I let them help till I got to my underwear. I mean, I *was* thirteen."

Betty laughed, her eyes softening as I continued on, telling her how once Hale and I were warmed up and dry, they had a steaming bowl of gumbo ready for us and hot cocoa afterward.

She shook her head. "How in the world is this a good memory?"

I drank the last sip of my wine. "Because Mom and Aunt Mary doted on us like kings. And even better, they didn't tell my dad, which would've landed us in a hell of a lot of trouble. He was fortunately out picking up a brisket from my grandfather's store." I held her gaze as I told her the real reason. "Most importantly, it proved to me in the few split seconds when

Hale's head went under how important he was to me. How important my family was to me. It solidified in my heart and head at a very young age that the people you love are the most important thing in your life. Not money, not ambition, not anything else."

Betty's expression warmed and softened even further. I wasn't saying these things to impress her. I was telling her because it was something about me that I felt deeply. And I wanted her to know me.

"Now you," I told her. "Give me a happy childhood memory."

She sputtered out a laugh. "Well, mine won't be as grand or have the long-lasting effects of a lesson learned. Let's see." She looked up, trying to recall something. "Okay, your story reminded me of one of my favorites at the same time of year. My sister Emma and I always wondered why people didn't go Christmas caroling anymore. We would see it in older movies, how people would just adore listening to the carols and give them treats and so on. So we decided to go caroling around our neighborhood."

"Can you sing?" I asked, wondering why she never auditioned for musicals.

"Not at all. I'm terrible. The reason I only do straight plays at BPAL." She heaved a sigh. Straight plays were non-musicals. "Anyway, Emma and I set off with some lyrics of Christmas songs. The first door we knocked on, they never opened. We went to another neighbor who opened the door and nearly jumped out of his skin when we launched into a very loud and awful rendition of 'Joy to the World.'"

I couldn't help but laugh, imagining these two young girls singing their hearts out. Very badly.

"That neighbor was Mr. Viator, and he was ornery to begin with. He listened to us sing one song then waved us away without a word and closed the door."

"But you two didn't give up."

"Um, not on your life. You have no idea the tenacity of the Mouton sisters."

"I can imagine."

She arched a brow at me but kept going. "Then we went to another neighbor, and they actually listened to us sing three songs. Then gave us each a candy cane. You'd have thought we won the lottery. Emma and I were ecstatic. Our plan to sing and bring cheer to the hearts of our neighbors while being paid in sweets was working."

I smiled, watching her face light up at the memory. Her laugh tumbled out as she told how they sang to every house on the block and had racked up two candy canes, a handful of Hershey's kisses, and five dollars.

"Plus," she added, "we brought Christmas joy to the whole neighborhood."

"I'll bet you did."

Her smile dimmed to something sweet rather than merry.

"To be honest, the look on Mrs. Peterson's face always comes back to me. She was a widow who lived with an old, blind toy poodle and six cats on the corner. She listened to every single one of our songs. All *seven*. And she just looked so happy the whole time."

I could imagine the elderly widow with two cute little girls on her porch, singing carols and giving her a little bright spot in her lonely world.

"She was the one who gave us the five dollars," added Betty. "I was glad we went caroling because Mrs. Peterson passed away before the next Christmas."

A sweep of melancholy clouded her features.

I reached over and lifted her fingertips in my hand, brushing my thumb over her soft knuckles. "I'll bet you brought Mrs. Peterson more happiness than you realized. I'll bet she smiled every time she thought of you two that last year."

She nodded, her gaze down at our hands. Realizing I probably overstepped, I let go of her hand.

"So, what about your dad? I never hear you mention him."

Her smile faltered, then fell away altogether.

"Oh, shit. I'm sorry. If it's a bad topic—"

"No, don't worry. My father was," she looked up again, trying to find the right word. "Absent," she finally added.

"I'm sorry, Betty."

Meanwhile, I was flagellating myself in my head for asking such a stupid fucking question. She didn't talk about her father for a reason. The conversation was so easy; I just asked without thinking.

"Seriously," she laughed a little uneasily. "There's not much to tell, really. He divorced my mom, left when I was ten, remarried some woman in Texas, and never looked back."

"What an asshole."

"Truly," she agreed with a softer smile.

I would've felt like a total loser for the fact she was comforting me while she was the one who'd lost an asshole of a father, but all I could feel was sheer relief. She didn't seem upset. Just surprised when I brought up the topic.

"It hurt a long time ago, Bennett," she said softly, "but I'm over it now. I mean, it was his loss for not knowing such an amazing daughter."

"You got that damn right," I said with more force than I'd intended.

Her smile widened. "And though he was little more than a sperm donor, Mom said he did give me one thing."

"What's that?"

"Good teeth."

"Come again?"

"I have *amazing* teeth, Broussard. Never needed braces or had a cavity in my life. Comes from my Dad's side, apparently. My sister Emma got my mom's side. Deep grooves and all. No matter how much she flossed, she always had a new cavity at check-ups." She laughed, then sipped her wine. "Used to drive her crazy."

Marveling at her unswerving spirit, I lifted my wine. "A toast then. To good teeth."

"To excellent chompers." She held my gaze over the rim of her glass, my heart squeezing at the softness there.

The waiter then stepped up to our table and set our appetizer down. I sat back.

We ordered our entrees. I recommended the filet mignon with asparagus, béarnaise sauce, and jumbo lump crabmeat. She took my recommendation, then we fell into a discussion of other memories. Lighter ones without any darker depths.

Still, I couldn't help but marvel at how Betty put on the toughest front. No, that wasn't right. It was never a front with her. She *was* tough. She was direct and forthright to the point of rudeness at times. And yet, beneath that prickly exterior was this sweet woman who once went caroling with her little sister to bring the neighbors hope and a smile. Who still remembered the dear old lady years later who gave her five dollars for being the bright spot in her otherwise lonely life.

I wanted this woman so goddamn bad.

I had to leash my desires, not let her see how much she affected me. Too afraid she was the kind of woman who might be skittish if I showed how much I wanted her. So I played the relaxed charmer.

Meanwhile, I was dying inside, desperate to hold her, kiss her. Lay her on my bed or on the ground or any flat surface I could find, then strip her bare and prove how I felt.

After dinner, as I led her out of the restaurant, she asked, "What time does the movie start?"

"We've got about thirty minutes."

Her eyes glittered like a midnight sky as she stopped in front of the passenger door of my truck. "Aren't you going to open my door for me, Broussard?" she teased, her gaze on my mouth.

Jarred for a minute, because Betty was giving me all the vibes that this was a real date, I stared down at her, frowning.

"Something wrong?" she asked like she had a secret.

Shaking my head, I opened her door, wondering if I only imagined it because I wanted her so bad.

"Get on in, Ms. Mouton."

As I rounded the truck to the driver's side, I made the decision that I was going for it. Whether Betty was ready or not, I was coming for her.

Chapter Thirteen

~BETTY~

THE GOLDEN OLDIES PLAYED OLD MOVIES, MOSTLY BLACK AND whites, like *Arsenic and Old Lace* or *The Philadelphia Story*. But occasionally, they played movies from the sixties, seventies, and eighties. I grinned when I looked up at the marquee that read *Barefoot in the Park—starring Robert Redford and Jane Fonda.*

"So awesome," I said, standing in front of the theater, Bennett beside me.

"Come on," he chuckled, ushering me toward the entrance with a hand at my back, his fingers coasting softly. I couldn't help but lean in closer to him, relishing his amazing scent.

His honey-brown eyes flashed fiercely at me before he purchased our tickets at the fifties-style ticket booth with room enough for one person inside.

I was still working up the nerve to tell him how I felt. I wasn't shy, but I was nervous that maybe I was misreading all the signals. Then his hot gaze dropped down my body again, and I knew I wasn't. Still, I wasn't sure how to say it.

Hey, I know I've been kind of a bitch to you, but I've decided I like you and your pretty face. Also, let's have sex.

Nope. I needed something more subtle and less desperate.

When we walked into the lobby, I marveled at the art deco. "This is so cool. I've never been here since they renovated."

"No? You've been missing out. They've got reclining chairs and even sell adult beverages now." He pointed to the snack bar that listed the regular movie snacks but also included beer and wine.

"Okay, now that's amazing." I looked up at him, hitching in a breath at the hungry look in his whiskey-gold eyes.

We held, simply staring. Then he stepped up to get us drinks and snacks.

I watched him, thinking of the story he'd told at dinner. I could easily imagine a rambunctious, daring adolescent, Bennett. I'll bet he was quite a devil to raise. But also, I loved hearing how the near-drowning of his brother had taught him early on that there were consequences to your actions. And he cared—very deeply—for his family.

It had opened my eyes to the man he truly was. One with depth and honor and loyalty. Not the man I thought I knew that first day at rehearsal.

His fierce loyalty to his family called to me most of all. Perhaps because I knew what the opposite felt like from my father. I could only imagine what it would be like to be on the receiving end of such devotion. The very thought set off a flock of flutters in my stomach. And fear.

I decided to ignore the fear for now.

"Let's sit in the back," I pointed to the back rows as we walked into the darkened theater. "I like to sit up high."

"Fine by me." He carried my glass of wine and a longneck beer for himself.

I opened my Milk Duds as we took our seats. I shook the

box, loving that rattling noise they made. I was weird that way. "You sure you don't want some?" I asked him.

"I'm good." He grinned, swigging his beer and handing over my wine.

I lifted the tray beside the seat and set my wine there. Two older ladies tottered in and sat down lower, closer to the screen.

"You know?" I said, popping a Milk Dud in my mouth. "My Mom and I used to watch *Barefoot in the Park* all the time growing up. It's one of our favorites."

He sipped his beer. "What is it you love so much about it?"

"The writing is perfect comedy. Neil Simon was a genius. Plus," I whispered, a little tipsy from all the wine tonight. I had that lovely, happy buzz fizzing through my body. "I might've had a serious crush on Robert Redford. And on Paul Bratter."

He turned his head, making me realize how close our faces were in these seats. The view of him up close made me feel even more intoxicated.

"How am I doing playing your childhood crush?" he asked in that low, intimate rumble.

"You're doing really, really good."

I was such a wordsmith after a few glasses of wine.

He licked his lips, gaze on my mouth. "I'm going to use my superior acting skills—"

"Cocky."

"Confident. And stop interrupting. As I was saying, I'm going to use my superior acting skills to make you fall hard for me, Mouton."

"So you can do what? Point and laugh, proving how awesome of an actor you are?"

"So I can prove how good we could be." Heated hazel eyes flicked from my mouth to my eyes. "Then I'll keep you."

My insides liquefied. My heart catapulted faster. Then the lights went out and the screen shined brightly as the reel started. I broke our hypnotic trance first, focusing on the screen and trying to calm my heart rate. He settled in his seat, calm and assured as always.

There were a few trailers for next month's features, *The Quiet Man* with John Wayne and *Breakfast at Tiffany's* with Audrey Hepburn.

When the intro music and credits started for *Barefoot,* Bennett draped his arm around me. Stiff at first, I managed to settle into his shoulder and watch Jane Fonda's rendition of Corie Bratter. She was excellent, even though I played her with a bit more edgy snark.

When Mr. Velasco picked up Corie on-screen to turn on the heater and Paul walked in, catching them in what looked like a compromising situation, I belted out a laugh and knocked the Milk Duds off my lap. They fell to the right of me.

"Oh, crap," I mumbled.

"Let me," said Bennett, leaning over and across my legs to reach for the box.

He paused when he was fully bent over my lap, his eyes snagging where my dress had ridden up to mid-thigh. I watched him, my attention no longer on the big screen.

He froze for a few seconds, then he was on his knees in front of me. Though there was more space in the aisles than in modern-day theaters, I was thinking how big and broad his shoulders were as he knelt before me, his fingers skating up the backs of my calves.

This *so* wasn't a fake business date.

I shivered. Then he lifted the glass of wine and set it farther away on his tabletop, turning to look in the direction of the two elderly ladies. They were laughing at the screen.

I wasn't. I was riveted to the man in front of me with ravenous hunger in his heated gaze. He folded the table down so that there was nothing between us.

Then those long fingers coasted up the front of my legs and thighs, so slowly, like he was waiting for me to push him away.

"Betty."

Mouth parted and breath coming faster, I managed to whisper, "Huh?"

"I want to kiss you."

Licking my lips, I nodded. "Okay."

He eased his body forward between my open knees, one hand sliding up my skirt. He bit my bottom lip and then slid his tongue along the hurt before he gently swept his mouth over mine. I made a sound of frustration, easing forward.

He smiled against my mouth, his thumb at my panty-line brushing lightly at the border as if seeking entrance.

"Betty," he rumbled again in that dominant tenor.

"Huh?" I repeated, wishing he'd kiss me properly.

"I want to kiss you—" he grazed the pad of his thumb over my damp panties down the center of my pussy—"right here."

His eyes were slits of fire as he watched me, waiting for my answer.

Swallowing my moan when he brushed his thumb again, a slow caress, I leaned back against the seat. "Okay."

A feral look hardened his expression as he pushed the hem of my dress all the way to my hips until he could see my red lace panties.

"Fuck," he muttered, closing his eyes, nostrils flaring. "Lift your hips up," he rumbled low, gaze back on mine, intense as he gave me a clear order.

I did, allowing him to shove my dress all the way up around my waist, completely exposing myself to him.

I wasn't sure if it was the wine or Bennett's commanding voice, but I was entirely intoxicated by the moment. By the man. Captivated in a trap of sensation.

He coasted his fingers along the line of my panties, up around my thighs, then back down. Nice and slow. Then he pushed my thighs wider, watching me for a reaction. For resistance? He wasn't going to get any. I was ready for whatever he had planned.

Apparently liking whatever expression he saw on my face, he hooked two fingers on both sides of my panties and pulled them down. It was a slow trek. He was in no hurry, petting me along the way, dragging his fingertips in the wake of the lace.

Once he slid them off and tucked them into his pants pocket, I let my knees fall wide. He chuffed out a grunt that seemed more animalistic, instinctual. Shaking his head, he licked his lips and scooped his hands under my ass to pull me forward.

Then he lifted my legs, his fingers under my knees, and propped them on the armrests of my chair, my body tilted at an angle, fully open to him. My palms were on the seat cushion, my nails digging in, waiting. The perfect angle for one thing.

He levered up on his knees, blocking out the movie screen. Not that I was watching. Then he slid his middle finger, palm facing my pussy, along my slit, finding me already wet and ready for attention.

His smile was nothing but savage, his expression so tight and ravenous I thought I'd combust from the sheer desire radiating off of him. His chest rose and fell more quickly as he watched his finger sliding and stroking.

"Bennett," I hissed in a whisper.

As if awoken from a trance, his gaze flicked to mine. Pure, fiery lust lit up his features while he continued stroking me. He leaned forward, bracing his other hand on one inner thigh, holding me in place. They were trembling a little.

His thumb swept a soft path over my fleshy inner thigh as he eased closer. "You know what I want?"

Goddamn. His voice was a dark rumble, vibrating in the air.

He stroked a finger along my sex, circling my clit before

returning to my entrance. "I want inside this sweet, tight pussy." He pressed inside me to the first knuckle. A teasing, shallow pump. Not nearly enough. "I want to bury my dick balls-deep inside you, Betty. See how long it takes for you to scream my name. I'm willing to fuck you as hard and as long as it takes."

Lord help me. Mr. Perfect had a filthy, fucking dirty mouth. My kryptonite.

To everyone else, he was the easy-going charmer. But that predatory, ruthless look skating from my face back down to my pussy was only for me.

Then he buried his head in my lap, and when he sucked my clit in between those pretty lips, I was totally, utterly lost. My head hit the armrest. I bit my bottom lip to keep from making a sound, burying one hand in his hair, fisting his thick locks.

He eased one of my thighs over his shoulder, giving me leverage to rock my hips. Then both his palms scooped under my ass and tilted me up so he could flick that talented tongue while watching me come undone...in a fucking movie theater.

Bennett Broussard was on his knees, palming my ass and licking my pussy like it was a juicy peach pie. And I was in pure heaven.

He fucked me with his tongue, then went back to nibbling and flicking my swollen clit. I bit back the heavy moans trying to crawl up my throat, which came out as stifled whimpers.

He grinned, loving that I was barely holding onto control. I let out a choked laugh right when the old ladies down front laughed at the screen. Mine was borne of complete, wonderful surprise.

Why had I resisted this for even one single minute?

His pussy-eating skills beat every guy who had his head between my thighs before him.

He slid a hand below his mouth, where he worked my

sensitive nub and pumped two fingers inside me. And that did it.

Squeezing my eyes closed, I clawed into his hair with both hands, holding him still while I rocked through my orgasm. I bit my lip so hard that I tasted a metallic drop of blood. He groaned a deep, satisfied rumble that vibrated against my clit, wrenching yet another orgasmic spasm around his fingers.

With his fingers still gently stroking inside me, he levered back onto his knees, leaned his broad chest against mine, and took my mouth in a sensuous kiss. He tasted of beer and Bennett and me. I whimpered into his mouth.

Wrapping my arms around his neck, I hauled him closer, relishing the afterglow endorphins of an orgasm I didn't have to provide myself. Besides, even my rabbit vibrator couldn't make me come that hard.

"I like the movies," I whispered against his mouth when he eased up.

His laughter shook his chest as he smiled against my mouth. "I like dessert in the movies."

"You sure do know how to woo a girl, Broussard."

"I aim to please, Ms. Mouton."

Before I could say anything else, my face cracking wide with the crazy smile I was wearing, he pulled my panties from his pocket and carefully slid them back on.

I shimmied my hips up so he could get them in place. When I went to push my hem back down, he shoved my arms out of the way and did it himself, seeming to enjoy redressing me as much as undressing me.

He picked up my Milk Duds and handed them over, then my wine, unfolding my tabletop from the side of the chair. Once satisfied I was completely comfortable as before, he sat back in his chair and exhaled a happy sigh, grinning as he swigged his beer and returned to watching the movie.

"Proud of yourself, aren't you?" I murmured, my eyes on the screen.

"Immensely."

"That was a devious move, Broussard."

"I didn't hear any complaints."

"Of course not. My vagina was too busy enjoying herself."

He barked out a laugh. "Very pleased to know that at least she's enjoying the date."

"This was supposed to be a business date."

"Something you should know about me." He turned to look at me, the light from the screen caressing his chiseled jaw and cheekbones, the other half in shadow. "I don't always play by the rules to get what I want."

Grinning, I focused back on the movie, popping a Milkdud into my mouth. "Cocky."

"Confident." Then he leaned sideways, his big shoulders pressing into mine as he asked, "Am I going to get a second date?"

There was no pretending now. Bennett was hotter than Hades, in all the ways. And I sure as hell wasn't about to stop now.

"Yeah. But I'm going to get you back for this."

"I hope so," he teased.

Laughing, I looped my arm through his, leaning my head on his shoulder while Corie Bratter did her "Shama, Shama" dance. I felt his lips coast over the crown of my head before he turned back to watch the movie.

A sensation I'd never felt warmed my belly. A tightening, sweet knot that kept a goofy smile on my face for the rest of the evening.

I'd hovered in the foyer when he dropped me off at the doorstep, watching him back out of the drive and touching my lips where he'd given me a slow, melting, but short kiss, then departed without asking to come in or even hinting that he wanted to.

I was both disappointed and relieved. We'd gotten to second or third or third and a half base; whatever the hell going down on me in a movie theater was on the baseball metaphor scale. And I didn't want to take it too fast, even if my body wanted to.

He seemed to be of the same mind, leaving me with a happy smile as he swaggered back to his truck.

I laughed as I closed and locked my front door at how worried I'd been, trying to figure out how to tell him that I liked him. Then he'd charmed the panties right off of me —literally.

"I guess he's aware now," I mumbled to myself, basking in my post-orgasmic bliss and the anticipation of date number two.

Chapter Fourteen

~BENNETT~

"WHY DON'T YOU PACE A LITTLE HARDER?" MOCKED MY BROTHER, stirring the giant pot of gumbo over the butane burner. They were set up underneath the Broussard Fresh Market tent, where Hale was using his crawfish boil pot, the only thing big enough to cook this massive amount of gumbo.

"Shut up, Hale."

I hadn't seen Betty since rehearsal on Thursday. I'd walked her to her car, where we'd made out in the parking lot for forty-five minutes like horny teenagers, then told her I'd meet her here at the Beauville Gumbo Cookoff on Saturday.

It was her idea for our second date when I told her I was busy Saturday manning our annual booth. I wasn't the actual cook for our tent. That was Hale's department. But we had a booth at the Gumbo Cookoff every year since its origin two decades earlier when my grandfather used to enter with his specialty meat shop.

When Pop had told me to take over the family tradition

with my own store as the sponsor rather than his shop, I nearly cried. It was like passing the torch. I'd tried to tell him no. That I could have my own tent right next to his.

"Nonsense," he'd said. "Who'd cook your gumbo then? You?"

It wasn't an insult. I wasn't the great cook of the family. Hale was. And my mother. Mom retired from being the Gumbo Cookoff chef when Hale was old enough to take over.

And as harsh as Pop was when he'd told me to stop being obstinate and arguing with him, he meant it with love. I could see the proud glint in his wrinkled eyes that he wanted this for me. Wanted the store to be a success, too. Being a sponsor at this event was fantastic advertising with the community. People from all over, including the surrounding towns of Acadiana, ventured to Beauville for the Gumbo Cookoff.

"You just worry about your gumbo," I told Hale behind me. "I don't want my first cookoff event to be a disaster because my brother's gumbo sucked."

I knew damn well it wouldn't. But I wanted Hale off my back and to get him talking about something else besides the obvious nerves wracking my body.

Betty had texted this morning to tell me her mom and her mom's boyfriend would be here today at the Tractor Supply booth, so I was officially meeting the parents. Or parent. I clenched my teeth, thinking about her asshole of a father. Who could abandon their own daughters? It boggled my mind.

I imagined little Betty with her bright eyes and brighter hair, how precious she must've been. I rubbed my chest, a tenderness aching beneath my rib cage. Especially when my thoughts wandered to a daughter she might have one day who would look just like her with a spray of freckles across her nose.

Then my thoughts jumped to whether or not her mom would like me. What if she didn't? And what if I was taking this too seriously too fast? What if Betty was just along for a bit of fun, and I was headed for major, gutting heartbreak?

Blowing out a breath, I tried to slow my mind down before I had a full-on panic attack but hell, I couldn't. This woman had me thinking about white dresses and churches.

These straying thoughts weren't exactly healthy because we'd been on one goddamn date. One that wasn't even supposed to be a real date.

Was I alone in these intense feelings?

At least my parents wouldn't be here today. They were on one of their weekend excursions to New Orleans. It wasn't Mom I was worried about. Just my father. He'd ruin my day by talking business, interrogating me about my new store, and putting me in a piss-poor mood. I didn't want Betty to see that side of me yet. I didn't want to scare her off before I'd even gotten her.

"Hey. You okay?"

I glanced back at Hale. "Fine, why?"

He chuckled and went back to stirring the pot. "I've never seen you this worked up over a girl."

My parents and Pop would also be around sometime today, so chances were I'd be introducing her to them, too. Plenty of girls I'd dated had met my family, but this was different. This was Betty. Her opinion mattered to me. I'd never cared what other girls thought before. That was another thing gnawing on my insides, tying my stomach into knots.

"You know, I remember Betty Mouton from high school," said Hale with one of his signature smirky smiles, leaving his post to lean on the table right behind me.

Serving didn't start for another thirty minutes. The other hundred gumbo booths sprawled in rows in Belle Teche Plaza down the center of town were prepping for the crowds. People were already milling around, checking out what each booth was offering.

Belle Teche Plaza was a giant square parking lot set between Main Street on one side and Bayou Teche on the other, which wound all the way through town. The plaza served as parking for offices and the Main Street boutiques, as well as the venue for all local festivals. The Gumbo Cookoff was one of many. When the weather was nice—or at least breathable— Louisianians liked any excuse for day drinking and eating good food outdoors.

Hale had made a duck and andouille sausage gumbo this year. My favorite. All ingredients were provided from Pop's shop and my store.

But my attention wasn't on the locals walking the aisles or the competition of the other booths. It was on Hale's fiendish grin when he said he remembered Betty. My Betty.

Just like always, I couldn't ignore the bait. Hale knew me too damn well.

"What do you remember?"

"She was in the class below mine."

I knew this already. I'd graduated BHS when Betty was a freshman, and I'd never noticed her back then. But since she'd gotten the role in the play, I'd done some snooping.

"She was on the dance team, did you know that?" he asked, that mischievous grin widening. "I didn't know her personally, but the whole damn football team enjoyed watching her dance. She was a tiny thing, but she sure could move that tight little body."

"Hale," I warned with a growl, unable to control my anger at the thought of a bunch of fucking football players ogling her back in high school.

"If she looks like she did back then, I can see why you've got your panties in a bunch. Hot as a firecracker, that one was."

"If you disrespect her in any way or make her feel uncomfortable with your usual rude behavior, I'll knock your teeth out."

Hale's green eyes widened before he let out a sharp bark of laughter. "You've got it worse than I thought."

Ignoring him, I turned to look up the aisle again, hoping to see that flame of red hair in the crowds. I was wound tighter than usual. Somehow, Hale's ribbing eased my nerves. Jealousy and anger had replaced the spiraling worry. I'm sure he'd done that on purpose.

"Yeah," he sighed. "I can see why you've got it so bad."

My gaze snapped to his, where he was looking in the opposite direction. Sure enough, Betty sauntered up the aisle in tight red jeans and a white long-sleeved top made of loose material that formed to her body when she walked. She'd kept her hair down, a curtain of fire shimmering past her shoulders.

"Damn, Ben." Hale whistled under his breath. "You sure you can handle all of that?"

Again, I ignored his not-so-subtle taunts. Hale lived to stir the pot and cause mayhem. We gave each other shit all the time. Usually, I was in a much better frame of mind to handle it. But I was having Betty withdrawals—yes, after two days.

That twisting sensation in my gut loosened and allowed me to finally breathe. The nerves melted away as I watched the gorgeous redhead coming my way and beaming a smile at me. As I watched her come closer, I could only think one thing over and over. *She belonged with me.*

As the woman who was the sole center of all my thoughts lately came within a few feet, I murmured to my brother, "Be nice, Hale. Or I'll beat the shit out of you later."

"Damn. It's like that, is it?"

"Just like that."

When he'd tormented me about girls in the past, which seemed to be one of his favorite pastimes, I'd always rolled my eyes and ignored him. I'd never threatened him with violence. Not that I thought Hale would say anything to scare Betty off. I just didn't want him accidentally offending her or hurting her feelings in any possible way. Hale could often come across as extremely offensive, even on his *best* behavior.

Then she was right in front of me, wrapping her slender arms around my neck and pulling me down for a kiss. "Hey there, handsome," she whispered against my lips.

"Hey, beautiful." I hauled her in tight and kissed her back, wanting to bury my face in her hair and lose myself. But my brother watched like a nosy pervert, so I eased her to my side and took her hand. "Betty, this is my brother, Hale."

"Ah. The home builder who doesn't like homebuilders." She offered her hand. "Nice to meet you."

Hale, taken aback at her greeting, had me grinning wide. He reached out and shook her hand, seeming to regain speech. "The teacher who plays actor in her spare time. Nice to meet you, too."

"Hale," I warned, scowling at this motherfucker.

But Betty only smiled bigger, completely unfazed. "Who is a fantastic actor in her spare time. The best in town, as a matter of fact. If we're going to be completely honest, I might as well set you straight now."

"Better than Bennett?"

"Hell, yeah." She squeezed my hand affectionately. I squeezed hers back.

Hale's smile widened to something akin to genuine respect when he turned to me. "She's a keeper."

Letting go of her hand, I wrapped my arm around her waist and hauled her against my body, squeezing her luscious hip. "I'm well aware," I said to her, not Hale.

Her brow pinched a little then she stepped up to the table. "So, what kind are you serving?"

"Come taste and see," called Hale, walking back to the pot. "I have no doubt I'll get the honest truth out of you."

Miss Lucille was stacking bowls, spoons, and napkins to prep for the lines on the other side of the tent.

"Miss Lucille, can you please pass me a bowl?"

The bowls were actually small tasting cups. Since locals liked to sample several different gumbos, they bought tickets for the same-sized tasting bowls at each booth. But they could also buy the leftovers by the pint at the end of the day. If there was anything left. We had very little in past cookoffs. Hale was a seriously good cook.

I tugged Betty around the table and under our tent, reluctant to let go of her soft hand when Hale handed over a bowl.

She took it with a smile and tasted a spoonful, her blue eyes widening. "Damn. That is really, really good."

"Does she lie often?" he asked me.

"She always tells the truth. Whether you want to hear it or not."

She scoffed. "There's no point in wasting breath, dancing around what needs to be said." She took another bite and closed her eyes in pleasure.

Fuck. Just like that, I was hard as a rock.

"Seriously," she added, "that's a winner."

Hale grinned triumphantly. "Well then, that earned you some time off, big brother. You two kids go have fun. I can hold down the fort."

"You sure?"

I'd asked Hale earlier if he'd mind. He'd whined and complained and told me no girl was worth me selling out the family's prestigious place in the top five at the last eight Gumbo Cookoffs. And now he was shooing me away like I was a nuisance. He liked her.

Grinning, I gave him a wave. "Thanks, man."

"No problem. Betty has declared me a winner."

"Your gumbo is a winner. Not you," she clarified.

"Potato, po-tah-to." Hale shrugged.

"Come on," I laughed, tugging her away before he changed his mind.

Lacing our fingers together, I hauled her closer so that we brushed shoulders when we walked. I couldn't help it. I wanted her against me, on top of me, underneath me. I could hardly handle this insane need to be with her nonstop. What was this mania?

Infatuation? Obsession? Something more?

"Let's go see my mom at the Tractor Supply booth. Her boyfriend Dan is a manager for them."

"Gotcha."

"This way."

We meandered through a long row. I read some of the other booths' gumbo signs to see what was on the menu for the day. As usual, there was a wide variety, from chicken and sausage to seafood to alligator and andouille.

Betty started bobbing as she walked to the tempo of a live Zydeco band that had just started playing. The stage was behind the last booth with a roped-off area for dancers.

"There they are," she called over her shoulder.

I exhaled a heavy breath as we stopped in front of the Tractor Supply booth next to a woman several inches shorter than Betty. Same creamy pale skin, her hair a shade darker, streaked with a little gray. Her clothes were relaxed, hippie-ish, her long hair twisted on top of her head. She wore the same carefree expression on her face as Betty but aged with soft wrinkles.

Betty was a strange combination of ornery and free-spirited and bold that made her so bewitching.

"Bennett, this is my mom, Karen Mouton."

When her mother's gaze turned up to me, they brightened with excitement. "Bennett Broussard. It's so nice to meet you."

Rather than stick out her hand to shake, she went in for a hug. I leaned over, awkwardly hugging a woman I'd just met who happened to be over a foot shorter than me.

"Just roll with it," Betty murmured.

"Here, y'all try this," said Dan, walking up with two samples for Betty and me. "It may not be Hale Broussard's gumbo, but it's pretty damn good."

I glanced up at their sign that read *Shrimp and Tasso*.

"Can't go wrong with that combination," I added encouragingly before I took a bite.

It was delicious. But most of these cooks out here meant serious business and knew what they were about.

"That's really good, Dan," said Betty, inhaling her serving cup before tossing it in one of the big trashcans set out in the lane for festival-goers.

"Yeah, we've got a team on it this year." He motioned behind him where cooks and helpers were shuffling around. "I'm Dan Bernard," he said, holding out his hand. "Nice to meet you."

We shook hands. "Bennett Broussard."

He chuckled. "Yeah, I know."

I frowned at Betty, who rolled her eyes. I wasn't sure how I was so well-known among her family, but I could only hope it was because she was saying nice things about me.

"Hey, Country," Betty called, looking over my shoulder.

When I turned, I had to look up at the guy she greeted walking into our circle. This was an unnatural experience for me. At six foot three, I rarely had to look up. But the man walking up into our circle was easily four or five inches taller. Tall and broad, not fat but fit. Looked like a linebacker for the Saints.

I couldn't help the flare of jealousy I had that Betty seemed to know him so well. Had they dated or something?

"Hi, Betty. Karen. Nice day for a cookoff," he rumbled in a deep voice to match his size.

"Come on and try ours," said Dan, ushering him forward. "We've got plenty."

"Thanks, Dan. I appreciate you getting me that new commission on the rockers, too. I'd wanted to tell you."

After a quick introduction to me, the giant named Country fell into a conversation with Dan while eating a sample of shrimp and tasso gumbo.

When I quirked my brow at Betty, she scooted close and said, "Country makes homemade furniture and sells on consignment at Tractor Supply. Dan helps him out with it."

"That's pretty cool. He doesn't want to open a shop of his own for something like that?"

I couldn't imagine starting a business and selling on consignment, giving away profits to another store. I'd been raised to think single-mindedly about business.

"Oh, no," Betty laughed. "It's not his livelihood. He's a sugarcane farmer. Has about a hundred acres off Broken Arrow Highway. The furniture thing is a hobby."

I angled a suspicious look down at her. "You know a lot about this guy. Just how do you two know each other exactly?"

Her mischievous grin spread wide. She faced me and wrapped her hands around my waist. I took the offer and hauled her in close, the tension easing at her open affection.

"Someone's jealous," she whispered.

I thought about blowing it off and pretending nonchalance, which is what I would've normally done. Hell, I don't think I'd ever been jealous of another man because of a woman. My jealousy tended to be only for those who seemed to have a better handle on their business.

I didn't want to hide anything from Betty. Especially how I felt about her. Or how I felt about the idea of her being with another man. Hugging her tighter against me, I said low for only her to hear, "I can't help it. I'm becoming territorial over you."

I stroked a hand down her spine, pressing her to me. She arched her back like a cat.

I whispered low, "The thought of another guy touching you makes me insane."

She was still grinning like mad. "Country and I never dated," she said, putting me out of my misery. "I've only met him once when Mom and I went to check out and buy a rocker she wanted for the back porch."

"Y'all want a water?" Her mom popped up beside us, holding two water bottles and smiling wide.

It seemed I had her approval, at least.

"Thank you, Ms. Mouton," I told her, taking the water and drinking a sip.

"Call me Karen, please. I saw you in last year's performance of *Chicago* at BPAL. Betty and I both did. You were so amazing."

"Thank you. I enjoy doing the musicals, but I've been really enjoying doing the straight plays, too. They're actually more challenging for me when I can't rely on a song to get me through the scene," I added.

"You sure can dance, too." Her eyes lit up. "Betty and I couldn't keep our eyes off you when you were on stage."

"*Mom*," Betty whined.

"Is that so?" I wrapped a hand around Betty's waist and pulled her against me. "Couldn't keep your eyes off me?"

"Shut up." She pinched my waist. "My mom is just being nice." Her face flushed pink.

"I am not," Karen protested. "I say what I think, and you know it."

"You seem to be quite the free spirit, like your daughter," I admitted openly.

She smiled right back. "Or a free bird."

"Mom, no, please," begged Betty, confusing me.

"Oakland, California," said the older version of Betty with a reminiscent gleam in her eyes. "July fourth, nineteen seventy-seven. The Lynyrd Skynyrd concert that rocked the world.

That's when and where my mother said I was conceived. Right during his performance of 'Free Bird.' That's why I'm a free spirit, as you say."

"Mom, Gran was probably lying to you just to have an interesting story to tell."

She chuckled. "Gran has a lot of stories to tell. And they're all true. There's a wild streak in the women of our family," Karen said to me with a wink. "Hope that's what you were looking for."

"Please stop, Mom." Betty looked mortified. And it was the most adorable thing in the world. She never ever got embarrassed. This was fantastic to watch.

"It's true," she defended. "He should know what he's getting himself into. You're as crazy as your grandmother."

"You're mistaking me with Emma," she said haughtily. "I'm a respectable educator in this community."

"And actor," I added.

"Exactly." She tightened her arm around my waist.

"Can't change the stripes on a zebra. Even if you put a saddle and reins on her."

"Mom, that is literally the worst metaphor I've ever heard." Betty looked up at me. "I'm not crazy like them anymore. Promise."

Suddenly, I couldn't help but remember how she let me go down on her right there in the theater at Golden Oldies. I had been so fucking turned on that I couldn't keep myself on a leash. And she'd been right there with me, ready to go.

For the hundredth time, I wondered what she'd be like in bed. Because Betty's mother was right. This girl had a wild streak. I had no intention of putting a saddle and bridle on her, but I sure as fuck wanted to ride her hard.

I coasted my hand under her silky fall of hair and wrapped my hand around her nape. "You're perfect just the way you are," I whispered against her temple.

She stiffened for a few seconds then shivered and smiled up at me when I straightened.

"See, look at her," Karen said, completely unfazed by our PDA. "She can't even keep her feet still. That's how Betty got all her extra energy out as a little girl. Dancing. I made her start lessons when she was five. Used to make me crazy, twirling around the living room all the time."

I'd noticed that she had kept bobbing to the Zydeco music in the background.

"A dancer?" I questioned, though Hale had already said as much earlier.

I didn't want to think about that, or I'd get pissed again about all the football players drooling over her. Which was fucking ridiculous because that was years ago.

Betty glanced over her shoulder to the stage where the Zydeco band was playing. "You want to dance?"

"Sure."

She grabbed my water and put both of our bottles on the table, then snatched my hand and dragged me toward the roped-off area where a few couples were dancing.

"Can you two-step?" she asked.

I didn't tell her that my own grandmother had taught me how to two-step when I was nine. I simply shrugged. "I think I can keep up with you."

"It's not hard. I'll show you."

We walked into the dance area in front of the stage, the music blaring loud. She faced me and took both of my hands in hers.

"Okay!" she yelled. "So just follow the music. You shuffle your feet twice this way. Then once the other." She showed me the basic two-step move, staring down at our feet and then looking up when I didn't move. "Come on, Broussard. If you can dance to Broadway tunes, you can do this."

Smiling wide, I hauled her close and whirled with her, two-stepping fast and hard among the circle of dancers.

Her eyes widening with shock, and gleeful surprise, was the prettiest sight all day.

"You tricked me," she yelled, still laughing, following my lead.

I grinned right back and twirled her to the beat of the Zydeco music, keeping in tempo with the two-step movement. Then I spun her out and spun her hard back in. She landed against my chest, but I kept our movement continuous, two-stepping in the circle, holding her tight.

She laughed, her head tipping back, her blue eyes reflecting the clear autumn sky. She was the most beautiful woman I'd ever seen, and I didn't want this dance or this day to ever end.

Chapter Fifteen

~BETTY~

"Act Three is where we need the most work," said Bennett as he flipped through his script, sitting on his sofa.

It was Sunday, the day after the best Gumbo Cookoff ever, and we'd decided to have a rehearsal at his house since we had to be off-script by tomorrow. I'd bathed and shaved, and primped in preparation for this *rehearsal.*

I'd been surprised—and not—when I first drove up to his house. Before I knew Bennett, I expected him to live in the fancy gated community near the Beauville golf course, Sugar Oaks. But now, I was pleasantly relieved to see that he'd bought an older home in one of the neighborhoods that wound next to the bayou.

It was a white Acadian style with dark-stained columns on the porch and rustic finishes, which he'd confessed he'd done mostly on his own over the five years he'd lived here.

It was charming with sweet lines and pretty but cozy, just like him.

I watched him, noting the pensive look etched in his forehead as he scrolled to the scene he wanted to rehearse next. His fabulous jaw was working hard on that piece of gum. When he was in this mode—work mode—he was so focused and stern. For some reason, it made me smile to learn his different moods.

But also, that edge of trepidation surged at the same time. No matter how much I told myself there was no reason to be afraid of liking him so much, I couldn't completely convince my heart that it was true. Shaking off that nagging voice, I watched him quietly.

The Bennett Broussard charm was ever-present, but there was also a fierce kind of determination set in his features. I'd seen him this way at the store when he was with his employees. I could only recognize it now because I'd come to know him so well.

"I say let's start on page eighty-eight."

He stuck his gum on the napkin on the coffee table, leftover from the raspberry chocolate tart he brought from the store. I loved his damn bakery so much it made me mad. Living so close to his store, I was going to put on a lot of pounds or be forced to work out.

Staring at his chiseled jaw, I mourned the loss of his gum and the scenery of watching him chew it.

He glanced up and frowned. "What?"

"Nothing." I didn't want to tell him how adorable I thought he looked when he was in all-business-Bennett mode. Flipping quickly to the page, I said, "Ready."

We'd been practicing lines on the sofa and only looking down if we got completely stuck. Peter was serious about his off-script deadlines, Bennett had warned me, and the rehearsal really was helping me. Beyond giving me the chance to ogle Bennett in a faded pair of Levi's and a T-shirt and barefoot.

I launched into the climactic fight scene where Corie was

demanding a divorce. Immediately, Bennett's expression shifted to his Paul Bratter face as he blazed through the drunk Paul scene.

Biting my lip to keep from laughing, I stood from the sofa, unable to sit still for the passionate scene. This was where Corie made a complete about-face from hating her husband to worrying about him. In his drunken stupor, he climbs out of their bedroom window and to the roof of their apartment to prove he's wild and spontaneous like her.

Hale did an excellent job on the set, creating the giant window in the ceiling where Bennett would cling during the final part of the play.

Bennett stood when I did, maintaining his Paul expression, but his words softened as his fear of dying and losing his wife became clear in the delivery of his lines. I couldn't help but step closer to Bennett, just like Corie inched closer to Paul on the rooftop, trying to save him from falling after behaving like a drunken fool.

Their vulnerability and love for each other were apparent in the lines on the page, and we were playing them to perfection. So perfect, in fact, that my throat thickened with emotion as I drew closer to him.

"Paul! Don't fall!"

Corie's feelings for her new husband, her beloved who had risked his life—albeit foolishly—to prove that he could be everything she needed, began to bleed into my own.

Or was it the other way around? I wondered as I stared up into Bennett's eyes, blazing with an intensity that wasn't Paul at all. But Bennett. The hungry, passionate man that made me shiver with anticipation.

"Oh, Paul," I said. It was one of the final lines when she meets him on the rooftop. I remained standing there, arms at my sides, wanting to bridge the short distance between us. But also afraid of the unbearable tension stretching like a steel line that could pop and lacerate with bleeding force anything in its path.

I'd had several sexual partners over the years. But none of them—not one—had my heart hammering out a warning that sex with this man would be different. That I might be changed from the experience.

And yet, I wanted him more than my next breath. I couldn't stop it if I tried.

We'd finished the final scene altogether but still stood there, staring, unmoving. Until he moved, tossing his script on the floor with a resounding slap against the wood.

He was mere inches from me, devouring me with his fiery gaze. He roamed my face then lower, snagging on my off-the-shoulder shirt that exposed the lacy strap of a bralette I'd worn for comfort. And to make him look at me just like this. With insatiable need.

He lifted his hands and cupped my face, fingers threading into my hair, his thumb coasting over my mouth. He brushed his thumb again across my bottom lip.

His expression was tight and savage. I'd almost think he was filled with rage if I didn't know his moods so well now. I recognized this one right away. I'd experience the onslaught of its intensity when he was on his knees in a movie theater, thoroughly eating my pussy and making me come in the dark.

What I found so intriguing about Bennett—well, one of the reasons—was that while he seemed predictable when I first met him, I'd discovered happily that I was wrong. Dead wrong. Right now, I knew what he was thinking, the same thing that I was. Still, I was shocked to my toes when he finally opened his mouth to speak.

"I've wanted a lot of women," he crooned softly, his minty breath from the gum he'd been chewing coasting over my lips.

With those words, a brutal pain crested at the center of my

chest, but then he held my face harder and went on, his words a barrel-deep rumble.

"But I've never in my life needed a woman the way I need you." He watched his thumb grazing my lower lip before he pressed softly. I opened at his silent command. His heated gaze remained fixed there, his chest rising and falling faster with each breath. "I feel like if I don't have you right now, if I don't find out what it's like to be buried inside you, I'll fucking go insane."

After wrapping my hands around his thick wrists, I squeezed, drawing his attention back to my eyes.

"Then take me to your bed."

The crushing force of his mouth on mine made me whimper in response. Just as before, his kiss was an onslaught of sensation, his tongue aggressive but in no way sloppy. Thorough. He kissed me the way he'd fuck me. I was sure of it. With sure, deep strokes, wrenching pleasure with each thrust.

Heat pooled between my legs, and I ground against him, moaning at the feel of his hard dick in his jeans.

"Fuck," he cursed. He curled his hand into the edge of my loose-fitting shirt and the strap of my bralette and yanked them both down.

My breast popped free. He groaned as he lowered his head and sucked my nipple into his mouth.

"Ah!" I fisted one hand into his hair, the other wrapping his nape to hold him there.

My nipples were my most sensitive spot, and the way he was sucking and nibbling gently with teeth, stinging then licking to soothe the slight pain, had me grinding harder against him.

"Your bed, Bennett," I rasped. "Your *bed*."

Growling like a rabid dog who'd been torn from his bone, he let go of my breast with a sucking pop. He was dazed for only a second as he stared at my reddened nipple against my fair skin before he grabbed my ass with both hands and hauled me up, aligning me with the big bulge in his jeans.

"Hurry," I panted, nipping his neck as he carried me out of the living room and down a hall on the first floor.

His long strides ate up the short distance. I arched my back, loving the sensation of my bare breast and sensitive nipple pressing into his tight chest, the warmth of his body seeping through his T-shirt.

"Goddamn," he ground out as he dropped me roughly to the mattress and reached behind him with both hands to yank his T-shirt over his head. I had no idea why I should be surprised that he was sporting an eight-pack. This was Bennett Broussard. Of course, his body would be honed and chiseled to magnificence. Everywhere.

I didn't mind because I was in a hurry, too. But apparently not as much as him. He had my jeans and panties off before I'd managed to strip my shirt and bralette. When I'd tossed both aside to the floor, I stared up at Bennett standing at the end of his bed—which was big and comfy with a dark bedspread—while he heaved breaths and consumed every inch of my body now exposed to him.

I squirmed under his inspection, not because I feared he didn't like what he saw, but because I knew he did. I never minded my smaller-than-average breasts or my wider-than-average hips. I loved my body. And the way Bennett looked at me with the wolf in his eyes told me he did, too.

"You work out," I remarked casually, feeling not at all casual about any of this as I drank him in.

"A little."

"Liar."

He worked out like a madman to get that body, but I was not complaining one single bit.

Scooting back till my head was on a pillow, I slid one hand down between my legs and ran a finger along my slick slit. I'd shaved smooth except for a small patch at the top of my mound. His tilted smile slipped. His jaw clenched.

"If you just keep standing there and staring at me like that," I told him softly, "then I'm going to have to take care of myself."

He huffed out a grunt of disapproval and went for his jeans. My breath left my lungs when he'd shed the rest of his clothes and stood to his full height again.

In addition to a model-gorgeous torso, he had that muscular vee low on his hips pointing to a perfectly proportioned penis, if not a little large. The tip glistened with his arousal as he gave it a hard pump. My mouth watered, and that was a first.

But good heavens, I wanted to taste him. Every single inch of him.

His next words sent a tantalizing shiver over my body.

"Tonight," he said, letting go of his erection which bobbed against his abdomen as he reached down to his jeans, "the only one who's going to make you come is me."

He then tossed a pack of condoms on the bed next to me. Must be four or five there.

Whoa. Someone was ambitious.

People could say a lot of things about me, but nobody ever said I was a quitter.

Chapter Sixteen

~BENNETT~

I VIBRATED WITH NEED AS I CRAWLED ON TOP OF BETTY AND between her spread legs, welcoming me right where I longed to be. My head spun with dizzying lust as I gripped my dick hard and stroked it to ease some of the aching pain. Knowing that I was going to finally be inside her was the only thing keeping me in check, from falling on her like a starving animal.

Instead of going for her mouth, I braced my weight on one forearm and licked a circle around the nipple I hadn't yet tasted. Those pretty little breasts of hers had me rethinking the fact that I'd always been an ass-man. And it wasn't big breasts that I wanted. It was hers—small, perky, nipples easily darkening after I'd barely sucked them. Taking my mark and jutting up for more.

Fuck, her moaning and squirming response was driving me mad. My dick was hard to the point of pain, yet I wanted to kiss and taste her more slowly. Her small patch of orange-red hair on her pussy, slightly darker than the hair on her head, sent my body into a maddening spiral of lust. I let go of my dick so I could touch her there.

I caressed two fingers over her mound then lower, petting and stroking, then sliding into the slickness between her lips. Lifting my mouth from her breast, both nipples berry-red from my mouth, I looked up. Her blue eyes were dark, pupils dilated, and her mouth parted as she panted and thrust her hips up while I stroked her teasingly.

"So wet for me, aren't you?" I slid two fingers inside her.

She squeezed her eyes shut and arched her neck on a mindless moan. "Bennett. Fuck me, please. Just fuck me."

Groaning and growing harder at her desperate begging, I leveraged up onto my knees between her spread thighs. "Goddamn, I wanted foreplay, but I can't fucking take it."

I ripped open a condom package, rolled it on, then gripped her hips and lifted her up till her ass was high on my thighs.

I wanted to watch my cock sink inside her sweet pussy. I *needed* to.

Gripping her hip with one hand, I used the other to wet my dick along her slit, hissing at the mind-hazing pleasure. Holding her steady, I watched her face as I sank the tip inside.

Her mouth fell open, her gaze fixed on me as I sank deeper, the tight sensation both agonizing and euphoric. She was extremely tight, making me withdraw and thrust, gaining an inch at a time.

It made me wonder, and I couldn't help but ask, "How long since you've been with someone?"

She didn't seem shocked or appalled at my question when she answered, "About a year."

Why that made me happy, I have no idea. It hadn't been that long for me, but none of them compared to her. This feeling of entering her body was brand new. Unparalleled. I'd never fucked a woman I'd admired so much and wanted this badly.

I wrapped my hands around her hips and held tight before thrusting hard to the hilt. She gasped, clawing her hands into the covers.

Closing my eyes briefly at the heady sensation of being buried deep inside her, I leaned forward and crushed my chest to hers, pressing her into the mattress. Scooping one hand behind her hair spread in fire-like tendrils across the pillow —*my* pillow—I cradled the back of her skull while also gripping her thigh.

I withdrew to the tip. When she whimpered, I slammed back home again. Her nails clawed at my back, one sliding down to my ass to urge me faster.

"This is where I belong," I whispered. Then pounded with another thrust. "Deep inside you."

"Yes." She pulled my head closer with the fist in my hair and murmured against my lips, "*More,* Bennett. For fuck's sake."

Kissing her deeply, I pumped inside her, moving in a quicker but steady rhythm. I didn't want this feeling to end too fast, so I dragged it out. I trailed my mouth to her throat, tasting her silky, pale skin, my cock stroking into pure heaven.

"This is the sweetest, tightest pussy I've ever felt," I murmured against her skin. "I could fuck you forever, Betty. Chain you up. Never let you leave this fucking bed."

"Then why don't you?" she teased.

Growling, I nipped her earlobe and pounded a little harder. "Fuck yes."

Her inner walls fluttered, her moans rising louder, warning me she was about to come. I kept my steady, pounding pace, but my mouth found her neck and shoulder where I bit and sucked, loving the reddened marks I made. I felt like some barbaric caveman hopped up on Viagra, grunting and sucking and biting with near-brutal force, needing to claim her on some primitive level.

That sent her over the edge. She clawed at my back as she

screamed and came. I fucked her through the orgasm, groaning as she clenched around me, sending me spiraling closer to my own. When I felt her pulsing lessen, I withdrew and flipped her over.

Scooping one hand beneath her hips, I cupped her pussy before I thrust back inside her, loving the feel of my hips hitting her plump ass each time I drove home.

She'd pressed one cheek to the mattress, her gaze toward the window where moonlight spilled in, outlining her delicate features and pale skin in soft silver. A possessive force tightened my chest and bled to my bones, making me pound harder, faster, wishing I could make her mine by fucking her senseless.

But Betty was a wild creature. And more beautiful because of it.

"Love the way you're taking my cock," I whispered in her ear, "squeezing my dick so tight." I nipped her ear. "You're so perfect for me."

She moaned, her inner muscles fluttering.

"That's my girl. Give me another one."

"Bennett," she moaned mostly into the bedding, sounding like a desperate plea.

My orgasm barreled up my spine till I pumped hard and held, pulsing inside her. Pressing my forehead to her nape, I knew I was lost. Unraveled and undone.

This woman had stolen my whole heart, and it scared the shit out of me.

"Bennett," she whispered.

I jumped, realizing I'd come minutes ago and hadn't moved. I held the condom in place as I slid out of her, and then went to the bathroom to take care of it.

I left the bathroom door open and turned on the lights as I threw away the condom and rinsed myself off. I tossed the towel in my hamper.

When I returned, she was lying on her side facing the bathroom. "I thought you'd fallen asleep on top of me or something." She laughed, a carefree, beautiful sound.

Pulling the covers down on my side, I popped her sweet ass. She squealed. I grabbed the condoms and dropped them on the side table. We'd be needing those.

"Get under the covers with me."

She grinned and did, burrowing her cheek into the pillow I never used. She looked so perfect there. A pang pinched my chest. I scooped an arm around her waist and hauled her nearer so I could study her up close.

"I'm not done with you yet. Neither one of us is going to sleep."

"Oh, really? So sure of yourself." She tucked her hands together like in prayer under her cheek and grinned at me, looking like both a devil and an angel.

"I am," I told her, then coasted my hand to one of her breasts and flicked my thumb over her nipple. It responded, automatically hardening.

"You don't play when it comes to the bedroom, do you?"

Relishing the vision of her red hair spilling across my pillow, I eased closer and abandoned her breast to glide a finger over her clit, still wet from our first time.

"I've wanted you for a long while, Ms. Mouton."

She lifted a leg, opening her thighs, and draped it over my hip, giving me full access.

"How long?" she asked, her hands still tucked under her cheek.

She watched me with half-hidden arousal softening her mouth and glazing her eyes as I stroked a slow circle around her clit. In no hurry, I massaged slowly and gently with hardly any pressure at all.

"Since the read-through." I glided my middle finger to her entrance and stroked languidly inside. "Since you mouthed off to me about my grand opening making you late for school."

She huffed out a shaky breath as I continued to pump inside her. "That was mean of me."

"Very." I pumped a second finger inside.

"Maybe you should punish me." Her eyes glittered with mischievous intent in the dim light from the bathroom.

My dick was rock-hard in a millisecond.

"Fuck, woman."

I threw off the covers, stood, reached for her ankles, and dragged her to the side of the bed.

She squealed with laughter. "Bennett! What are you doing?"

"You can't put a thought like that in my head and think I won't use it."

I maneuvered her hips to the edge of the mattress and flipped her over.

"Put your knees on the edge of the mattress. Ass up." I grabbed her hips and lifted. I could hear the edge of raspy arousal already saturating my words.

She said something that was muffled in the sheets, but she obeyed.

"That's my girl," I crooned, palming her ass in a soft circle.

Then I reared back and spanked her on her right cheek, loving the jiggle of beautiful flesh and the bright mark my hand made. She squealed with laughter.

I ground my teeth together at the possessiveness taking hold again. What was it about seeing evidence of my hands and mouth on her that sent me into a spiral of domineering need?

"You're right," I said lightly, belying the heavy emotions churning in my gut. "This was a good idea."

"I was kidding!" she said right as I smacked her again on the left cheek this time. "Mother fucker!" she screamed, but then she was laughing again.

Smiling, I smoothed over the sting with my palm then

drifted back to the right, letting my fingers dip in her crease but not linger there. I could already see her glistening, evidence that this was turning her on as much as it was me.

"How many do you deserve?" I asked as I spanked her again, immediately smoothing and then trailing my fingertips lightly over her slit in a teasing caress.

She made a muffled moaning sound, no longer laughing.

"Two more should do it," I said, hauling back and spanking her a little lower this time, closer to her pussy.

"Oh, God, Bennett." She arched her back, presenting more of her ass to me.

Fucking hell, she was beautiful. In every possible way. To have her submit to me on something like this, wanting more, was enough to make me come before I was even inside her again.

"One more, baby," I growled, caressing her right cheek and heating it with my palm.

Then I hauled back and spanked her the hardest on the fleshiest part of her ass. She moaned, her pussy growing wetter.

"Don't move," I ground out.

Spreading her wide with my thumbs, I sucked on her clit and fucked her with my tongue. She moaned and squirmed but didn't move forward. Instead, she arched even more, spreading her legs wider, letting me do whatever I wanted.

With a nip of her ass, I stood and ripped another condom from the pack, suiting up in seconds. "Keep your head to the mattress just like that," I told her, lining my cock up.

When I pumped inside, she reached both arms above her and clawed at the covers.

"Yes, right there," she rasped. "Just like that."

Encircling my hands around her slim waist, I groaned in pleasure at the sight of my hands on her creamy, pale flesh, at her reddened ass, at the hickey I'd put on her exposed throat with her hair flying wide across my mattress.

I'd intended to go slow this time, but I couldn't. She felt so fucking good. I drove hard and fast, the sound of flesh slapping and her whimpering moans the only sound in the room.

When she started to rock backward to meet my hard thrusts, I knew I couldn't hold out for long. She was too fucking perfect.

Falling forward, catching myself with one arm, I reached underneath her and found her clit, rubbing in fast circles.

"Need you to come. Goddamn, Betty, you're so fucking beautiful," I groaned, watching her profile contort into pleasure, her eyes closed, her mouth open. "Come for me."

I pressed harder on her swollen clit, pounding harder inside her.

When her mouth opened wider in a wailing cry, and I felt the first flutter of her orgasm, I crushed her flat to the bed, trapping my hand on her pussy as I ground out my own climax. Circling my hips in a slow grind, I groaned in bliss as her pussy milked my cock.

What the hell was happening to me? I wondered if I'd been too rough. Both times. A sliver of unease slipped into my mind that I was behaving like a psychotic animal.

Then she turned her head and pressed a kiss to my wrist where my forearm curved by her head. "This has to be what heaven is like," she murmured, almost sleepily, as the waves of our orgasms ebbed.

Closing my eyes in relief, I whispered a thankful prayer, pulled out then flipped her. I cradled her face, kissing her lightly, tenderly.

"I hope I didn't hurt you," I admitted, ready to somehow beat the shit out of myself if I had.

Her brow furrowed. "When? When you fucked me to a second orgasm while I screamed in ecstasy? No, Bennett." She lifted and pressed a chaste kiss to my lips. "You didn't hurt me." Then she wiggled underneath me. "I never thought I'd like spanking, but I did."

I had been fairly sure myself by evidence of her arousal, but I didn't want her to regret or feel ashamed of our sex play. Because I wanted this for a long time. For a very long time.

Settling her closer and tighter in my arms, I kissed her cheek, her closed eyelids, and her other cheek.

"Bennett?"

"Mm?"

"Are you hard again?" Her voice went high in disbelief.

I chuckled. "Yeah."

Her eyes snapped open. "How?"

"Not all the way there. Just yet."

"I need a break."

Laughing, I said, "I do, too." Then I kissed her lips, sweeping my tongue in a slow exploration of her sweet mouth. "Stay the night with me."

I didn't hide my vulnerability or my need for her to stay when I asked her, more like I softly begged her to stay with me. I let her see my need, for once not feeling like I had to hide. Not from her.

She had work in the morning, and if it had been me, I'd be thinking of all the things I had to do the next day and how sleeping at someone else's house would only throw a hitch in my daily ritual. So I'd expected her to say no.

Instead, she brushed her fingertips into my hair and smiled, whispering softly, "Okay." Without a word of protest.

Where had this girl come from? Where had she been?

Heaving a relieved breath, I took care of the condom again in the bathroom, then returned to bed, where my beautiful girl was going to sleep in my arms.

When I slipped under the covers, she instantly rolled away and then backed up, letting me haul her close, spooning her from behind. My whole body and mind were completely relaxed. Not a worry or concern niggling me as it usually did before sleep.

Now that I thought about it, these past couple of weeks with Betty had been much less stressful when it should've been the opposite, opening the store. Interesting that I'd also avoided my father during this time when I normally never would. Never had.

He wasn't a terrible man. He was a good man, actually. But a stern father who expected a lot. Especially out of me since he'd given up on molding Hale into the perfect businessman.

Releasing a heavy breath, I pulled her closer, tucking her tight against me. A sense of belonging and lightness filled me.

"You're a cuddler," she murmured on a soft, throaty laugh.

"Never have been before," I confessed, hoping that didn't scare her off.

After a minute, she hugged my forearm tighter where it wrapped around her waist. With a contented sigh, I fell asleep faster than I ever had.

Chapter Seventeen

~BETTY~

BENNETT HAD WOKEN ME IN THE MIDDLE OF THE NIGHT, HIS mouth between my legs. I didn't complain. Before I came again, he slid inside me for the third time and rocked us both to a slow, mind-tilting orgasm. At least, it was for me. But maybe that was because I'd been half asleep.

When morning light filtered through his shutters, I'd woken this time to a freshly showered and grinning Bennett bringing me coffee in bed. He was also fully dressed in his business attire best, ready for work.

"What time is it?" I asked, exhausted, considering calling in a sick day.

What would I put on my excuse card? *Thoroughly fucked by the local grocer* wasn't on the check-off list of excuses.

"Six-fifteen. Get a shower, and I'll have breakfast ready when you're finished. You'll still have time to get home and uh..." His gaze roamed to my bare breasts when I sat up, letting the covers fall.

I blinked innocently at him, lifting the coffee cup and taking a loud sip. His mouth slack-jawed, and his perkiness fell away as he stared openly.

"Get home and what, Bennett?"

"I have no idea what I was saying."

I couldn't help but laugh, setting the coffee cup down. I pushed off the covers to walk the few steps to him. His throat worked as he swallowed, and there was a tent in his perfectly pressed pants all of a sudden.

"You were saying I wouldn't be late if I hurried and showered and put my clothes on." Grasping his tie, I straightened it, though there was no need. I just did it to torment him.

"I could call in sick," he offered, his hands landing on my hips and squeezing.

I pressed my forehead to his starched shirt, laughing at the both of us, already wanting to skip work so we could fuck like bunnies the rest of the day.

"I'll go get a shower. You go cook me breakfast."

He squeezed me closer and pressed a kiss to my temple, letting out a small groan. "It was worth a shot."

He had no idea how tempted I was to take him up on that offer. But I fought against breaking the rules to spend more time with him. My feelings were growing at an astronomical and possibly non-healthy pace. I remembered the old adage by Shakespeare himself: *violent delights have violent ends.*

That familiar tremor of trepidation skittered across my subconscious, but I pushed it away. I didn't want this to go too fast and burn out too soon. I wanted to enjoy this as long as possible.

Of course, it was hard to go slow after I knew what his tongue felt like inside me. And his perfect dick. And the way he ground into me at the end of each thrust.

Shakira was right. *Hips don't lie.* Bennett sure knew how to use his.

"Did you take dance lessons when you were younger?"

He was still hugging me, fully dressed while I was completely naked, his big hand sliding softly up and down my back. I was seriously getting turned on by his gentle strokes.

"What?" He chuckled. "Why would you ask that?"

My hands fell from his waist to his ass, where I gave him a good squeeze. "You've got some loose hips in bed."

Then his own hands fell to *my* ass. "We don't have to use the bed." His lighthearted veneer had completely vanished. I was looking at his devilish demeanor that promised skin-tingling, bone-melting orgasms.

My phone alarm went off, which I had set for every weekday to remind me to get out of bed and get my butt to work. I made a whiney groan.

He smiled and dipped his head to my neck, sliding his hands to my hips again. "There's always tonight," he promised. "Go get a shower."

Then he popped my behind and walked toward the door.

"Hey!" I rubbed my butt cheek while walking to the bathroom. "You did enough of that last night."

"You loved it," he said in that low rumble, grinning as he walked away.

Yeah, I did.

I sauntered into the bathroom and gasped at the state of my hair and the hickey on the curve of my neck and shoulder. "Damn, Bennett."

Needing to get a move on, I jumped in the shower and used his men's shampoo. Ooo, this was where the woodsy smell came from. After rinsing off, I stepped out and wrapped a fluffy towel around myself, tucking it at my breasts. Then wrapped another around my hair. Even his towels were soft and smelled good. They even matched.

I snort-laughed. He would probably run screaming from my nightmare of a laundry room. While he was neat, I found that he wasn't obsessively so. There were some gym shoes scattered around. A little clutter on his nightstand and dresser.

Smiling at the old-fashioned straight razor kit on the counter, I picked up the fancy brush and grazed the soft bristles over my chin.

Feeling extra nosy, I opened his medicine cabinet, finding some mint mouthwash and Advil and…a prescription bottle.

Frowning, I started to close the door but stopped.

"Shit," I muttered, trying to make myself close it all the way. But I *couldn't.*

When I picked up the scrip bottle, I winced, knowing it would be something like this. I knew exactly what sertraline was—Zoloft—and what it was used for. Finn's therapist had prescribed it for him when he was going through a darker period at the beginning of college when he came out and was figuring out what to do with his life.

He no longer needed the medicine on a regular basis, but I wondered if this was something Bennett needed all the time. My heart squeezed in anguish.

Before I could be any nosier, I put it back and shut the cabinet. Quickly dressing in what I wore last night—minus the panties, because gross, I'd rather go commando—I towel-dried my hair, ran a brush through it, then headed into the kitchen.

"Something smells good."

"Hope you like French toast," he said, placing a plate with a fluffy stack in front of me, dusted with powdered sugar and a drizzle of syrup.

"Damn, Broussard." I sat down and forked in a delicious mouthful. "Someone's really trying hard to impress me."

He freshened up my coffee and set the creamer on the table next to my cup.

Arching a brow at him, I said, "Next thing you know, you'll be waking me up with cunnilingus."

He coughed on the sip of coffee he'd just swallowed, then belted out a laugh when he could breathe properly.

"Oh, wait, you already did that." I smiled, loving this side of him. The soft, sweet side. So different from the cocky charmer. Then I thought of the bottle in the medicine cabinet.

"What is it?" he asked, a frown pinching between his brow.

I wasn't the kind to hide my thoughts and feelings. That was for damn sure. But I didn't want to admit I'd invaded his privacy.

I ate another bite, and he waited, seeming to know something was up. When I set down my fork and wiped my mouth, I said, "I accidentally, but not really, found your scrip bottle in the bathroom."

His expression fell, his mouth tightening into a line. He walked over to the kitchen sink and rinsed his cup.

Immediately, I was up and behind him, wrapping my hands around his waist. "Please don't be mad. I didn't think I'd find anything embarrassing. Or if I did, I thought it would be like Clearasil or hemorrhoid cream."

He didn't laugh like I'd hoped he would. He grasped my hands and unclasped them from around his waist.

No, no, no. I didn't want him to push me away. Not yet, *not yet.*

"I'm so sorry, Bennett. Look, it's not a big deal. Lots of people take meds for anxiety disorders and depression and stuff. I'm sorry I snooped. I shouldn't have done that."

Rather than push me away like I was afraid he would, he turned and took both of my hands in his. But he didn't look at me right away, staring down at our hands instead.

"I wish you hadn't done that." The fun, flirty Bennett was long gone, and it was all my stupid fault. The tone of disappointment made me want to cry.

"Please, Bennett. I'm so sorry," I said softly.

I bit my bottom lip, afraid I'd ruined this before it began.

We were only a few hours past our first night together. I wanted it to last a little longer.

"I wasn't going to hide this from you, Betty." He finally met my eyes. "I just wasn't prepared to share my demons with you just yet."

"It's not a big deal. My friend Finn has had to take them for some past anxiety. Is it—" I paused, staring at our hands where he cupped mine gently—"is it something you need all the time?"

"No," he assured me. "Only on occasion. My anxiety is mild. I'm taking them now because the opening of the store has me stressed right now." He clenched his jaw as if to say more. I wasn't going to push him.

"I'm sorry I was so nosy. In addition to my judginess, my curiosity is crippling apparently."

He smiled, his hands coming up to cup my face. "I lo—" he cleared his throat, "like everything about you, Betty."

"I like everything about you, too," I said, wrapping my hands around his wrists, "except for the gluten-free area of your bakery."

He laughed and shook his head.

"I mean, there's just something very wrong about baked goods without gluten."

He leaned forward and pressed his forehead to mine. "You are something else, Betty Mouton."

Relieved that he was smiling, I wrapped my arms around his waist and pressed my cheek to his chest.

He hugged me tighter against him. "The anxiety can get the best of me sometimes, but I'm handling it."

"You definitely are. I'd never have known. You're always so charming and perfect and…."

"Cocky?"

I giggled and squeezed him tighter. "Always." Then I tilted my head to look up at him. "Maybe it truly is confidence."

He leaned down and coaxed my lips apart. He took his time, stroking his tongue into my mouth with reverent slides, slowly exploring. At the same time, ravenous need had me pressing closer and his body hardening against mine.

He pulled away, glancing at his watch. "You need to go."

"Right. So that kiss means you're not mad at me?" I whispered, feeling uncomfortably vulnerable.

He shook his head, looking at me with that worshipful intensity that made me want to strip my clothes back off and climb him like a tree.

"Finish your breakfast and get going," he said sweetly. "I don't want to hear complaints at rehearsal this afternoon that you were late to school because some guy made you sleep in his bed last night."

I pushed off of him with a teasing look. "Made me sleep in his bed and forced multiple orgasms on me. All night long."

"What a terrible guy this guy is."

"Awful," I whined as I sat and stuffed another bite of French toast in my mouth. "And then he made me eat the most delicious breakfast I've ever had. I mean, who the hell does this guy think he is?"

He laughed as he cleaned around the kitchen while I took five more minutes to inhale my breakfast. By the time I kissed him and backed out of the driveway, he gave me the smile that made my heart sing again. The one I wanted permanently branded on his beautiful face.

Only after I'd driven away did my thoughts wander to this morning. The level of pressure Bennett seems to always be under with the business, yet he holds it together so well. From what I'd seen anyway.

The nagging thought that he wasn't as perfect as I'd thought should reassure me that he was actually human. Humans had flaws.

But sometimes, those flaws made people do unpredictable

things. It was the unpredictability that made me so uncomfortable…and scared.

I was falling for Bennett. And short of being a serial killer, I was willing to accept his flaws. So what was this sour sensation churning in my gut?

Bennett didn't know one important thing about me. I might not have many friends, but those I did have remained so for life.

Like my roommate and college bestie, Lola Landry. She moved back to her hometown in Tennessee, but we still kept in touch. I'd actually even found her a job lead not too long ago. Though she ended up turning it down, I supported her no matter what.

That was me. Supporter and friend for life.

Bennett was moving well beyond just a friend. He was becoming much more. This realization should make me happy, not shoot an arrow of doubt through my heart.

But it did.

Chapter Eighteen

~BETTY~

To say I couldn't concentrate at school was an understatement. I'd been rereading an essay test from first period's honor class for all of fifth period, and I still hadn't gotten past the second paper.

My mind kept wandering back to last night. To Bennett's hands and mouth and other admirable body parts. I was in such an insanely good mood I'd even scared Lily this morning.

Her eyes bugged out when I greeted her in an abnormally chipper manner, then declined the apple fritter she offered me since I'd already had homemade French toast by a man who knew his way around the kitchen as well as the bedroom.

And then that raincloud in the back of my mind flipped my mood to stormy, thinking about how serious Bennett and I were getting so fast. Too fast.

Since the day I'd decided I didn't hate him so much and let the blazing lust between us flare, I'd become consumed, obsessed with him. This passion was burning too bright, like wildfire ravaging too hard and too fast to quench.

In an attempt to distract myself from my thoughts, I pulled up my lesson plans on the desktop, determined to at least get something done while my students took their tests. Someone knocked on my door before I'd gotten through Monday's lesson.

Finn sauntered in. This wasn't unusual. He interrupted my class at least once a day during his off periods.

"Hello, kiddos," he said as he strode to my desk.

A few "hellos" were returned before they frantically went back to their papers.

"They're taking a test," I fussed in a whisper. Meaning, don't disturb them.

Finn had a way of taking over my class and entertaining them with his sparkling personality. He especially loved to do this when we were in a deep discussion of *Pride and Prejudice*, mocking Darcy's stoic character and suggesting that Lizzy should've gone for Bingley since he was much more fun to be around. He did things like this only to get a rise out of me.

He grinned as he plopped his cute ass on the edge of my desk and whispered, "I actually need something."

"What?"

"I know you're busy with *Barefoot*, but I really do need your opinion on *Much Ado*. The current blocking. Your boy Trace got the lead."

I beamed, knowing that he would have. He'd been prepping for auditions for the past month, and he was a natural when we role-played Shakespeare and other classics in the classroom.

"I can't today."

Katherine stood from the back and walked to the side table where I kept supplies the kids could use if they needed them. She picked up the dispenser roll of scotch tape, sniffling as she returned to her desk with it. She never looked up, but I could tell that she'd been crying. Or still was.

"What day do you have off of rehearsal this week?" he asked, still whispering like a good boy so I wouldn't blow a gasket.

"Thursday," I replied, still watching Katherine doing something with her copy of *Jane Eyre.*

"Terrific. Do you mind stopping by just a few minutes after school? I need a second opinion. And I chose this play for you, after all."

Much Ado About Nothing was my favorite comedy by Shakespeare. Not just because the plot and banter were stellar, but because the leading female had my name, Beatrice.

"Sure," I said, turning my attention back to him.

"Not getting much done today, I see," he remarked, lifting my one graded paper from a stack of thirty ungraded.

I slapped his hand and arched a brow at him. He knew damn well not to bring up last night in front of the students. I'd been late again and forced to tell him why since I couldn't keep my post-orgasmic euphoria to even a dim glow when I got to my classroom door this morning.

The first thing he'd said as I swaggered in was, "You finally got laid."

And he'd said it almost within earshot of a student. After punching him and telling him we'd discuss it at lunch, he'd valiantly strolled back to the Fine Arts wing. I'd had to make copies and do some teacher stuff at lunch, so I still hadn't given him the details.

"Do you have time for a cup of coffee after school? So we can *talk*?"

"Yes," I hissed. "Now get out. My kids are testing."

He rolled his eyes as if that were ridiculous. He thought I took academia so seriously. But as I'd told him, we couldn't all play drama games and dress up for a paycheck.

After he closed the door, my attention went back to Katherine, who was hunched over her desk, fiddling with her book. I tried to return to my lesson plans, but I knew something was wrong.

When the bell rang ten minutes later, the last few who hadn't turned in their essays stacked them on my desk as they headed out. Katherine was sniffling loudly again and taking her sweet time packing things up.

When she sauntered up and dejectedly dropped her essay on the stack, I said, "Hold on just a minute, Katherine."

She glanced at me, her eyes red-rimmed, evidence of her crying. "Yes, ma'am."

Once everyone had filed out, I stood and leaned on my desk. "What's wrong?"

"I didn't finish the essay, and I know I'm going to fail it." She let out a quiet sob, staring at the floor.

I was glad I had the next hour off so no one would interrupt us. Katherine was a sensitive student. She made straight As and was on her way to being valedictorian of her senior class. She was quiet and introverted with a few friends who spent most lunches in the library. Most of the time, she was sweet and smiling when she wasn't ignoring the world with her nose in a book or last-minute cramming for a test. This was definitely out of the norm for her.

"You can have more time to finish," I offered. "If I send it home with you, I trust you to complete it on your own."

She looked up at me in shock. "But that wouldn't be fair to the other students."

Katherine was very attuned to what was just and right. She had aspirations to become a defense attorney as a public defender for those who couldn't afford a high-profile attorney. She wanted to be the best defense attorney for the underprivileged in Louisiana history since she saw how unjust and lopsided the law could be if you didn't have enough money to fight your battles. She was an idealist with a charitable spirit and a giant heart.

"If other students needed more time, I'd give it to them, too. However, I wouldn't trust all of them to finish it outside my watchful gaze," I teased.

She smiled and sniffled.

"So, what's going on with your copy of *Jane Eyre*?"

Her face crumbled and her mouth turned down as she lifted the paperback. Everything seemed fine to me. Then she set down her backpack and opened her book to the middle where a page had been torn and taped, obvious damage done by a foot since there was a dirty footprint of a sneaker imprinted on the page.

"What happened?" I asked, taking the book, but still not sure why she was quite this devastated as she sobbed again.

"I was studying in the Commons this morning and needed more space, so I spread out on the floor against the wall near the three-hundred hall." She had to stop and inhale shakily every couple of words as tears poured again. "Then that jackass Emmitt Sanders came running down the hall with one of his dufus friends and stepped right on it."

I grabbed a tissue and handed it to her. While she collected herself, I took a closer look at the retaped page. Other than the footprint, she'd managed to stitch it back together fairly well. Minimal damage, really.

"You've mended it pretty well."

She dropped her hand with the tissue, exhaling a frustrated sigh. "But look how it's all messed up with my notes in the margin. And his dumb footprint all over my page. It was perfect before, and now he's ruined it!"

First off, Katherine never cursed or talked badly about anyone. If she thought uncharitable thoughts, she kept them to herself or shared them only with her group of friends. So for her to blast Emmitt, who happened to be a jackass a lot of the time, she was quite upset.

"You can still see the notes pretty clearly," I added, still not understanding why she was so upset about this.

"You don't understand," she hiccupped.

Apparently not.

"Katherine." I handed back her book. "Explain why this has you so upset."

"I just—" she started, then paused to take a breath. She finally met my gaze, looking absolutely destroyed over this.

My heart clenched, wanting to somehow make this anguish go away but not knowing how.

"It sounds stupid, but I love my books. Like I *love* them. And this class, this unit, has been my favorite of all. I recognize so much of myself in Jane Eyre, and I've loved every second of studying this in your class."

I gave her an encouraging smile to go on.

"I've preserved all of my books from this class and when you taught me sophomore year. I love that we take notes in the margins, and I can go back and relive our discussions when I reread the book. I love how perfect they all are, and now my favorite book is absolutely ruined. And I couldn't calm down enough, so I did badly on the essay. And now my GPA is going to fall and I won't be valedictorian." She was working herself up again into a frenzy.

I put a comforting hand on her forearm. "Hey. These things happen." I wasn't about to say "it's just a book" because obviously, to her, it wasn't. "Sometimes things get ruined. I'm sorry that this one isn't perfect, but—"

Then I stopped, dawning realization slapping me in the face.

The signs had always been there for Katherine, but I'd never internalized it because it had never upset the apple cart.

She was a perfectionist. Every quiz, test, and essay was

completed flawlessly. When she'd miss an answer or I'd take off a point for her elaboration not being entirely correct, she'd stay after class and ask me a hundred questions to be sure she got it right the next time.

She reminded me of myself back in school, actually.

While perfectionism was an amazing catalyst for self-discipline and inner drive, I knew it sometimes got the better of a person and could cause emotional harm like this. I'd been the same way in college, pushing myself to be the absolute best because I needed all the hard work and money I was investing to be worth it.

When I was a freshman at LSU, Lola had to give me tough love and physically take my books away when I'd stayed up on a 24-hour bender of caffeine and energy drinks to study for finals. I was to the point of weeping at my bedroom desk, and she'd had enough. Thankfully, she made me realize that I was hurting myself and that it was okay if I missed some questions. It was even okay if I failed a test.

I decided to go for it anyway, not knowing if this was the right thing to do with Katherine. I turned and shuffled the papers around until I found my copy of *Jane Eyre*.

Turning to the page where hers had been torn, I ripped out the same page.

Katherine gasped, her eyes wide. I didn't think she was even breathing.

"Why would you do that? That's your teacher copy. Your *notes*."

"Nothing remains perfect, Katherine. Nothing. Now I'll tape mine back up, and it'll look just like yours. Minus Emmitt's big, dumb footprint."

She let out a shocked laugh. "I don't understand."

"I just wanted to make my point clear. Look." I took the tape dispenser, taped the page back together on the front and the back and showed her. "Can I still teach effectively with this?"

She nodded.

"Am I going to do a less than brilliant job lecturing on Jane and Rochester with this book now?"

She shook her head.

"It's okay if things get screwed up sometimes, but what's in here"—I tapped on her forehead—"and in here"—I tapped on my heart—"will still be perfect. And by perfect, I mean intelligent and kind and giving. Perfection is unattainable. For humans or anything else in life. Nothing and no one can ever be flawless."

She nodded, her smile wider and genuine. Grateful, even.

"I have an extra assignment for you tonight when you finish your essay. You can think of it as your penalty for not finishing in class if it makes you feel better." Because she was the kind of student who might feel she deserved an extra assignment for having the privilege of finishing her essay at home. "Research the Ruins of the Glastonbury Cathedral in England and write a short, one-paragraph explanation of why these ruins are more beautiful now than they were when the cathedral was built."

I'd had the chance to visit Glastonbury years ago when I traveled to England one summer. It was the most beautiful place I'd ever been, the way the sunlight filtered through the broken arches stretching toward the sky. It was old and tarnished with age, crumbling into ruins, yet it was magnificently beautiful. More so with the natural light of the sun streaming onto every stone.

"Not all things need to be fresh and new and *perfect* to be beautiful," I told her.

"Thank you, Ms. B." She leaned forward and hugged me, which I wasn't ready for.

I settled back at my desk and heaved a sigh at how I'd once

been so much like Katherine. I'd even had sessions with a therapist while at LSU. Her words floated back to me from one of our last sessions. It had brought me both a heavy dose of self-actualization and bitter heartache.

"Perfectionism is innate, Betty. There is nothing wrong or bad at all with this part of your personality. It's what gives you drive and tenacity."

"Then why do I allow it to take over and cause me harm?"

"That part is from another source. It can be a fear of judgment or disapproval of others. Something from earlier in life. Do you think that your father's abandonment may cause you to strive for perfection so that no one has cause to abandon you again?"

I sucked in a breath, watching a drop of water fall to the essay on my desk. Not water. A tear. Wiping the back of my hand across my face, my mind drifted to the memory of my father walking down the driveway with a suitcase, not even looking back as I cried at the window, calling for him to come back.

Wiping my face with a tissue, I shoved that memory to the back of my mind, determined to forget my father.

Rehearsal was tonight. If anyone could cheer me up, it was Bennett.

Chapter Nineteen

~BENNETT~

I LOVED MY FAMILY. I TRULY DID. BUT SOMETIMES, THEY COULD drive me batshit crazy.

Mom had asked me to stop by this afternoon after work to pick up some of the leftover gumbo from the cookoff so I could freeze it.

What she really wanted was to interrogate me about Betty, then chastise me for not introducing her to the family sooner.

I definitely wasn't going to tell her that I was waiting as long as possible to put her in front of the Broussard welcome wagon. Because my family wasn't exactly welcoming. They were more like a league of scientists inspecting a foreign organism to determine if it was allowed to mingle with its host. And I wasn't ready to terrify the living shit out of Betty.

Then there was my brother, who also happened to stop by our parents' house this afternoon.

"Ben, you've got that constipated look again."

My loving, supportive brother.

Then again, Betty held her own with Hale just fine. Maybe it wouldn't be such a nightmare for her to meet the family.

Pop walked into the kitchen. "Who the hell took my Imodium?"

Yeah, I made the right decision to hold off a little longer.

Pop had lived with my parents since my grandmother passed away about eight years ago. My parents' home, the one I was raised in, was a six-thousand-square-foot home in the gated community next to the golf course Sugar Oaks. It was my mom's idea for Pop to move in so she could be sure he was fed properly.

Never mind that Pop owned a specialty meat shop and could cook pretty damn well on his own. Hale used to follow him around in the kitchen when we were little. But Pop wasn't going to argue with Beth Broussard. She was a force to be reckoned with when she had her mind set on something.

Besides, he had a giant wing of the house all to himself, including a kitchenette and patio.

Pop was slamming cabinets when Mom said, "I bought you a brand-new bottle on Thursday. It's in your kitchen above the coffee pot."

He grunted, turning to face me where I had parked my ass against the counter, both hands gripping the marble behind me. I clenched my jaw tight.

Everything was revving me up more than usual. Maybe it was because all I could wonder was, what would Betty think of this insanity? She seemed so skittish sometimes like anything might send her packing. Would she decide I wasn't worth the annoyance? Or would she laugh them off?

Probably laugh them off.

"Now you're making a creepy clown smile," said Hale, eating a bowl of chicken tortilla soup from a stool at the big island, shoveling food like a goddamn gorilla into his maw. "You look weirder than normal today."

"He needs a woman," said Pop from next to Hale, eating one of the tortilla strips used to crumble on top of Mom's homemade soup.

"He's got one," offered Hale, "and she's a firecracker."

I wanted to punch that shit-eating grin right off his face because now I had to deal with—

"Oh, ho!" bellowed Pop, turning his full attention on me.

Sighing, I rolled my eyes and crossed my arms.

"What's she look like?" Pop waggled his bushy, white eyebrows.

Before I could answer him, Hale jumped in. "She's a redhead. And a hottie. With a smart mouth."

"I like her already." Pop nudged Hale with his elbow then asked him, not me, "What about her gams? She got nice ones?"

"Lovely stems. And a perky ass."

I swear Pop and Hale acted like two middle schoolers. Even though I knew they were purposefully poking the bear, I couldn't fucking keep my mouth shut.

"She's also smart and funny and amazing in every damn way. Stop talking about her like she's a piece of meat," I snapped back, trying not to lose my cool. And obviously failing.

The room went silent as three pairs of eyes focused on me. Mom with a sweet, knowing look. Hale's grin widened. Pop looked confused.

"What?" I practically shouted.

"We got him," murmured Hale to Pop.

"No, sir," he grumbled. "*She's* got him."

Before I could grab my quart of gumbo and storm from the room and off to rehearsal, where I couldn't wait to be, Dad walked in still in his business clothes. "Who is *she*?"

He read the room in the three seconds of the conversation he'd overheard as he walked in.

"Bennett's new girlfriend," said my mom. "Are you hungry, Peter?"

Dad grunted. Whether it was about me having a girlfriend—though I wasn't sure Betty would agree with that title, I didn't correct my mom—or about whether Dad was hungry, I had no idea.

It didn't matter. Tension tightened every muscle in my body as Dad got that calculating look when he found me in the kitchen.

"I wanted to talk to you about the store," he told me, gesturing to the kitchen exit, then walking out and down the hallway leading to his office.

Why the fuck hadn't I left when I'd had the chance?

I didn't even look at Pop or Hale, knowing they wore identical pitying looks on their faces. Mom gave me her reassuring smile.

Heaving a sigh, I followed in my dad's wake toward his office, feeling like I did when I was sixteen, working at his appliance store. He'd often lecture me on how to handle customers or when to upsell a new model or how proper salesmanship led to a gratifying, successful business career but came with lots of hard work.

By the time I stepped into his office, my muscles were strung tight, my lips compressed to keep my mouth shut. I'd been edgy all day.

Something about that conversation with Betty this morning had rubbed me wrong. I'd just wanted to wait a while longer before she started seeing all of my faults, say when she was as obsessed with me as much as I was with her.

Obsession wasn't the right word. It was much more profound, much more life-changing. More heart-changing.

I rubbed my chest, remembering her sweetness as she apologized for being nosy.

Simply the thought of her eased the throb of stress pressing in on my temples as I stopped beside Dad's desk.

He'd been sending me article after article for the past two years, ever since I'd started researching and planning to open my own business. Originally, he'd balked at the idea of a Whole Foods-type supermarket in Beauville. But he backed down once I'd researched the town's demographics through the Chamber of Commerce. When I'd given him a detailed chart of my data, I had the triumphant honor of proving that I knew what I was talking about.

Thank God for my grandfather. If Pop hadn't helped me out, investing in me financially, I'm not sure I could've pulled it off. Pop had believed in me.

Now my father? His high expectations were the ones that kept me up at night. The ones that made me doubt whether I actually knew what I was doing. The ones that had me balling my fists in my pockets as he pulled up whatever he was going to show me on his computer.

Dad clicked open an Excel spreadsheet. I scowled at what I was looking at. Then the anxiety retreated, replaced by fury.

"How did you get those numbers?"

My father frowned up at me, recognizing the anger in my voice. I didn't spare him a glance as I zoned in on the receipts of my store since opening day. They were accurate because I checked them daily, almost obsessively.

"Don't get bent out of shape," he told me. "I got them from your new bookkeeper."

Sylvia Theriot. The woman I'd recently hired whose son was in Betty's class. Of course, he'd go to her and demand information he had no right to, knowing she'd give him whatever he asked.

I didn't blame her. My father could be authoritative and persuasive, one reason he'd been so successful as a local businessman. But I would be having a discussion with all of my employees and drive home the fact that my father, though his name was Broussard, does not, in fact, have permission to give any orders at my store. Nor does he have the right to take vital information, like my incoming/outgoing receipts.

I inhaled and exhaled, trying to calm my boiling blood. But it wasn't working.

"I wanted to show you that if you stay on this course, you won't even come out even next month. You've got to cut back on these imported products from overseas that are costing a fortune. And what the hell are you hiring a Michelin-star chef from Lafayette for? It's a grocery store, not a restaurant, Ben. If you—"

"Dad." The rattling rage in my voice cut him off.

His mouth spread into a thin, tight line as he recognized I didn't appreciate his advice.

If I wasn't so fucking furious, I'd laugh.

My father had stepped over the line plenty of times, all in his efforts to *help* me. But this was beyond that. This was not only illegal but was damaging to my psyche. If I was going to fail, I wanted to fail all on my own. I didn't need him trying to throw me a life raft. And the thing was, he had no fucking idea what he was talking about.

Dad," I started again, marginally more civil, "you own appliance stores. While yes, it is a retail business, it is far, far, *far* different than my own. I'm not simply running a grocery store. I'm attempting to offer something new and different for Beauville and local residents. A lifestyle change to better their quality of life. This isn't just a mini-Walmart."

"Exactly. And you're in way over your head, Bennett. I can see with the numbers that—"

"Don't ever presume to come into my store and steal my receipts again."

He stopped talking, finally realizing the level of anger

riding me hard. He didn't even defend himself; he wasn't stealing, just trying to help or some similar bullshit.

"You know appliances," I continued, slowly gaining control of my temper. "You don't know anything about what I'm doing. I've done my due diligence for longer than the two years I've been planning and building this store. I've been considering this since I graduated college and saw the upward trend in healthy foods and realized that there was very little of that offered to residents in Beauville and within a thirty-mile radius."

He leaned back in his chair and crossed his arms defiantly, but he didn't say a word.

"I am well aware that my expenses extend beyond sales this month. I expected it. I planned for it. It's an investment in the community to build a different kind of experience and draw the kinds of customers that will come back again and again when they see what I have to offer at Fresh Market."

I felt compelled to defend myself to my father, the man I respected more than anyone, even when he made me want to throttle him.

"You don't understand these numbers or how it will change dramatically after the initial costs because this isn't your business. This is mine. I know *exactly* what I'm doing. I've modeled my store after several highly successful similar ones across the country that I've researched in finite detail." I scoffed. "Dad, when have you ever seen me do anything without extreme, detailed planning?"

His own irritation with me—his stubborn son—subsided. He heaved out a sigh. "I was only trying to help. I don't want you to—" He stopped himself, not saying what I clearly knew he was about to.

"I know, Dad. You don't want me to fail. Neither do I," I stated the obvious. The fear that he could be right tried to raise its ugly head, but I stomped it down. That was when my anxiety spiked and let those demons into my head. "You've got to trust me. I know what I'm doing."

His gaze dipped down as he nodded, then he looked back up at me. "Fine." He stood and exhaled another sigh, apparently completely frustrated with me.

Laughable. I'd wanted to punch him in the face when I first saw those numbers on his screen. And he was exasperated with *me*? I realized he did everything out of concern for me, but this was beyond crossing a line. I was done being Dad's pet.

Something inside me eased at the thought.

"And delete those," I told him as I turned for the door.

"Fine," he grumbled. "You're coming to the fundraiser next Saturday."

A command, not a question. The tightness returned in a millisecond. Every time I thought I was out from under his thumb, he reminded me I wasn't.

I'd been attending the local fundraisers since I was a teenager. They were good for business, mingling with the money of Beauville. And seeing as my store catered to a lot of clientele in those circles, I'd have to keep attending.

"Sure," I said, "but I'll be bringing someone."

"Good, good. I'd like to meet this new girl."

I heard his indifference, even if he didn't mean it. But I couldn't blame him. No girl I ever brought around lasted very long. I wasn't about to get sentimental with my dad and tell him this girl was different.

This girl was everything. She made the shadows go away when she smiled. She made me happier than I'd ever been in my entire life.

"I've gotta get to rehearsal," I told him as I walked out, knowing he didn't understand why I wasted time volunteering with community theater.

What he didn't understand was that the stage was my joy, my escape from the mundane and the hard work of everyday life. Yes, I'd longed to open this business. But it was work. A living.

The theater was play.

And I wanted to be there more than anywhere else these days because a beautiful redhead was waiting there for me.

I was practically running when I walked back into the kitchen. I kissed Mom, grabbed the gumbo, and tore out of there before Hale or Pop could make another comment. All I could think about was getting to the theater and getting to *her*.

Chapter Twenty

~BETTY~

Something was wrong. Even though Bennett had pulled me in for a tight hug the second he stepped on stage at rehearsal, the hug lingered longer than expected with our small audience of Peter, Trish, Frank, and Meredith.

One of his arms scooped underneath my long cardigan that hung down to my thighs to cover my butt in my comfy tights I was wearing. Since my hair was up in a messy bun out of my way, his nose grazed my neck as he inhaled against my skin. I shivered. Right when I went to pull him tighter, he let me go and abruptly settled into studying his script, avoiding eye contact with me.

I thought maybe he didn't want to show PDA or something, especially since we hadn't let the cast or directors know we were dating. Not that it would make a difference. Peter milled around the stage, showing Trish where he wanted a small set of stairs and landing built upstage, paying zero attention to us.

I stepped closer and whispered, "Is everything okay?"

"Of course." He gave me a big smile, but my instincts told me otherwise. After several years of analyzing teenagers' mood swings based on body posture and facial expressions, my Spidey senses were pretty damn attuned to when something was amiss.

"Is it about this morning?" I whispered as we walked backstage to our opening positions where no one could see us.

He turned, eyes wide with concern. "No, no." He cupped my face, giving me the eye contact I'd been craving since he walked in. "Just work stuff. And my Dad. Nothing to worry about." Then he kissed me softly right as Peter yelled, "Action!" from the audience.

We launched into Act One, nailing every scene without missing a beat. We even had Trish cackling so loud we had to pause in the group scenes that included Corie's mother and Mr. Velasco's characters, who served as the comic relief of the play. We'd have to pause for laughter with a live audience, so it was good practice.

Peter was so proud we'd remembered every line and the blocking that we went full steam ahead into Act Two.

Meredith blundered an entrance with the blocking—sitting on the sofa instead of the chair downstage—but still knew all her lines, so we kept going.

It was when Bennett made his second entrance in Act Two that we started having trouble. Or actually, Bennett did. He jumped ahead a line in our dialogue. After a short pause, I kept going, trying to make up for the little mistake.

Then he overstepped one of Meredith's lines, which was a cue for me.

"Wait, did I miss something?" Meredith asked frantically, breaking character in the scene and looking out at Trish.

"My line was coming up where she tells her mom about the man living in the attic," I added.

"Oh, I thought that was after…?" She trailed off, looking at Bennett.

Bennett frowned. "Oh, sorry." Then he bellowed, "Line!"

Trish was our line-deliverer as assistant director, but she'd only give it if we got lost and couldn't figure out where to pick back up. It was often better for us to struggle through the scene and work through it on our own.

Trish called out Bennett's line that we skipped, that he'd forgotten.

"That's right," he murmured to himself, then jumped back into character and delivered the line, frustration apparent in his voice.

We moved on, making our way a little more roughly than we'd rehearsed Act One. Then we came upon a scene where I got mixed up, thinking I'd missed something.

I turned to Trish. "Line? Was that me?"

"No," said Trish, looking down at the script in her hands. "It was Bennett."

"Shit," he muttered.

It wasn't the cursing that made me wince; it was the obvious aggravation in his voice and the tightness of his jaw and mouth. I barely heard what Trish was saying, recalling that part of the scene. But Bennett was in obvious distress.

"Can we take a short bathroom break and look at our scripts really quick before we continue on?" I asked.

Bennett's expression softened on me, a look of gratitude washing over him before he exited the stage without a word toward the lounge, or Green Room as we called it.

"Sure, let's take five, then we'll back up to Mrs. Banks's entrance," said Peter before turning to Trish.

Frank grabbed his script and sank onto the sofa on the stage while Meredith did the same, pointing out something to him.

I didn't wait another second. I immediately strode backstage to find Bennett.

He was sitting on the loveseat in the Green Room area, his arms at his sides, his head back on the sofa, his eyes closed.

Oh, boy.

After sitting quietly beside him, I put a hand on his knee. His muscle tightened beneath, but he didn't open his eyes.

"You okay?" I asked softly.

He swallowed hard, his throat working before saying, "Sometimes, things just trigger my anxiety, and I can't think past it. Through it. It fucks my head up so bad."

Brushing my hand on his knee comfortingly, I asked, "What triggered you this time?"

"My dad," he answered quickly.

"You've never talked to me about your dad," I said softly.

He'd mentioned Hale in several conversations and talked about his mother admiringly, such as how she was a Broadway actress in New York when she was young. And he'd told me about his Pop, but I don't think he'd ever mentioned his father to me.

"Do y'all not have a good relationship?" I asked when he wouldn't answer.

He lifted his head, gaze on me, stress carved into the set lines of his face. I wanted to wipe it all away, but I didn't know how.

"My father..." he started but then paused, covering my hand with his own on his knee. "He's a good man. I know his intentions have always been good."

"But?"

"But he never knows when to just leave me the fuck alone," he grated. "I got my MBA from LSU so that I could start my own business and hopefully, finally, be out from underneath his thumb. For fuck's sake, I deliberately told him two years ago, well in advance, that he needed to find another manager for his stores when mine was built because I'd be leaving Broussard Appliances for good."

His chest rose and fell more quickly.

"And how did he feel about that?"

He shrugged, his eyes not on me but on some distant point in the room in front of him. "He wasn't happy, but I didn't expect him to be. But then the grilling of my plans started and all of his fucking advice started rolling in. The problem is that it doesn't matter what I do. I'll never be good enough." His gaze snapped to mine, a feverish, tormented look shining in his hazel eyes, his words catapulting my heart rate faster. I knew that feeling well. "Do you know that he didn't even congratulate me on the grand opening? You know what he told me that night?"

"What?" I asked softly, trying not to show my own anguish at the sight of his pain.

"He told me, 'Now the real work begins.'" He scoffed. "He can't just be happy for me. Or accept that I might know what the hell I'm doing. Or, for fuck's sake, just support me even if I fail. It's always about what I'm not doing good enough."

"Have you ever told your dad how you feel?"

His head swiveled to me, an expression of shock wiping away the pain that had been etched there a second ago. "Uh, no. We don't have those types of conversations."

"The kinds where you share your feelings."

He shook his head and stared down at his lap, taking my hand in his and brushing his thumb over the veins in my wrist. "We don't have that kind of relationship. Our house isn't like yours."

He didn't say it as an insult but a simple observation.

"You mean like my hippie mom who talked to me about birth control, condoms, and clitoral orgasms at thirteen?"

He huffed out a laugh and looked over at me. "She didn't."

"She most certainly did. She wanted to be sure we knew

that we could explore our bodies and have safe orgasms without the help of a man. But she also wanted to provide safe sex options for us if and when we decided to include boys in the mix."

He looked at me dazedly, a small smile quirking his mouth. "I can't even imagine." Then he chuckled.

"What?"

"My dad caught Hale jacking off once in the downstairs bathroom when he was fourteen. His only advice was, *do that in your own bathroom or lock the goddamn door*. That was the only sex talk he or I ever got from either of my parents."

"Your mom never offered any?"

He laced our fingers together. "Before my first date, my mom said, 'Be nice, Bennett. Remember that all girls have fathers and brothers.' She was basically telling me to treat them like I would a sister or imagine how I'd feel if my date's father or brother knew what I was doing."

I laughed. "That's twisted."

"It was her way of making me keep it in my pants."

"And did it work?"

He gave me a devilish look, his smile curling in a way that had my heart rate quickening for a different reason.

"A little. I engaged in lots of oral sex in high school, telling myself I was kind of obeying her. I didn't lose my virginity till I was nineteen and in college, so I'd say it was partly effective."

Laughing again, I squeezed his hand. "And how about Hale?"

He blew out a breath and rolled his eyes. "Nothing ever stopped Hale from doing what he wanted. Least of all his conscience or bad parental advice."

Unable to stop myself, I climbed onto his lap, draping my legs over his right thigh and looping my arms around his neck. "I don't think it was bad advice from your mom. She wanted you to respect women. It was sweet, actually."

He wrapped one arm around my waist underneath my cardigan and draped another hand on my thigh, hugging me tighter. The warmth of his hand seeped through the tights I was wearing. I could feel the tension and rigidity loosening from his frame.

With my forehead pressed to his neck where I could smell how utterly delicious he was, I started to softly sing the Disney song "Let It Go."

His chest shook with silent laughter when I stopped after one awful chorus. "What are you doing?" he asked, stupefied.

"Making you laugh. Making you let go of all that stress." I looked up at him, our faces inches apart. "Did it work?"

His smile slipped as he homed in on my mouth. "You are something else, Betty Mouton. And you really are a terrible singer."

His hand squeezed my leg, his expression tender.

"Told you I was. I don't lie." I basked in his softening mood, his sweet side coming out. "Wanna sleep at my house tonight?"

He leaned in and pressed a soft kiss to my lips. "Fuck yeah, I do."

I wrapped my arms tighter around his neck and pressed my forehead to his. "You don't have to go to the store after work tonight?"

Because he seemed to live there when he wasn't at rehearsal.

"Not tonight," he whispered against my lips, grazing his nose along mine, his palm running a soothing pattern up and down my spine. My heart squeezed at the tenderness of his touch and the look in his eyes.

"Okay, guys, Peter's ready—oops! So sorry." Meredith was halfway down the ramp. "Uh, Peter wants to get started." Then she headed quickly back up the ramp toward the stage.

"Cat's out of the bag now," I told him.

"That we're dating?" he asked, brow raised.

"Uh-huh."

"So we *are* officially dating?" His smile widened, his grip on me tightening.

I snorted a laugh. "Of course, we are dummy. I would never introduce a guy to my hippie mom otherwise."

"How many guys have met your mom beside me?"

I thought about it for a second. "One."

His jaw tightened, a frown pinching his brow. "Who?" His voice dropped to a dangerous vibration. It made me smile.

"Finn," I finally answered on a laugh, putting him out of his misery.

He growled and kissed me hard, gripping the back of my head so I couldn't get away. Not that I was trying to.

Then his kiss turned gentle and we were gazing at each other in a way that we never had. The moment wasn't consumed with heat, but with a softer warmth that resonated straight through my chest, electrifying my heart to beat faster.

He held my nape but pulled away, the intensity of his gaze sending a shot of adrenaline through me. No man had ever looked at me like that. Like I was precious and so very important…to him. It both amazed and terrified me. But most of all, it called to me, wanting me to fall deeper into this feeling of wonderment. And sweet belonging.

"Come on, lovebirds," Frank called down the rampway.

We both jumped, as if snapping out of a trance.

For a few seconds, Bennett still held me in place, then he gripped my waist and lifted me to my feet. Before I could take one step, he grabbed me around the waist and hauled me back, wrapping his arms tight.

He pressed a kiss to the side of my neck. "Thank you," he whispered.

I wrapped my arms over his. "For what?"

"For cheering me up." He kissed my temple. "For being so good to me."

My pulse tripped faster. “I like being good to you.”

“Oh, Betty.” He huffed out a little laugh, hugging me tighter. “Where have you been?”

He buried his face in my neck and we simply swayed in place, him holding me from behind and me melting into the sweetness of the moment. The sweetness of this man. This gentle emotion blooming inside me was new and lovely, and a little scary.

Peter’s voice rang out from the audience, yelling our names, breaking the spell.

Bennett’s hands slid to my waist, gripping and giving me a tight squeeze before he gave me a soft kiss on the cheek and let me go.

When I glanced over my shoulder as we headed onto the stage, he still had that hypnotic look, the one that did more than turn me on. The one that pulled me toward him with a force I wasn’t sure I could fight against, even if I tried.

Chapter Twenty-One

~BENNETT~

BETTY HAD SUCCESSFULLY DISTRACTED ME FROM MY MELTDOWN, flipping a switch I usually couldn't turn back off until the panic attack subsided.

She had worked magic on my brain, dislodging the stressor of the incident with my dad so I could concentrate on the script. Interestingly enough, after our break in the Green Room, it was Betty who kept fumbling over lines and missing cues.

I knew why. Something shifted between us during that break. The attraction between us was heavier now, magnetized by something stronger than lust. I knew it. And she knew it.

Meredith opened her mouth to say a line when a thundering boom rattled the rafters. A second crash of thunder quickly followed the first. Meredith yelped.

"Okay, guys," said Peter, glancing down at his Smartwatch. "I didn't realize we had bad weather rolling in. Let's stop there before the rain hits."

Everyone gathered their things quickly. Frank walked Meredith out through the back exit, leading directly to the parking lot.

"Y'all go ahead," said Peter, walking toward the reception area. "I parked out front. I'll lock up and set the alarm once you all leave through the back."

"Bye, guys," said Trish, hurrying for the back exit. "Careful driving home!"

I waited for Betty to find her purse in the third row where she'd dropped it, then she hurried in front of me, giving me a small smile. "Finally," she said.

Grinning, I nudged her at the small of her back toward the side curtain that led past the Green Room and to the back exit.

By now, my body was vibrating, needing her like I needed my next breath.

Ever since she'd calmed me with her sweet side, I'd been dying to sink inside her. I needed her tight warmth all around me. Her soft sighs as she clung to me and came apart.

We shoved out the backdoor, straight into a deluge of pounding rain.

Betty squealed as we took off for our cars, holding her cardigan over her head. Though it did little good in the heavy downpour.

She was parked right next to me. Rain soaked us through. A crash of lightning made Betty jump, and she dropped her purse between our cars.

I picked it up, but instead of handing it to her, I jerked open the passenger side of my truck and yelled over the rain, "Get in!"

She didn't hesitate, jumping up into the cab of my truck. I climbed in after her and tossed her purse to the driver's side before hauling her onto my lap. Without a word, she dropped the cardigan and straddled me, then ground herself down on my soaking jeans.

I fisted a hand in her wet hair and pulled tightly, arching her neck. Licking a line up her throat, I tasted fresh rain and salty skin. I groaned as I jerked the loose shoulder of her blouse down. Loving that she wore these loose-fitting lacy bras, I tugged the delicate strap down and wrapped my mouth around her entire breast.

"Ah!" she cried out, lifting up and thrusting her chest out for me while grinding her pussy against me. "Feels so good. So good."

It did. That need for connection, to be so deep inside her, was driving me mad. I'd never wanted a woman like this.

Groaning, I flicked her tight nipple back and forth with the tip of my tongue then sucked it one more time, admiring the berry-red color before I nipped my way back to her mouth.

"So fucking beautiful," I murmured against her lips, kissing her hard and sucking on her tongue.

Her moans escalated, our body heat fogging the windows as lightning crashed and thunder vibrated the cab of my truck.

She pulled off my shirt and scraped her rounded nails down my chest, tweaking my nipple as she went.

"Fuck! Need you, baby," I breathed on a hot huff of air, sliding a hand between her legs and rubbing her swollen clit, her tights hot and wet from her arousal. "Fucking need you now."

"Yes, yes," she moaned, reaching down to the hem of her blouse and stripping it off. She then pulled both straps of her bra down, revealing the other breast, the nipple a pale rosy color, begging for my full attention.

On a feral growl, I lowered my head and took her neglected nipple into my mouth. Her hips bucked off of me as she cried out.

"Ah, God, so good, sweetie. Keep sucking me."

My brain hazed at her pleasure-filled cries, her pleading for me to suck her. Without even thinking, I grabbed hold of the material between her legs and jerked, ripping it wide.

She whimpered while working at my snap and zipper. I lifted up enough to shove my jeans and briefs down, still latched to the tender peak of her nipple, suckling it hard.

When my cock was free, she gripped my neck as she rose above me, her other hand clenched in my hair. I rolled on a condom faster than I ever had in my life, and while I held her gaze, I gripped my thick dick at the base and slid her panties aside, wetting the tip in her soaked folds.

Her eyes glazed over then slid closed. I loosened my hand in her hair to get a better grip on the wet strands at her nape.

"Open your eyes, baby."

Midnight blue slits slid open, dazed with arousal. But more than that. I wanted that look she'd given me earlier, the vulnerable one. I wanted that fragile moment to stretch between us as I took her tonight.

"Want to see those beautiful eyes when I sink inside you," I growled, thrusting up slowly to the hilt as I pushed her down with a hand on her hip. *"Fuck."*

She gasped, mouth falling open, but didn't close her eyes. Simply held my gaze as my hard dick throbbed deep inside her. She squirmed, trying to move, but I held her still.

"You feel that?"

I wasn't talking about my dick for once. I was talking about that deeper connection. She stared back at me, brows pinched as she nodded.

Then I slid my hand between us, gliding my thumb through her folds to slide her juice around her clit.

"You're soaking wet for me," I murmured. "You know how fucking crazy that makes me?"

"Bennett," she moaned, pressing her forehead to mine. "Stop torturing me and fuck me."

I braced my legs wider, boots flat on the cab floor and

pumped up inside her sweet pussy with deep thrusts, circling her swollen clit with my thumb.

"So hot and tight." I nipped and licked her lips, holding her gaze. "Wanna fuck you forever."

Her nails dug into my scalp as she clenched her inner muscles around me.

"That's right. You squeeze my dick. Milk all your pleasure. I want you to take what you need and come hard." I bit her lip. "Only from me."

"Bennett," she whimpered. "Stop or I'm going to come too quick."

"No such thing," I whispered in a low, steady voice, still working her clit. "Come all over me, baby. Whenever you're ready. I could fuck you all night like this. For forever."

She clawed one hand down my chest again, groaning, her eyes open on mine.

"You think I'm kidding, don't you?"

Suddenly, the words were spilling, and I didn't even care. Maybe it was that her own honesty battered down the walls I kept so firmly in place. Her openness, her sincere compassion, her wild beauty. It all called to the deepest part of me, screaming for me to lay claim to this magnificent woman.

Holding her gaze, I kept fucking her with hard, steady thrusts. "You make me ache. You make me want you so bad, I could go insane thinking about getting inside you." I gripped her hair tighter and surged against her mouth for a brief, tender kiss, keeping her lips against mine so she could feel the words I was about to press there. "Sometimes, all I can think about is spreading you wide and fucking you long and hard, coming inside you so deep that you're marked as mine. So good that you won't ever even think about giving it to another man."

She made a desperate sound in the back of her throat, half-lidded eyes watching me while I made my dirty confession.

"I want you to crave me pounding you deep, knowing it's the only one you'll ever feel again." I licked her bottom lip, which was trembling with heady emotion. "Need you to know that this sweet, sweet pussy"—I lifted my hand and sucked her juice from my thumb then pressed my thumb between her open lips—"this pussy is mine now, baby. Only mine."

Whatever she saw in my eyes or heard in my words sent her over the edge. Her neck snapped back and she let out a growling scream, filling up my cab as she pulsed around my cock.

"Yes, just like that," I murmured, planting my feet hard and lifting my hips off the seat.

Holding her by the waist, I pistoned inside her through her orgasm, groaning at the fluttering sensations, pulling me toward my own climax.

"That's it. Squeeze me tight. I'm all yours."

"Oh, fuck, Bennett." Her head fell to my shoulder as she came again, a pulse of ripples squeezing me.

"Mmmm," I moaned then buried my face into her neck.

Thrusting twice more before embedding myself deep and holding hard, I came inside her with a shivering orgasm that barreled down my spine, tightening every muscle in my body.

When the rolling waves subsided, I eased my hips back to the seat, wrapping my arms tight and holding her torso to mine, loving her small, bare breasts against my chest.

She breathed heavily, brushing a hand through my hair. Finally able to see straight, I kissed a line up her throat and along her jaw till I found her mouth. After a long, languorous kiss with more lips than tongue, I pulled back to see if I saw fear or hesitation in her gaze.

There was none. If anything, she looked at me with the deep emotion I craved. Longed for.

Still, I didn't think Betty wanted to talk about this new

emotion floating between us. It was still too new and raw, untried.

The rain had started to lessen, still sprinkling steadily but not the same downpour. The thunder rolled farther away. The windows were steamed up, so if anyone strolling by had tried to get a peek, they certainly wouldn't have seen anything.

Not that it would've stopped me from fucking her in my truck anyway. When I'd gotten my hands on her, I couldn't stop. This feverish need barreling through my blood with blinding speed and alarming determination was almost terrifying.

"Did I scare you?" I finally asked, wanting to know for sure if I'd frightened her away with my declaration. Maybe she hadn't understood it. Maybe she didn't think I was serious. Just my filthy mouth saying meaningless words to get her to come.

Not one word I'd said was meaningless. I meant every single one.

"What?" she asked softly. "That you kind of just told me you wanted me and only me. Forever?"

Softening my hold but not letting her go, I said without a hint of hesitation. "No 'kind of' about it, Betty." I eased my head back so she could see my expression and know I was serious. "I've been around long enough to know what I want. To know what I need whenever I see it. Whenever I hold her." I squeezed. "You're it for me."

The thought that I could possibly have a woman like her. That she might be able to overlook all of my faults and work-a-holic tendencies. I held my breath, waiting for her reply, a shock of fear blanketing me at the thought she might say no.

It was too soon to tell her things like that. I should've waited, kept my feelings to myself. Even though I knew, without a doubt, that my feelings were real. That this didn't come along often. For some people, it never did.

She coasted her fingers through the wet bangs falling

across my forehead, keeping me in agony for at least thirty seconds before returning to my gaze.

“Okay,” she finally said, seeming nervous, her eyes wide.

“Okay?” It wasn’t a declaration of love. Of course, I hadn’t said the words either, though I felt it growing between us.

“I’ll be your girlfriend, Bennett Broussard,” she said cheekily with a big smile.

My heart clenched; my pulse pounded. Then I smiled and kissed her again.

Girlfriend seemed a paltry label for what I wanted, for what I felt, but I was happy with this exclusive label.

For now.

Chapter Twenty-Two

~BETTY~

Trace was reading aloud Byron's poem "She Walks In Beauty." Like most poetry, it was meant to be read aloud, the words, rhyme and rhythm savored. And Trace's sonorous, articulate voice was doing it justice.

Caroline seemed to notice. Her gaze wasn't on the page but on him with dreamy wonder, her attention riveted. So was Heather's, Naomi's, Sarah's, and every other girl in first period. I couldn't blame them.

Trace wore the combination of bad boy, intelligence, and swagger that would have most teenage girls swooning. I couldn't help but smile as he finished the poem's final lines, followed by audible feminine sighs from multiple corners of the room.

"Indeed," I murmured, drawing their attention. "Byron was a lover. He knew how to use words to woo women. Can you tell?"

"Yeah," agreed Sarah in the first row next to Caroline.

"Byron lived in an age where romance flourished. And poetry was one of the best art forms to express romance."

"Romance is dead nowadays," added Sarah on a huff.

"Is that all it took?" Emmitt frowned down at his textbook. "Because if you ask me, that was a bunch of sappy nonsense. All he said was 'you're pretty' in a bunch more words than necessary. Seems like overkill to me."

Emmitt might've been in a grouchy mood because I told him he owed Katherine a new, pristine copy of *Jane Eyre*. I'd even given him a link on Amazon for a beautiful hardbound book with gold embossing if he was feeling extra generous. He'd frowned but had screenshotted the Amazon page anyway.

"Of course, *you'd* think that," said Heather. "But I bet girls in his era didn't think so."

"I don't think so either," agreed Naomi, her petite friend next to her.

"What happened to women's rights? Feminist equality and all that?" asked Trace.

"What do you mean?" asked Caroline with a little laugh.

"I thought women wanted to be recognized for their brains and their strength nowadays. Not something as superficial as their looks."

"It's not just what he's saying," Caroline bristled. "It's how he's saying it." She looked back at Emmitt sitting behind Trace. "It's not just that he told her she was pretty. It's that he took the time to put his thoughts into a poem. A little work of art. Just for her."

"So now women need to be worshipped with words." Trace grinned. "I thought the twenty-first-century woman was above all that. That you wanted straight honesty and respect. Not flattery." He was being antagonistic on purpose, but I'd discovered over the past couple of weeks that this was his and Caroline's love language. Argumentation.

"This isn't flattery," snapped Caroline. "This is admiration and eloquence."

"So if I were to write a poem about a girl, telling her with *eloquence* all that I admired about her besides her looks, she'd go to Homecoming with me?"

Emmitt snickered, but Caroline didn't. There were some other chuckles in the room. Caroline's fair face flushed pink. Trace simply held her gaze, waiting for an answer.

Oh, boy. Time to step in.

"I'm glad you brought that up, Trace." All eyes swiveled to me as I flicked on the Smart Board at the front of the room with the new assignment listed for the day. "Today, you'll be writing your own three-quatrain poem, following the rhyme scheme of Byron's 'She Walks In Beauty.'"

Emmitt grumbled then banged his head on his desk. Someone laughed.

"However, you don't have to write about romance. Especially since Sarah thinks romance is dead. Your subject matter can be—"

Knock, knock, knock.

We all turned toward the door. Through the narrow rectangular window, all we could see were…flowers.

Then the door opened and someone stepped in with a giant bouquet. I sighed because the Homecoming theatrics had been in full swing for weeks.

I didn't mind the wild, sweeping gestures some guys were implementing to get the girl they wanted to go to Homecoming. Though honestly, to quote Emmitt, I thought it was overkill. Just ask the girl and don't make it so high pressure for her. It was kind of hard for a teenage girl to say no—even when she wanted to—when a guy got the band to serenade her in the cafeteria and then asked her to the dance with a bouquet of balloons.

"I'm not sure who you're here for, but I'm in the middle of class," I said irritably.

Then the flowers were moved to the side, and Bennett's beautiful face was smiling back at me. It was so unexpected to see him at my workplace that I hadn't even noticed the all-too-familiar lower half of the flowers-bearer at first.

A feverish blush rushed to my cheeks when my gaze landed on the jeans I'd seen him in after our last rehearsal. In the rain. And in his truck.

"Bennett," was all I managed to say on a breathless whoosh.

"Hi." He met me where I'd frozen in front of the class and handed over the bouquet of stargazer lilies and other exotic-looking flowers I couldn't identify. They were stunningly beautiful.

"What are you doing?" I asked, staring at the heavy vase of flowers.

"I was thinking about you. Wanted to come by and say good morning."

My gaze flitted to his, my body heating under his mischievous glint. He'd already told me 'good morning' with his head between my thighs, his favorite alarm system apparently. And now mine.

There was dead silence in the room. Bennett turned to his young audience. "Morning, kids."

Some of the girls giggled. Heather said rather loudly, "Good morning, Mr. Broussard."

I set the vase on my desk, took Bennett by the forearm, and dragged him toward the door. "You have your assignment," I told the class. "Get started."

There was some shuffling around and low chuckling amongst them as I pulled Bennett into the hallway and closed the door but stayed where I could watch the students through the window.

"I just saw you this morning," I whispered, though no one

was in the corridor, a strange panicky feeling fluttering in my chest.

"I missed you already," he confessed, lacing a hand with mine.

My stomach did that triple somersault it did every time Bennett looked at me like that and said something sweet, but also, this was moving really fast. Flowers at work?

"Me, too," I admitted, glancing away.

He gripped me around the waist and hauled me away from the window, bending to latch onto my lips. I couldn't help but sink into his kiss, savoring the scent of citrus shampoo, his aftershave, and the addicting scent that was uniquely him.

He was so delicious and so sweet I couldn't help but wrap my arms around his neck and hug him close. While little, baby alarm bells were ringing in my head, my heart soared.

When he was the one to break our kiss and ease me back, he said, "I don't want to get you in trouble. Just had to see you and tell you how beautiful you are."

So, apparently, Byron wasn't a total idiot because hearing those words from a man I was obsessed with made glorious things happen inside me. Like a starburst exploding in my chest, I hitched in a breath at the massive blast of *feelings*.

He cupped my face and looked at me like I was the most important person in the world. Being the center of that sort of attention from him was a heady sensation. I swear, he was going to kill me with his swoony charm.

"Thank you for the flowers. They're beautiful."

"You're welcome."

"What's with the casual wear? You take the day off?"

He glanced down at his jeans, black T-shirt, and casual jacket. "No. Hale needs an extra hand this morning finishing up the set for *Barefoot*." He huffed out a breath. "Figured I'd better volunteer some time so we can get that apartment window finished for the final scene."

Waggling my eyebrows, I added, "You're going to be bending and stretching those muscles all day? Working up a sweat?" I sucked in a hissing breath. "Hot."

He smiled, watching his thumb sweep across my cheekbone, enjoying my teasing. "You can wash me off when we get home. Maybe take a soak together in that big claw-foot tub of yours."

There was a sudden intimacy in our conversation. As if it were self-evident that we would end up at the same home. The vulnerability between us was only broken by the fact that all of this was still so new. I felt like I'd known Bennett forever but also that I barely knew him. It was a strange, scary paradox.

"I wanted to ask you," he broke in before the silence grew too heavy, "to see if you'd come with me to the Broadway on the Bayou fundraiser."

Broadway on the Bayou was an annual dinner soiree to raise money for BPAL, typically held downtown at the posh reception hall for weddings and big parties but sometimes at one of the sponsor's homes. I'd never attended, choosing to donate to BPAL anonymously when I could. That fundraiser wasn't my kind of scene.

"Please," he begged. "I have to go or my dad will blow a gasket."

"When is it?"

"This Saturday."

I started to tell him yes when I remembered. "I can't," I apologized, loosening my arms from around his shoulders to hold his hands. "I'm chaperoning the Homecoming dance."

His face fell, and I wished I'd never signed up for duty at the Homecoming dance. All the teachers had to pick one event each year, and I liked to get mine out of the way as early as possible.

"I'm sorry," I whispered.

"It's okay." He smiled, obvious disappointment marking his face. "Maybe we can meet up after the dance?"

He didn't have to voice what he was thinking. We'd barely spent one day apart since that night of the thunderstorm, since we'd basically declared that we wanted each other exclusively. It had somehow given us permission to obsess over each other ridiculously. We'd seen each other at rehearsal and then fallen into bed together at his place or mine every night since.

"Yeah. We can do that. It might be late."

"I don't care," he admitted without hesitation. "As long as I can be with you by the end of the night." He squeezed my waist.

I nodded. "I better get back."

Across the hall, there was a sudden boom of music, then spiraling colored lights flashed in the room.

Bennett chuckled, "Is she playing 'Staying Alive' by the Bee Gees?"

"Sounds like it." I smiled at whatever Lily was getting up to. "She's got her disco ball going too."

"Is that part of the curriculum?"

"Nah. Lily has freshmen. She uses a lot of alternative teaching methods. She has to do whatever it takes to get their attention. And keep them awake."

"And you don't?"

I scoffed. "Of course, I do. I have seniors. They're worse." I beamed up at him and batted my eyelashes. "I just use my sparkling personality."

That made him laugh, then his smile softened. "I hope you have a great day."

Still reeling from seeing him unexpectedly, I gripped his shoulder with one hand, the other on the doorknob of my classroom and planted a quick kiss on his lips. "How could I not now?"

His sweet smile was firmly embedded in my brain when I

went back inside. Of course, every single student had settled down. Some had actually started the assignment. But then a few like Emmitt still didn't even have their notebook out.

"Continue with the assignment," I snapped.

"So you and Mr. Broussard, huh, Ms. B?" asked Trace, the only one brave enough to say it aloud.

"Yes," I declared, folding my arms over my chest. "Me and Mr. Broussard."

Emmitt nodded his head toward my desk, where the giant bouquet of flowers stood. "Guess romance isn't dead."

I turned my attention back to my desk, a melty sensation fluttering in my tummy. Funny that I'd never considered myself the romantic type.

I remember this guy had brought me roses on our second date back in college. I'd been polite, but I'd inwardly cringed. He was trying desperately to get me to date him and him alone, and I'd already told him I didn't want anything serious. I never did.

Still, I'd thanked him and put them in the kitchen window of the apartment I shared with Lola. We'd forgotten them till they were nothing but dry husks. We spritzed the dry petals with cheap perfume and used them as potpourri for the bathroom. College girls on a budget.

But this, Bennett delivering an exotic bouquet to my classroom when we'd spent all night and this morning together?

Somehow, that had my entire body giddy with excitement. I wouldn't even acknowledge that this kind of gesture typically made me uncomfortable. He was my boyfriend now. This was totally normal.

Finally, I dragged my gaze back to the classroom, most of them with knowing smirks on their faces. I'm sure I was broadcasting my feelings loud and clear.

But I simply arched a brow and finally replied, "No,

Emmitt. Romance is not dead. And if you know how to do it right, you just might get the girl *you* want."

That had all the guys, including Trace, turning back to their notebooks with vigor, scribbling away.

I pretended to not be affected while I roamed the room and helped whoever needed it, smiling goofily at every whiff of floral scent throughout the day.

Chapter Twenty-Three

~BENNETT~

STANDING IN THE HOME OF THE GIBSONS, THE HOSTS OF THE fundraiser, I was completely bored out of my mind. More so than usual. Any other time, I'd be networking with businessmen and women of the community, chatting it up with someone from the Chamber of Commerce, or simply laughing with my brother in the corner. Like children.

Yes, we tended to do that. But currently, Hale was flirting with an older attractive woman across the room, and I was watching the clock, waiting for the opportune time to get the hell out of here. Dad would be pissed if I made my escape before the performers had done their thing.

The entertainment hadn't started, which would be a few short solo performances from regulars at BPAL like Mandy Harper.

I'd never wanted to perform at one of these, especially when my father liked to play the charitable local businessman, not the doting father of a volunteer thespian. He'd never understood my need to *waste time* at the theater. And quite frankly, I'd never bothered to tell him why I did.

What was the point? He wouldn't understand. Or care.

I was about to get another drink when Mandy spotted me. She sashayed over to me in a floor-length red dress.

"Hey, Bennett." She reached up to hug me.

I gave her a one-arm hug in return. Then she smiled up at me and angled her cleavage toward me, broadcasting her assets and her intentions.

I needed to get out of here.

"It's so good to see you," she crooned.

She looped an arm through mine to survey the party with me, but really she just wanted to press her breasts against my arm to get my attention.

Mandy hadn't exactly been shy in telling me what she'd wanted. Her showing up in my dressing room—topless—after the last night of *Chicago* last year was evidence enough.

I was glad I'd never encouraged her or taken her up on her offer. It was hard enough to make her understand I wasn't interested even when I'd point-blank told her in that dressing room that we were just friends.

She'd laughed it off but hadn't stopped giving it her best shot ever since.

"How's *Barefoot* going?" she asked, bitterness evident in her tone.

"Great." I downed the rest of my Bourbon, trying to subtly dislodge my arm from hers with no luck.

"Is Betty holding her own? She's never had a role this big before."

"Betty is phenomenal," I told her honestly.

She laughed as if I'd said something funny. I hadn't. I wasn't even remotely smiling, her nasty jealousy so obvious.

"You don't miss me at all on stage. We've been playing the

leads together for years, Ben," she practically cooed as she faced me, sliding one hand up my bicep.

I cringed at her use of the nickname only my family had ever used. And petting me like I was her lover. Knowing Mandy wasn't the type to take subtle hints, I carefully took her wrist and removed her arm. That alone caused her smile to slip.

I'd always allowed her flirting before to avoid hurting her feelings. But that was before my heart belonged to someone else. That realization hit me hard. Yes, my heart did belong to Betty.

I wouldn't appreciate some guy pawing all over her. As a matter of fact, the very thought made me want to break bones. So I surely didn't think she would like the way Mandy was behaving with me.

"Betty is more than my leading lady on stage," I told her emphatically. "She's my girlfriend." Before the shock could even register on her face, I said, "Excuse me," and took off for the bar.

Hale sidled up next to me as I waited for my drink, grinning like a fiend. "Ol' Mandy giving it another go?"

"Not anymore." I caught sight of the hostess flitting around the room, apparently nowhere near getting the show started. "When the hell is this thing going to get started?"

"Damn." He shook his head at me. "I honestly never thought I'd see the day you'd fall this hard."

"Well, you're looking at the day, brother. I'd rather be with her than this cesspool."

His gaze turned more serious. Something rare for him. "You've never been quite so bitter about these fundraiser things before."

"Yes, Hale, I always have. I've just never voiced it because these *things* were beneficial for business."

"And they aren't anymore?" he asked curiously.

"My priorities are different."

"Your priorities being Betty Mouton."

"Yes," I found myself snapping. "Is that a problem?"

"Not at all." He took the drink the bartender slid his way, and I took mine. "I've just never seen you like this over a woman. Let me ask you this." He narrowed his gaze like he was inspecting a new species. "In your list of priorities, what else would you put behind Betty?"

"Everything," I answered easily.

Hale laughed, but then his eyes widened. He shook his head knowingly at me. "You're in love with her."

And there it was. My heart responded to his words, quickening at the truth laid bare.

As the hostess finally made it up to the stage she'd erected in her giant living room, I told him, "I need some air," then strode out onto her back patio.

It was lit with white lights around a pagoda, tiki torches all the way down to the bayou behind her house. I caught sight of a familiar silhouette closer to the water, sitting on a wrought iron bench under a heavy oak tree. Pop.

Exhaling a heavy breath, I made my way down to him and took the seat next to him in silence.

"Why are you here?" I asked. This wasn't Pop's scene. He preferred his sofa and NCIS to a night out with the Beauville socialites.

"I'd ask you the same thing." He raised the longneck beer he had propped on his knee to his lips.

I frowned, a little confused since I was always at these things. Rather than clarify his comment, he answered mine.

"Your mother won't leave me alone," he added on a sigh. "Wants me to get out and meet someone."

My chest pinched. Everyone knew how much Pop had loved MawMaw. She'd been gone several years now, but he'd never hinted at wanting to find another partner.

"And you're listening to Mom?" I teased. Because Pop rarely listened to anyone.

He snorted a laugh. "No. I heard there was free food and booze."

I laughed. Pop had more money than most people here, but he was always penny-pinching.

We both gazed out at the slow-moving bayou, visible in the reflection of the torches along the bank. My mind wandered back to my conversation with Hale.

"Pop, can I ask you something?"

"Of course."

After taking a deep swallow of my Bourbon, I cleared my throat. "What does falling in love feel like?"

He didn't make light of my question. Or tease me. He took another minute to contemplate, gazing up at the stars in the cloudless night.

"Feels like dying, son." He turned his head to me, fixing me with that grave expression Pop wore only once in a while. When he wanted me to listen good. "Then being brought back to life again. Both terrifying fear and pure ecstasy in one."

I gulped hard. "Yeah," was all I could manage. "I guess it does."

"Hurts when you're apart, doesn't it?"

All I could do was nod tightly.

He gave me a small smile. "It's rare. Trust me when I tell you, don't waste a minute of it."

Standing abruptly, I looked out at the water, suddenly needing to see her like I couldn't breathe if I didn't. This aching sensation when we were apart would only go away the second I held her in my arms.

"What am I doing here?" I mumbled.

"That's what I was saying earlier." He laughed and stood with me, giving me a clap on the back. "Get out of here. Go see your girl. Stop wasting time."

Without a thought, I jerked Pop into a rough hug. "Love you, Pop."

He laughed, surprised by the sudden affection. "Love you, too, Ben. Now, go."

Not needing any more encouragement, I raced up the side of the house and into the cul-de-sac to find my car. The tension of the night instantly eased, washing away like water down the bayou. My heart thrummed faster in a much happier rhythm. All because I was running to her. The woman I loved.

Chapter Twenty-Four

~BETTY~

I WAS COMPLETELY BORED OUT OF MY MIND. WITH THE exception of Mr. Burke trying to be cool with the kids by dancing a few moves to some hip-hop song, which was mildly entertaining, this dance was dragging ass.

Usually, Finn would amuse me with mocking jokes to keep the night rolling on, but he'd opted to chaperone Prom since he was going out with that stuck-up surgeon tonight. That guy was all wrong for Finn, but he wasn't listening to me.

The decorations were pretty impressive though, I surmised, looking around the romantically lit gym. No overhead fluorescent light, only cozy, warm lanterns centered on tables for sitting and enjoying refreshments around the dance floor.

I had to give it to Lily. She was head of the Homecoming Committee, something you couldn't make me do under threat of death or dismemberment.

The theme was fairytales or happily-ever-after or something. I never kept up with those things.

Around the gym were life-size cutouts of Disney scenes like Cinderella's castle, Snow White's wishing well, and Jasmin's flying carpet. There were a few Disney couple cutouts for kids to take pics with, putting their faces through the open ovals of the hero and princess. But that wasn't what was so spectacular.

Gossamer fabric draped over the dancefloor from a pergola-style structure at the center. It gave the students a focus for their dancing and chatting, the cutouts framing the pergola, so they had a more intimate space since the gym was so big. And it looked like the ceiling had vomited glitter on the whole scene. Everything sparkled. I half expected unicorns to come prancing out any minute.

Of course, I'd already caught one couple making out behind Belle and the Beast, but that was to be expected.

Lily sidled up beside me and handed over a bottle of water. "Here you go."

"Thank you. I have to admit this is the best this gym has ever looked. Including when I went here."

"Really?" She beamed. "Have the dances always been in the gym?"

"As far back as I know. Except for Prom, which they hold at the reception center in town."

She nodded, inspecting her hard work. "It was fun. I didn't mind."

This was where I realized Lily needed a new hobby. Or a man. She was younger than me. She couldn't be more than twenty-two. I knew she'd gotten the job at BHS straight out of college.

"Is your family from here?" I asked, genuinely curious.

Lily was the eternal optimist, but there suddenly seemed to be something a little sad in her demeanor that I'd never noticed before.

"Uh, no," she replied softly. "I have a foster family in Texas, but"—she shrugged—"we don't keep in touch much."

My heart squeezed painfully. It's interesting how little you truly know about people. Or how you can easily block out other people's problems because, well, they aren't your problems. After that self-flagellating thought, I suddenly wished I'd been a little nicer to Lily. I was never mean to her, mind you, but no one would ever accuse me of being overfriendly or welcoming to someone new on the block. I was a stay-in-your-lane kind of girl.

"Your last name is Breaux," I pondered aloud. That was a very Cajun name. "Were your parents from here?"

She nodded, watching the students dancing. "My dad was from here. But he died in an offshore accident while working on a rig."

"I'm so sorry. I don't mean to pry."

She smiled at me, and I realized something about Lily. She was the kind of person who never faked her emotions. She was also filled with an overabundance of sincerity and sympathy. Or maybe, by comparison, I just found myself lacking.

Like right now. Compassion radiated out of her like a beam from the sun. Even while I was poking my nose in her personal business—a bad habit of mine—she was eager to share. Rather than telling me to shove off, she fed my curiosity.

"It's fine. I was two, and I don't remember. My mom was from Texas, so we moved back out there. Unfortunately, she only had a great aunt still living. So when my mom was killed in a car accident when I was nine, I was sent into the foster care system. Her aunt was already suffering from Dementia."

I stared at her, completely baffled. "How in the world are you so goddamn happy all the time?"

She laughed, her smile amused but her gaze serious. "We don't get to pick the cards we're dealt. All we can do is make the best with what we're given."

That was the moment my respect and admiration for Lily Breaux escalated to the top tier of my esteem. She'd been dealt the shittiest hand there was. All jokers and deuces, it seemed. And still, she was the kindest and happiest person I knew. Outwardly, anyway. And she shared her joy and creativity with open arms. She deserved a little reciprocation.

"I bought my first house recently," I told her, changing the subject abruptly.

"Oh, wow! That's amazing! Congratulations."

"It's not my dream house. Not yet. Teacher salary, ya know?" I quirked a brow.

She nodded and laughed in understanding.

"Anyway..." I unscrewed the cap of my water bottle. "I'll be having a housewarming party pretty soon. I'd love it if you'd come."

"Me? Really?" Her blue eyes rounded with surprise. "I'd love to. That's so sweet."

"Great. I don't have details or anything yet. I want to get past Homecoming and this play I'm in first."

"At BPAL? What play?"

"*Barefoot in the Park.*"

"I love that movie! It's so funny and cute. So you're playing the wife? One of the newlyweds?"

"Yep. Corie Bratter. It's my first lead role, and I'm nervous as all hell. But I'm having a blast, too."

"I bet you're amazing. You're so confident and good at everything you do."

Was I? I never saw what others saw when they observed me. I was always finding the imperfections.

"Who's your male lead? Wait, excuse me." She snapped her fingers at two boys who passed. Football players. Twice her size. "No, sir." She shook her head at the biggest one and held out her hand. "Give that to me right now, Preston."

"Aw, come on, Ms. Breaux. I'm seventeen."

"I don't care. No tobacco products on campus. You know the rules."

He rolled his eyes and reluctantly handed over a can of snuff.

Damn. Little Miss Lily had a spine.

I took back my earlier observation: she was now at the tippy-top of my tier of admiration. Hell, we should totally be friends. And that was not a light sentiment coming from me.

She tucked the chewing tobacco into the pocket of her blue dress. "You were saying?" she asked, all politeness again.

I tried to remember where our conversation ended. But before I could answer who my lead male was, she gasped and said, "Bennett Broussard."

"What?" I asked, incredulous. "How'd you guess?"

"Guess what?" she asked, gaze still on the dance floor.

"Who my stage partner is for *Barefoot in the Park*?"

She turned to look at me. "He is?"

"Yeah."

"Did you have rehearsal tonight?"

"No," I answered with a laugh. "Of course not. Why would you ask that?"

"Well, he isn't here for the fruit punch, that's for sure."

Oh.

I followed her gaze to see the man himself, dressed fine as ever, stalking across the gym. The students didn't pay much attention, but the other chaperones—mostly young, single teachers—followed his progress across the room.

It didn't matter because his attention didn't waver from me. Not for one second. As a matter of fact, he'd better stop giving me bedroom eyes in the middle of the BHS gym where teenagers would definitely know what that look was about.

I glared at him, giving him my warning face, which only seemed to urge him on. He took long strides, eating up the distance with a leisurely grace, his heated gaze devouring me from head to toe.

I'd worn a plain black mini-dress with a silvery-white

cardigan on the dressy side. An outfit I actually kept in my closet for events like this that required an actual dress. It wasn't fancy. Or exceptionally pretty. But the way Bennett looked at me like he wanted to rip it off me said otherwise.

When he finally stood in front of me, he slid his arms around my waist and bent down to kiss me on the cheek, but then grazed his nose along my jaw to my ear where I heard him take a deep inhalation of breath.

"Easy, tiger," I whispered, grabbing hold of his forearms and stepping back.

"Sorry," he murmured, grinning down at me, looking anything but sorry.

"What are you doing here?"

"I had to see you," he blurted out so fast I think it shocked even him. His hands skated down my arms till he gripped me by both hands. "I missed you."

My heart responded to his tender words, pounding faster and faster. "I missed you, too," I murmured low, realizing I'd never said those words to another human being.

Except when Emma went away to horsemanship camp for a week without me the summer she was in the fifth grade. And those were a child's feelings. These were very adult. And very real.

"Hi. I'm Lily Breaux. I'm Betty's hall buddy."

Bennett broke his devouring stare to face Lily and shook her hand with the one not still holding onto me. "Bennett Broussard."

"I know who you are. I saw *Chicago* last year," she beamed then promptly blushed. "I loved it. But I heard you were even better in BPAL's performance of *Grease* a few years ago. I wasn't living in Beauville then, though."

Lily looked genuinely disappointed. But then, so was I. "When was this?" I asked him.

He looked up, trying to remember, "That was three years ago for the spring musical, I believe."

"You had to play Danny Zuko, didn't you?" I asked.

He nodded, smiling shyly.

Then I was right there with Lily, wishing I'd seen him strut around stage in a leather jacket, singing his heart out for Sandra Dee.

"Let me guess who was Sandy," I said, a tad bitterly, "Mandy Harper."

He gave a little nod, his smile dropping, looking around the gym. "You wanna dance?"

The DJ had just switched it up, playing a slow song, Adele's "Someone Like You."

"I'm not sure I'm allowed."

Lily snort-laughed. "Of course, you are. Mr. Burke always dances with his wife at these things."

Somehow, knowing that the ogling Mr. Burke enjoyed dancing with his wife made me like the man a little more. Or disdain him a little less.

Without another word, Bennett tugged on my hand and pulled me a few feet away, off to the side of the dancers near the cutout of Ariel and Eric. I ignored Trace and Caroline slow dancing together while smirking at me. I gave them the wide-eyed look that said *mind your own business*, but they just laughed before turning to look at each other.

I'd been jittery and annoyed all night, not quite sure why. But when Bennett swept me into his arms, one hand on my waist, the other pressed against my back, holding me close, my sour mood vanished instantly.

Honestly, it had vanished when I saw him walking across the room. Some tender nascent feeling I'd never known spread its wings inside my chest, flapping wildly to break free. With both my arms around his neck, fingers playing in the edges of his hair that curled the tiniest bit, I stared up at him.

We were barely dancing, hardly moving, just staring and holding each other like lovestruck teenagers. How fitting.

"I thought you had a fundraiser," I finally said.

"I did. But I didn't want to be there."

"Why?"

"I wanted to be here."

Again, my stomach fluttered with excitement.

"No hot chicks there who could keep you away from me?"

His face remained serious as he clutched me tighter and shook his head.

I arched a brow, "But there were hot chicks there."

He rolled his eyes.

"Tell me who."

"Mandy Harper was there," he admitted.

Suddenly, my sweet, floaty birdlike feeling transformed into something ragey with teeth and talons.

"I'll bet she was all over you."

The thought of it made my blood boil.

He shrugged, which was a yes. I looked away, not liking this wretched feeling that inspired murderous thoughts. He redirected my gaze back to his with a finger under my chin.

"Are you jealous?" There was a definite gleam of utter glee shining in his whiskey-warm eyes, his face lit from the sparkly lights overhead.

"You find this funny? That bitch better keep her hands to herself."

He chuckled at my harsh threat. "Or what?"

"Or I'll break them," I said sweetly, meaning it and wondering where this violent streak had come from.

He burst out laughing and hugged me tighter when I tried to wiggle away.

"No, no, no," he murmured into my temple. "This jealous side of you is fascinating."

I was so riled up, spitting mad, that I was about to pinch him to get out of his hold when Lily popped up beside us.

"Hey, Betty. You guys get out of here."

That stalled my temper tantrum. Bennett loosened, and I glanced down at my watch. "I have thirty more minutes left for my duty."

"I'll cover you," she said, handing me my purse where I'd stashed it with the others at the refreshment stand. She glanced at Bennett with a knowing look. "Go on."

I reached over and hugged Lily, and I wasn't really a hugger. "You're my new best friend. And I actually mean that." When I pulled back and grabbed Bennett's hand, I added, "But don't tell Finn. He'll pitch a girly fit."

She shook her head and shooed us away. I wasn't going to argue because my blood was pumping hot and I had a new mission on my mind.

Dragging Bennett through the throng, I pulled him out the back exit toward the parking lot but then took an abrupt right toward the football field. I kept close to the gym in the shadows so people hopefully wouldn't see us meandering off. If they did, I kind of didn't care.

"Where are we going?" he asked, amused at my obvious determination. He had no idea what was coming.

"To take care of some business," I told him cryptically.

"Business? On the football field?"

I didn't answer, the voices of a few students milling in the parking lot growing more distant. I pulled him through the gate then up on the bleachers, our shoes loud as we clomped our way up the short flight of steps.

"Betty, what are we—?"

I spun around and pushed him. "Sit down."

He complied, his face in shadow, but I could feel him fully focused. Bennett had that sort of power over me. When his eyes were on me, a hot sensation filled my chest to bursting, making me want him even more.

Stripping off my cardigan, I dropped it between his knees then kneeled on it, reaching for his belt and unbuckling swiftly.

"Baby," he whispered darkly, "what are you doing? There are people right over there." Yet he made no move to stop me.

"I owe you one, Broussard, if you recall. From the movie theater."

He hissed in a breath when I'd gotten his zipper open and wrapped my hand around his thick, throbbing cock.

"Also," I added, stroking all the way to the base then back up, one hand on his muscled thigh. I squeezed my body closer, "this cock is mine. And I'm about to prove it to you."

The low rumble in his chest was feral, almost menacing, then I swallowed him all the way to the back of my throat. His hips bucked in shock. *"Fuck. Betty."*

He opened his legs wider for me, then leaned his big torso on the bleachers behind him.

Yes, you just get comfortable, I thought as I pumped him with one hand and then deep-throated him in one swift move.

His whole body tensed as an agonizing groan left his lips.

We couldn't see each other's faces, only the shadowy silhouettes of one another. There was something naughtier but intimate about doing this in almost complete darkness, even while we heard voices and laughter echoing not too far away.

"Yes, baby." His hand was on my jaw, just cradling, not holding me to keep me from moving. "Suck me just like that." His hips thrust up with slow pumps. I matched his languorous rhythm, growing wetter between my thighs when he said, "Take my dick deep. Show me who owns it."

I moaned, sucking at the head then letting him pop free to lick the tip and slide my tongue down the underside.

He groaned like a dying beast, his hand shifting to clench in my hair. "You're trying to kill me, aren't you?"

"Maybe," I murmured, lips against the slick head of his dick.

"Baby, baby," he murmured, more to himself, his breaths coming quicker. "*God*, I'm about to come," he warned, probably thinking I didn't want to swallow.

I never had, to be honest, much preferring the guy to come outside my mouth when I gave head. But some deep, carnal side of me wanted all of Bennett. Every last drop.

So I sucked him deeper when his cock thickened and started pulsing into my mouth. He let out a shocked cry in the back of his throat, trying to restrain himself since we didn't want teenagers coming to check out any strange noises.

"Fuck, fuck, fuck," he murmured on repeat as he came. "Love this." His hand tightened in my hair. "Love you."

I went a little numb at the words as he finished, suddenly scooping me up under the arms and into his lap.

His mouth was on my neck. "Let me take care of you." His hand skirted up my leg, but I stopped him.

"No, I'm good." I snatched my cardigan up and tried to force levity into my voice. "This wasn't a tit-for-tat thing. Like at the movies."

I laughed lightly while smoothing my dress. He was quiet as he buckled up his pants. I could feel his eyes on me, even in the semi-dark.

"So," I said cheerily, pretending my brain wasn't whirring and my heart wasn't about to beat right out of my chest, "how about dessert?"

After he buckled his pants, he took my hand. "Sure."

Shit. He knew I was panicking.

"I need chocolate, to be specific." I squeezed his hand and giggled.

He nodded without saying a word, guiding me back toward the parking lot. Fortunately, the parking lot was empty now.

"I know just the place," I added lightly. "A grocery store nearby has a hell of a chocolate cake with Bavarian cream filling."

He pulled me to a stop at my car, forcing me to face him.

"What's going on, Betty?" His jaw clenched, he scowled down at me, still holding my hand tightly. "You're freaking out because I told you I loved you, aren't you?"

"No! Not at all." I blew out a breath. "I mean, maybe. Just a little."

"Not a little. You're freaking the fuck out right now. I can feel it."

"Don't get mad."

He nodded and looked away, seeming to calm himself. "I'm not mad."

"Look, I get it. It was the heat of the moment. I'm totally amazing at giving blow jobs." I dropped his hand and poked him playfully in the ribs.

"Don't even make light of this," he grumbled. "And sure as hell don't remind me you've had practice. It makes me want to murder people I've never met."

"Okay then." I crossed my arms and leaned back against my car.

His gaze hardened as he watched me. Then he shook his head. "No fucking way."

He unfolded my arms and cupped my face, pressing his body close, his grave expression intense. Even so, his voice remained steady and calm but low and deep.

"Listen, Betty. I don't want you putting up defenses and playing this off. I don't expect you to say it back. But I need you to know that it wasn't a slip-up in the heat of the moment."

He drew closer, his face inches from mine, burning me up with those hazel-gold eyes.

"I love you. I know I do. And I'm fine waiting for you.

Just..." he shook his head, brow pinching again. "No pushing me out because this scares the shit out of you. I know it does."

"How do you know?"

"I'm a good people reader. I've seen the signs that you're a bit of a commitment-phobe."

"I am *not*," I lied.

At that, he smiled sweetly and pressed a kiss to my lips. "You are."

At first, I didn't respond but then he slid his tongue along my bottom lip and I couldn't help myself. Curling my hands into his hair, I kissed him back. He kept it gentle and soft before finally pulling away.

"You did scramble my brains on those bleachers, though."

My smile broke wide. "I'm good, huh?"

"Fucking amazing." He leaned over and opened my car door for me. Then he slapped my ass as I climbed in.

"Ow!"

"I'll get the chocolate. Meet you at your place."

"Yes, sir." I winked then slammed my car door.

The hard, hot look he gave me promised he'd be getting me back for that BJ in the bleachers. As long as we didn't have to talk about the L-word, that was fine by me.

He was right. I was scared shitless and didn't know what to do with that. For now, I'd tuck it away and not think about it till I had to.

Chapter Twenty-Five

~BENNETT~

"Here, let me help you," said Brittany, taking the mic wire from me.

Brittany had been stage manager on several productions, and though I liked her, she seemed to like me a little too much.

I'd attached the mic receiver to my pants at the small of my back and had been trying to weave the wire up the back of my white T-shirt I'd wear under the seventies-style shirt and suit as my character Paul.

I didn't mind her helping me, but I did mind the way her knuckles were stroking along my spine more than necessary as she threaded the wire up and out the neck. When she'd finally extracted her hand from inside my shirt, I turned to take the end of the mic.

"I can do it for you," she offered, grabbing the mic tape with her free hand, still holding the end of the mic with the other.

When she went to thread the wire behind my ear, her fingers trailing intimately over the shell, I took a step back and grabbed the mic from her hands. "I've got it, Brittany. I appreciate your help."

"You sure?" She blinked up at me, flashing me a flirty smile.

"I'm sure," I said, turning toward the mirror on the wall next to the stand where we kept all the mics.

In the reflection, I spotted Betty standing at the doorway of the back entrance, her pretty face set in a deep scowl.

"Hey," I said, turning as I taped the mic wire near my jaw. "You running late?"

She walked in, gaze sliding where Brittany had just headed back up the ramp toward the backstage area. Then she arched a brow and sashayed closer.

"Apparently not late enough to catch some chick feeling up my boyfriend."

I couldn't help the warm feeling that swamped me at her jealousy. It was absurd for her to be jealous because no woman could turn my head away from her. Not even close. Still, I found some sick joy in seeing her seething with envy at Brittany's touchy fingers.

Especially after last night. She'd freaked out when I told her I loved her. I wasn't going to pretend I didn't, but I decided to pull back a little and give her time to come to terms with it. I didn't mind holding my tongue, but I couldn't stop how I felt about her.

I met her halfway and swept her against my body, pressing a kiss to her stiff lips, which she didn't return. Just scowled up at me like it was my fault.

"Do you honestly think I want Brittany?"

Arms still at her sides, she shrugged, looking indifferent while also looking annoyed. It was the cutest expression I'd ever seen her wear.

I dipped my head and slid my hand down to cup her ass before I rumbled into her ear, "I came in your sweet, tight pussy three times last night. And I want to get back in. I guarantee you that I don't want the stage manager."

She finally reacted, latching her little claws onto my biceps. "I know you don't. But that doesn't mean I'll tolerate her sticking her hands up your shirt and copping a good feel."

"Then we should make it official and tell everyone you're my girlfriend."

She rolled her eyes. "That's so dumb. Like what? We wait till our backstage huddle when Peter gives us the break-a-leg speech then announce we're girlfriend and boyfriend?"

I laughed rather than answer, kissing her again on her unresponsive lips.

"Why are you mad at *me*?" I asked incredulously when she still glared up with accusing eyes.

"Because you're too fine for your own good. Is this what it's going to be like to date Bennett Broussard? I have to beat women off with a stick?"

Oh, God, I was so in love with this woman. Every grumpy, scathing word that came out of her mouth made me want to throw her on the Green Room sofa and tickle and hug her then fuck her into the cushions.

I cupped her other cheek and hauled her against my body, rocking us back and forth. "We could take out an ad in the Beauville newspaper."

"Oh, please. No one reads that. Not even the online version."

"There's a billboard at the main bridge crossing of the bayou. We could blast it across there."

"You think you're funny, don't you?"

"I think you're funny." I kissed her cheek then her jaw. "I think you're beautiful when you're angry." I kissed her neck.

She angled her head to the side to give me better access.

"I think I'd rather take you back to my place and tear your

clothes off rather than go through a three-hour dress rehearsal with Peter at the helm tonight."

"That reminds me. We're not going back to your place after rehearsal tonight."

I pulled back, my mood dropping instantly. "What do you mean? You're not spending the night with me?"

She grinned. "Now who's all grouchy and defensive?"

The thought of being without her for even one night sent me into a little bit of a panic. That should be a warning that I needed to get control of my feelings. But that was the thing. I was in tight control of basically everything in my life *except* my feelings for the fiery redhead in my arms.

She made me crazy with need, with lust, with heart-aching longing. Simply spending a ten-hour day at work, which I'd done without any trouble at all before, was now agonizing torture akin to being stretched on the rack. Because I constantly checked my watch, counting down the minutes till I could be with her again. Till I could get my Betty fix. Till I could look at her pretty face, the delicate arch of her brows, the sassy angle of her sweet mouth, the tilt of her head when she laughed.

Until I could touch her, hold her, fuck her till we were both panting and spent, tangled in my sheets. Or hers.

I wasn't particular. As long as we ended up together in either her bed or mine by the end of the night. But now she was saying we weren't spending the night together? *Hell yes, I was grouchy.*

She reached up with her two index fingers and pressed them into the creases on either side of my mouth, trying to make me smile. "Turn that frown upside down, Broussard. I have a surprise for you."

"I hate surprises."

"I kind of figured that," she laughed. "But we're still doing it."

"Doing what? Where are we going?"

Her teasing expression turned sweet and tender. She cupped my face. "You'll just have to wait and see."

"But why aren't we spending the night together?"

"I said we weren't going back to *your* place. You'll still be sleeping in my bed tonight. But you have to let me take you on our little surprise adventure."

"We're going to be exhausted after this rehearsal."

"Actually, I think it'll loosen you up for what I have planned." She blinked sweetly at me. "*Please.* I just want to do something fun, to forget about the stress of grading papers or inventory or memorizing lines." She glanced down at my chest then added quietly, "Or your dad. And everything."

A tender look softened her features and shimmered in her sapphire eyes. She was worried about me. But the *and everything* made me think of her reaction to my confession in the school parking lot. This seemed like a sort of apology.

"Fine." Then I let go of her waist but took her hand and dragged her toward the mic station. "Now, let me stick my hand up your shirt and help you with your mic wire."

"My pleasure, Broussard."

"No, it's mine." I smiled. "Trust me. It's all mine."

Once everyone had mics on, Peter called us into the Green Room for his first of many pre-show speeches. Though this was merely a dress rehearsal, a few of the board members would be in the audience tonight to give us a good test run.

"If you drop a line, don't worry about it and just keep going. Most of all, remember the props. We've got a lot of prop changes. Brittany, do we have the knichi ready?"

"Yep. Sure do, Peter."

"What are we using as knichi?" asked Frank.

"Calamata olives," Brittany replied.

"Ugh." Betty shivered next to me. "I hate olives."

"What's wrong with you?" I asked, pinching her sexy, bare

thigh—exposed from the seventies mini-dress she was rocking. "Olives are delicious."

"Ow! Stop hating on my taste palate, Broussard."

"I cannot wait to watch you do the knichi scene now."

"Good thing I'm a fabulous actress. I'm the only character who likes the damn things in the scene when, in reality, I find them disgusting."

Betty and I were smiling, lost in our own little world when we realized everyone was quiet. We faced them all to find some questioning looks except for Frank, who looked devilish and pleased. With his fedora hat on and the sleek moustache in place, he looked every inch the wily, charming Mr. Velasco.

"Oh, sorry," said Betty. Though I wasn't sure what she was sorry about exactly.

I decided it was time.

"We should probably let you all know that Betty and I are girlfriend and boyfriend."

When she backhanded me in the abdomen, I pretended she hurt me. "Though it may not last long if she keeps abusing me."

"You pinched me first." Then she leaned in close. "I can't believe you just said that."

Shrugging innocently, I faced our audience yet again. Trish was grinning from ear to ear, but Peter just rolled his eyes.

"That's all fine and dandy, but I need you both on your game tonight. Focus, people. I want our board members to see the fruits of our labors. Now, let's put our hands in. Break on *knichi*."

As we all shuffled off sofas and chairs to put our hands in the middle of our huddle, I leaned over close to Betty and whispered in her ear, "I'd like to sample your fruits in this dress later."

She backhanded me again in the stomach and gave me a warning glare while fighting to smile.

I can't believe you, she mouthed. I knew it was about the girlfriend/boyfriend announcement rather than my sexual innuendo, which only made me laugh louder.

"All hands in," said Peter. "One, two, three..."

"Knichi!" We yelled simultaneously.

For some reason, I had zero anxiety about tonight. Usually, I'd be pacing and needing alone time to get my head together before the curtain rose. Not tonight. My thoughts were full of Betty, and my heart brimmed with the heady sensation of being with the woman I loved. None of my normal anxieties reared their ugly heads at all.

Maybe it was the surprise Betty had in store. Or the fact she hadn't run for the hills when I'd told her I loved her. It was hard not to say it now that it was out there, but I knew one thing. Betty might be one hundred percent into the hot sex and fun and girlfriend/boyfriend labels. But she was scared shitless of the L-word.

It was fine. I'd wait as long as I had to for her to love me back. I wasn't going anywhere.

Chapter Twenty-Six

~BETTY~

"THIS ISN'T HAPPENING." BENNETT STOOD OUTSIDE THE DRUNK Pelican, arms crossed, staring up at their digital marquee that read: *Improv Night!*

"This is absolutely happening," I told him. "You're going to love this."

"You mean I'm going to love watching you up on stage doing improv? Sure, now *that* might happen."

"Come on, Broussard."

"I'm not spontaneous. I don't like spontaneous," he spat the word like it was poisonous.

"But it's *fun*. You sure seemed to enjoy being spontaneous in the bleachers the other night."

He gave me a withering look, then glared up at the sign as if it had offended him.

Laughing, I pried his stiff arms away from his body and wrapped them around my waist. Then I laced my fingers at the nape of his neck and pressed my breasts to his chest. "I'll make it worth your while."

"Yeah?" His hands slid to bracket my waist, giving me a squeeze.

"If you get up on stage," I told him, scraping my nails lightly on his nape, feeling him shiver, "I'll let you do anything you want to me tonight."

His irritated look grew dark, primal. His voice dropped. "That's not fair."

"I don't play fair. You should know that about me right here and now."

"I just spent three and a half hours under the scrutinizing eye of Peter. I don't have the energy for this."

"No? Then I guess you don't have the energy to spank my ass before you fuck it tonight."

He flinched, fingers digging into my waist. "Are you playing with me right now? Because if that is on the table..." His words drifted away, his pupils dilating at the prospect of what I'd suggested. I could already see him imagining what I'd just planted in his brain.

"It's totally on the table." My voice had gone a little breathy. Husky. Because I wasn't totally unaffected by the idea myself. "But if you want to get in there, you've got to get up on stage for improv."

He clenched his jaw, his eyes narrowing at the wickedness of my offer.

I didn't know Bennett would be so against doing improv, but it made sense. He liked being prepared for everything. I just wanted to break away from our everyday routine, cheer him up after arguing with his dad last weekend and what seemed to be nonstop stress from work.

Also, I was aware I'd been weird since he told me he loved me. I had deep feelings for this man, but how did you know when it was actually love? I mean, I admired him and I was obsessed with his body and what he did to me in bed. I shivered at the thought of letting him take my ass and the look he was giving me right now.

His hands coasted down to cup my ass and then squeeze. He closed his eyes and groaned. "You're the devil."

I pulled his head down so I could whisper, "Come have some fun with the devil, my angel."

"Oh, I know it will be fun."

"I was talking about the improv," I laughed.

He hauled me closer, his hard dick pressing against my belly. "You can't tease me and take that offer back later."

I nodded, biting my lip. "I've always wanted to try it."

Another couple walked past us, the laughter from inside growing louder then fading away as the door opened and closed. Neither of us cared that we were basically blocking the entrance while he cupped my ass territorially.

I couldn't look away from Bennett anyway. I'd seen him look feral before, but it was nothing compared to how he looked at me now.

"You never have before?"

I shook my head. "I've played a little there during sex, but no, that's the final frontier. Where no man has gone before."

He clenched his jaw and blew out an angry breath. "I don't even want to think about you and another guy."

"Well, you asked." I pinched the hairs at his nape and tugged. He hissed in a breath before I added, "I told you, I'm brutally honest. To a fault sometimes. So don't ask me something you don't want an answer to."

"All I need to know is I'm going to be the first." He glanced up at another couple passing us by, his hands sliding to my waist when he muttered under his breath. "And the last."

"What was that, Broussard?"

"No take-backs." His voice was deep and seductive, his hazel eyes molten with desire.

"I'm not that kind of girl. What I say, I mean. But it's a trade. You have to do your part first."

He huffed out a laugh. "I can't believe I'm doing this." Then he took my hand and hauled me inside.

The Drunk Pelican was known for three things: insanely delicious fried shrimp po'boys, cheap draft beer, and their weekend nighttime entertainment. It flip-flopped each weekend, Trivia Night one weekend and Improv Night the next.

According to my sister, Emma, Trivia Night was hella competitive. She liked to join her friends and beat the crap out of everyone else. I'd never been to Trivia or Improv Nights, patronizing the Main Street café solely for the fried shrimp po'boys and jalapeno cheese fries.

A short, scuffed, well-worn bar sat on the exposed brick side of the café. The dark-stained beams in the ceiling and wrought iron light fixtures set the ambiance level to cozy/casual. The round-top tables were scattered around the smallish pub-style room. The "stage" was no more than a ten-by-ten raised dais about a foot off the floor.

Bennett and I settled at an empty table off to the left. I could already see his brows pinching with anxiety. As soon as the waitress stopped, I ordered a couple of beers and reached for Bennett's hand under the table.

"This is going to be fun. Just relax."

He looked at me as if I'd lost my mind.

"I promise." I couldn't help but laugh at the absolutely miserable and sour expression on his handsome face.

"You don't have to get up there," I reminded him.

His gaze turned sharp, predatory, "Oh, I'm going to. I have a bet to win."

The waitress returned with our longnecks as the MC walked onto the stage and picked up the mic.

"Welcome, everyone. Looks like we've got some regulars." A

hoot came from the right side, where a ten-top was filled with a rowdy group. "And some new faces."

Bennett's thigh tensed underneath my hand.

"Awesome to see you all for Improv Night. Why don't we start with a warm-up of one-minute monologues? This will be a round of celebrity impressions. All volunteers raise your hands."

Bennett's hands were firmly on the table and strangling his beer. Several from the ten-top shouted and raised hands.

The MC told them all to come up. The volunteers drew slips of paper from a mason jar on a stool next to the stage, apparently each choosing a celebrity to reenact. We were then entertained with a mediocre impression of Deadpool, a fantastic one of Ron Burgundy, and a terrible one of Professor McGonagall.

"I could've done a better Deadpool," Bennett murmured as we clapped and they exited the stage, his expression relaxing.

"Well, you missed your chance on that one."

"Now it's time for our 'awkward situations' portion of the night," said the MC. "Any volunteers?"

I shot my hand into the air.

"Shit," Bennett hissed before blowing out a heavy breath and raising his as well.

I beamed at him.

When the MC pointed to us, I clapped with a little hoot and grabbed his hand to haul him up there. Bennett joined me easily, smirking down at me as I bounced in place, waiting for whatever assignment we were about to be given.

The MC greeted us and tucked his mic into his side. "So you guys are new to this, right?"

"To improv, yes," I blurted giddily.

Bennett rolled his eyes at me.

"So, you'll pick a scenario from the hat, then you have three minutes to reenact. There are no limits. Improv Night is adults only. So cursing, sexual references, whatever you want is a go."

"Got it," I told him. The MC stepped over to pick up a different mason jar.

"How about spanking? Is that a go?" Bennett asked me under his breath.

"Save that for later." I winked up at him.

He blew out a breath and shook his head. "You're going to kill me, woman. I swear you are."

The MC held out the jar. Bennett gestured for me to go ahead and pick for us. I pulled out a slip of paper and opened it up. Then laughed while Bennett read it over my shoulder. It read: *blind date where one person is formal and awkward and the other has a hearing problem.*

"Which one do you want?" I asked him.

His head was bent next to mine, his brows scrunched together as he read the paper. "The formal, awkward guy."

"Get ready." I nudged him in the ribs with my elbow then we each took our places and waited for the MC to set a timer.

"Aaaaaand go!" He pointed to us.

Bennett went from smirky hot guy—his normal self—to stiff and terrified-looking guy in a split second.

"Pardonnez moi, mademoiselle," he said with a stiff bow, using an English accent while speaking French. "But I believe I have the pleasure of your company this evening."

"What?" I asked in a high falsetto voice. "Oh, I'm not that kind of girl. No pleasure on the first evening."

A few snickers from the audience didn't break Bennett's character. Nor mine.

"May I say that your perfume smells of hyacinths in bloom. It reminds me of my Aunt Gertrude."

More laughter.

"I'm sorry? When was I rude? I'm just saying I don't do sex on the first date."

He reeled back in fake shock while a ripple of laughter filled the room. His flustered Englishman impersonation threatened to make me break character, but I somehow held it together.

"You've got me all wrong. I would never undermine the fairer sex by assuming such a thing."

"Dude, if you proposition me one more time, I am out the door. But I really want my steak dinner, so keep it in your pants."

The laughter grew louder as we continued on for two more minutes, neither of us even flinching or falling out of character. When I mistook his word "ratio" in reference to his riveting divorce statistics for the word "fellatio," the audience fell out in hysterics. We had to pause for five seconds before continuing with our act.

By the time the MC rang the bell to end the round, I was high with the exhilaration of performing without any script and simply following instinct.

What made it even better was that I was sure it rolled so easily for both of us because we did it together. Bennett and I just matched. We fit. In every possible way. That familiar pang squeezed inside my chest.

We gave a quick bow to the applause then stepped down hand in hand back to our table. As soon as we were in our seats, Bennett scooped his hand under my hair and wrapped my nape then hauled me close and kissed me hard. A well of emotion burst inside my chest.

"What was that for?" I asked when he finally broke the kiss.

"For making me do that." He laughed. "That was awesome."

"I told you it was fun!"

He then scooped me out of my chair and plopped me in his lap, then the oh-so-controlled, straight-laced Bennett Broussard kissed me and held me close in front of a room full of strangers.

"It was terrifying, though," he said, chuckling in my ear. "But you did it. And it was awesome. See! Not everything has to be planned to perfection."

His laughter ebbed, his eyes glittering with a new emotion. Something deeper. Darker.

"I think it's time to go home." His hold on me tightened. "I recall we made a bargain."

"We did," I agreed, pulse pounding.

Without another word, he lifted me off his lap, pulled a twenty from his wallet, slapped it down, grabbed my hand, and hauled me home.

Chapter Twenty-Seven

~BETTY~

By now, I'd seen all of Bennett's faces, his many expressions that catalogued his complex emotions. Whether it was a slight tilt of the mouth, quirk of the brow, or slant of his gaze. But I wasn't quite sure I'd seen this one.

He was silent when we got back to my place as he pulled me into the bathroom, undressed me, then washed me in the shower with tender, sensual touches. He'd stroked and soaped me, sliding his middle finger along my cleft till he breached my ass just barely, all while kissing me hot and deep.

He didn't linger too long, but his expert hands had massaged and caressed and squeezed me into pliant flesh and bones, willing and ready for anything. Even what I'd promised him back at the Pelican. Or bargained for.

What I hadn't bargained for was the intensely carnal and possessive heat in his gaze as he kneeled above me on the bed in all of his naked glory.

I have to say, I might mock and tease him for being so disciplined, but right now, I was so grateful for his regular workout regimen. Whatever he did in his home gym had molded him into a powerfully muscled specimen of a man. One that was locked and loaded, ready to pleasure me with his hard body.

He lazily stroked his hard cock while I remained on my back, nude and waiting for his next move.

He didn't ask me if I was sure or for permission anymore. I would've given it freely, but whatever was going on inside Bennett's head, he'd already determined that I was his for the taking.

He'd be right.

His gaze never left mine. "No condom tonight."

We'd texted about it this morning. I was on the pill, and both of us had been checked since our last partner.

"No condom," I agreed.

"Bend your legs and spread them wide till your knees hit the mattress."

Oh, boy.

So it was going to be like that.

As I maneuvered to do as he ordered, he lowered himself to his forearms, scooping his hands under my open thighs to wrap and hold them tight.

My hips came off the bed when he opened his hot mouth on my slit to kiss me hungrily. He groaned and squeezed my thighs tighter to keep me still. I watched him, moaning and rocking my hips against his greedy mouth.

He alternated suckling my clit between his lips and flicking circles with his tongue. Right when I felt my orgasm spiraling closer, he'd lift the pressure and lap softly. Too softly.

"Harder," I groaned, reaching down and clenching a fist in his hair.

He eased farther down, grabbing my thighs and bending my knees up higher, licking me from hole to hole, slicking me good.

My head fell to the pillow. "Oh, fuck. That feels so good."

His mouth was driving me insane. Every time I felt my orgasm edging closer, he'd move on.

"Stop teasing me." I hissed in a breath when he fucked my pussy with his tongue.

Then he was gone, standing up from the bed. "I'm giving the orders tonight."

A whimper slipped from my mouth. When he got dominant like this, I was nothing but a melty, pliant woman.

"Where's your vibrator?" he asked, voice deep and steady.

"Huh?" I was panting and aroused and confused. "How do you know I have a vibrator?"

He chuckled as he opened and closed drawers in my dresser.

"Bottom drawer on the right," I told him.

He returned with my favorite, the medium-sized one that felt like heaven against my clit. I heard the tell-tale buzz of my old friend, the one who'd kept me company more nights than I cared to count.

But not tonight. Tonight I had a warm, hard man. And not just any man. The one who unwound me with soft touches and dirty words and then put me back together with his confident hands and talented mouth.

"Lay on your side and bend your leg," he commanded, grabbing my hip and urging me over.

As I did, he took a pillow and stuffed it underneath my bent knee.

"Yeah, baby. Just like that," he purred. "Now relax. I'm going to give you a massage."

I huffed into my coverlet, my head propped on my outstretched arm. "I want more than a massage, Bennett."

"I know what you want," he whispered against my shoulder, then trailed his lips to the base of my neck. "I know what you need." He nipped and licked a line up to my ear, inducing a shiver that tightened my nipples. "I'm going to give you everything."

The way he said *everything* curled my insides into a warm, tight ball. There was something else buzzing between us tonight. More than lust. It was a mutual connection on an intimate level that I'd never felt before. Not with anyone.

He'd taken my bottle of baby oil from the bathroom and set it on the nightstand after our shower. I heard him pour some into his hand before he massaged my shoulder and along my spine, pressing into the muscles as he stroked down to the small of my back then up again.

"Just relax," he murmured, voice rumbling deep.

"Bennett," I muffled into the pillow as he kept his hands far away from the hot zone, "that's not my butt."

I felt him laugh more than heard him, then those magical hands kept caressing and pressing, wiping all the tension from my muscles.

I moaned at the luxurious feel of his hands on my back, sinking deeper into oblivion. It was as if he were slowly prying me open. The strong, sure strokes of his palms and fingers seemed to reach deeper than my skin, like he was caressing my soul, petting me, plying me to give him what he wanted.

The word *everything* kept pinging in my head. While I yearned for everything he could give, I was afraid of letting go, letting him have too much of me. I clung tightly, trying to focus on just the physical sensations, but something was happening inside me against my will. My heart hammered in my chest, trying to break free of its cage, but I forbid to set it free.

After a few minutes—or maybe it was hours, while I drifted in that sensual, dreamy state—he poured more oil into his hand and massaged lower, sliding the oil along my clit, then pumping two fingers inside me. He then moved to the back entrance, rubbing in slow circles around and around until I was arching my spine, begging for him to give me more.

He continued kissing my nape, the scruff of his jaw scraping against my skin. He scooped his arm over my shoulder to cradle me close while his hand mounded my breast and he plucked gently at my nipple.

His slow, steady, tender strokes drove me mad, making me writhe back against him till I pressed my ass back on his finger, breaching myself.

"That's it," he murmured, slowly sliding in a little deeper.

I froze at the pinprick of pain. He didn't move forward. Just kept nibbling and biting along my throat, pinching my nipple a little harder.

That had me moving again while he moved his finger with me, edging deeper. There was still a smarting pain but also pleasure. I couldn't fathom it would feel this way. My emotions spiraled at the intensity of it, the clash of pain and pleasure given to me by the only man I'd ever take it from. The only man I'd ever truly trusted.

Then he removed his finger from inside me, leaning back to get more oil. He somehow did it one-handed because his other was still massaging and teasing my breast and nipple.

"Hand me the vibrator," he said, holding out the hand that had been at my breast.

I reached over on the mattress and gave it to him while he maneuvered his free arm under my body and around my waist. He pulled me toward him till my back was pressed to his warm, broad chest and flicked on the vibrator, sliding it through my wet folds and clit.

"Bennett!"

I rocked harder. He rubbed a heavy amount of oil into the cleft of my butt then pumped his finger back in. This time, it didn't hurt nearly at all. He worked me like that for a long time, amping the tension, the need, sliding the vibrator down to my entrance then back to my clit while working a second finger inside my ass.

There was stinging again, but the pleasure overrode everything. I wanted the sensation of him filling me up inside. Only him. Then my emotions climbed higher, suffusing me with a longing I'd never known.

"Please, Bennett. Fuck me. Please, *please*."

He gripped me under the knee of my bent leg and lifted it higher, wider, then I felt him at my entrance, slowly sliding inside me, the oil making me slick and ready.

"God. Damn," he muttered through gritted teeth, hissing in a breath. "So tight, baby. Take me. Yes, just like that. Take me in."

"Unh." My moans became incoherent and loud.

I was barely conscious of my rocking because he'd slid the vibrator down between my legs and glided it inside me as he penetrated me from behind. Reaching back, I gripped his thigh, clawing my rounded nails into his flexed muscle.

"Fuck, yes, baby. You scratch me up. Mark me all you want. Because I'm going to go deep inside you," he rumbled low and rough. "Where I belong." He bit my neck, stinging with teeth.

Then he did what he said. Fucking me in a steady, deep tempo with his hard cock and my vibrator at the same time. Not too hard, but just enough to override the pain with dizzying, drugging ecstasy.

I moaned louder, practically sobbing with each thrust.

He nipped my earlobe then sucked hard on the curve of my shoulder and neck, definitely leaving a mark.

"Mmm," he groaned, his chest vibrating, slick with sweat against my back. "This pussy and this ass is mine, isn't it?"

I moaned in response.

"Tell me. Fuck, you feel so good. So tight and perfect, Betty."

Fucking hell.

"Tell me this pussy is mine." He bit my shoulder. "This ass is mine."

"Yours," I muttered in a shaky voice, hardly recognizing myself.

Bennett was the dirtiest talker I'd ever had in my bed, and it wound me up so much I was already coming. The orgasm was almost violent, my inner walls clutching around the vibrator and my ass clenching around his dick.

I screamed out his name. Another first. I couldn't help it.

He rumbled deep, groaned my name, and said, "I've got you, baby."

He clutched me tight, no longer thrusting as I shook through a cataclysmic orgasm. The overwhelming sensation forced tears to my eyes, but I squeezed them shut, a little embarrassed by how much I was feeling.

As I relaxed into his arms, he pulled the vibrator out of me, cupped my pussy, and rolled me onto my stomach, never pulling out from behind. Rather than stroke deep, he pressed me into the mattress and ground against my ass, giving me the weight of his chest, his mouth hot at my ear, his fingers in the slickness of my slit.

"So sweet and perfect for me." He dipped two fingers inside me, holding me not pumping them. "Taking me deep like a good girl."

My inner walls pulsed around his fingers like a mini-orgasm, reacting to his filthy mouth, and he wasn't stopping.

"You love my cock in your ass, don't you."

I whimpered in agreement.

"I want the words." His other hand slid around my throat, holding me firmly, his weight on one elbow while he poured wickedness in my ears and kept pumping inside me. "Tell me you love it. Tell me you need it."

"I need it," I whispered, raw emotion bursting inside me as a tear slid free. "Need you."

"That's right." His thrusts came faster, harder, and his fingers slid deeper. "Because you're mine, baby. All *mine*."

His knees spread my thighs wider as he grunted and fucked my ass. Then he stiffened and held himself deep. I felt his swelling and pulsing inside me as he came on a long groan.

All I could do was lay there and hyperventilate. I closed my eyes, the muscles in my body going completely lax.

He lifted up, pulling out gently, and rolled me over. Cupping my face, he held himself above me with his weight on one forearm. He stared down at me with a look I could only describe as wonder. I was fairly positive I was returning that same expression.

Combing my fingers into his hair, I swallowed the thick lump lodged in my throat. *Where did that come from?* Blinking quickly, unable to hold it back, another tear slid into my hair.

Bennett's eyes widened. "Oh, shit. I hurt you, didn't I? I'm so—"

"No." My voice broke as I shook my head, trying to smile but unable to.

Sex had never made me feel so defenseless and vulnerable.

His concern softened into a knowing look. I couldn't look at him anymore; I was so undone. I turned my head to the side and closed my eyes, crying silently and feeling ridiculous at my reaction.

He fell to my side and turned my body till my back was against his chest. He pulled me close and wrapped his body around mine, holding me tight.

"It's alright, Betty," he murmured softly.

I couldn't say a word. But I wrapped my arms over his and squeezed further into his embrace.

"It's alright."

I fell asleep to his quiet reassurances in my ear and his mouth pressing soft kisses against my neck.

Chapter Twenty-Eight

~BENNETT~

"My family is here," I told Betty as I strode back to my dressing room to get my jacket, the last piece of Paul's costume for Act One that I wasn't already wearing.

Betty flounced into my dressing room where Frank was gelling his moustache. He'd gone all out as Mr. Velasco and grown a longer moustache that he could style into what might've been considered suave at one time. With his fedora and seductive European accent, he played the part of the charming, eccentric older gentleman perfectly.

Now, if I could just worry about my own part, that would be great. But I'd been distracted all day. To be honest, I'd been distracted a lot longer. Apparently, I'd completely forgotten to approve the order for truffle oil needed for last night's guest chef, who I'd hired out of Baton Rouge. He'd come a long way to teach and cook for Cajun Cuisine Night.

I'd made it my own priority to be sure I had stocked whatever the chefs needed, and usually, this wasn't a problem for me. When I corralled Lucille this morning to find out how the couples' cooking night had gone, she said it went well since I'd left her in charge because of my dress rehearsal. Except for the truffle oil incident. She'd figured out that I carried truffle oil in a special cooking section of the store for serious cooks.

The chef was delayed in getting started because of that, but otherwise, it had gone well. But all I could think about for the rest of the day was that I'd slipped up. Pissing off well-known local and regional chefs was not good business. My little enterprise to bring something special into Beauville could die on the vine if chefs found out I wasn't running on the level of professionalism they expected.

Chefs were typically very particular and high maintenance to begin with. Not having all their needs met could be considered a slight, like their job wasn't important enough to me if I didn't remember to provide all their ingredients.

Not only that, Hale would kill me. He wasn't a chef, but he enjoyed discovering top-tier new restaurants and forcing the chefs to be his friends. Yes, this was something that he did with frequency and great success. Strangely enough.

So my brain was buzzing all day, especially when the chef wouldn't take my calls till late this afternoon when I could finally apologize for the blunder.

I also realized my distraction was because of the beautiful redhead leaning back on the doorjamb of the men's dressing room. Not that I blamed her for my addled brain. But she'd been subdued ever since the other night when she cried after we had sex.

At first, I thought I'd hurt her but quickly realized she was emotional because her heart was so in it. Perhaps too in it for her liking.

So I didn't say a word. I'd let her come around and accept what was happening slowly. I didn't mind waiting, especially now that I knew she was experiencing the same hardcore feelings I was.

But right now, I needed to focus on today's Sunday performance, where all the regular season ticket holders showed up. My family was also in the audience. None of that really bothered me, except I always wondered if Dad was here solely because Mom had dragged him kicking and screaming to show his parental support. Not that I needed it at my age. Much.

"Is that what's got you so frowny today?" Betty asked, crossing her arms then her ankles. Her lime-green minidress fit her to perfection, showing the full length of her luscious legs.

"What do you mean?" I asked.

"Are you nervous about me meeting the parents?" she asked, quirking an auburn brow.

"What? No." I huffed out a laugh and finger-combed my hair to the side to look like the put-together attorney of Paul Bratter.

"You need more than that," she said, squeezing in front of me, her back toward the wall-to-wall counter and mirror that went to the ceiling.

"Five minutes," Brittany called into the open door of the dressing room.

"Thank you, five!" we all called back in unison, a stage technique to keep us aware of our time and keep the stage manager happy that she knew we were ready.

"See you out there," Frank said with a wink in the mirror before slipping out.

Betty picked up a comb and worked on my hair. "You seem on edge."

"I'll be fine." I tried to convince myself more than her.

She set the comb back down and wrapped her arms around my waist, tiptoeing up to give me a kiss. I slid my hands to her waist while she kissed me softly, quieting the barrage of noise in my head.

"Better?" she asked when she pulled back.

"Much."

"Let's do this."

I followed her to our entrance point at stage right in the wings. Frank and Meredith were already there. Frank, in full Velasco character, lifted his hat to us. Meredith was clutching her old lady handbag, muttering lines to herself. Funny that Meredith's character wasn't too far from the nervous character of Ethel Banks.

Brittany was in the wings, her headset on. "We're at places," she told one of our tech crew, Mike, at the soundboard.

The lights went up, the music dimmed, and Betty sashayed on stage for the opening scene. I watched her through the curtain.

Good God, she was beautiful.

The stage lights only enhanced her beauty—her coppery hair shining, eyes glittering, milk-pale skin looking soft and silky. I was so entranced that I almost missed my cue.

"Psst. *Bennett,*" whispered Brittany, pointing toward the door where I was supposed to stumble through, panting like a dog.

As soon as I was on stage, I fell right into being Paul Bratter, an exhausted and penniless young New York attorney with a quirky, free-spirited wife who'd bought an apartment on the top floor with no elevator and a hole in the roof.

I loved this play, I thought, as we journeyed through each scene seamlessly. It was amazing. The crowd was fantastic, laughing and reacting in all the right places. Audience participation makes a huge difference for stage actors. It keeps the energy up and lively. And they were giving us everything. By the time we passed the knichi scene, I thought the woman in the first row was going to hyperventilate from laughing so hard.

All of this was outstanding. That was why I was so utterly shocked when Betty forgot her line in the middle of Act Three.

I stayed in character, fumbling with my briefcase, as I realized Betty had drawn a complete blank. It rarely happened, but it wasn't unheard of in a play where we had hundreds of lines, many of which were similar. The fear on her face had my gut clenching.

I was about to say a line a little ahead of time when she finally she spit out a line, skipping *two pages* of script. The heat of the lights seemed to intensify, my heart rate tripling and growing too loud, pounding in my head. I wasn't even supposed to be on this part of the room for that scene. I had to be near the sofa. I moved quickly and picked back up, trying to smooth it over. We fumbled through the rest of the scene, a little off since we were both trying to get our bearings.

Betty skipped ahead another line or two and flounced around the apartment, slamming things since this was our getting-a-divorce scene.

I caught up relatively quickly and fell back into place, but the damage was done. Her missing lines had me second-guessing my lines even as I said them. Because I was thinking so hard about screwing up, I bungled a line that cued Betty's exit.

She overcame the error and exited anyway. We were near the end, and I was able to recover enough to do the final scene with all the energy I'd been doing during dress rehearsals all week.

When Betty shimmied out onto the makeshift ledge where I was dangling and singing the "Shama, Shama" song, she cupped my face and looked at me, an apology in her gaze. I shook my head slightly at her.

We delivered our last lines, she kissed me, then the curtains closed and applause and hollers filled the theater.

"That was a nightmare," she whispered.

"Curtain call," hissed Brittany from down below.

"Come on," I told her, urging her back down the backstage steps.

We hurried down to the wings right as the curtain reopened and David headed out, taking his bow as the TV repairman. Then Frank swept on stage, bowing with his fedora in hand before he stepped to the side for Meredith.

When Betty and I stepped out together from opposite sides of the stage, took hands, and walked down the middle, the audience leaped to their feet, cheering and whistling.

We took our bows and clapped for Peter and Trish, who poked their heads out of the side curtain then pointed to our sound and light crew in the balcony. Then it was done.

This was when we'd step down in front of the stage and receive congratulations from audience members. Normally, I loved this part of acting, riding the euphoric high of being on stage and a job well done, chatting it up with locals who appreciate live theater.

But that third act was a shit show, and I was seriously irritated. I didn't blame Betty. It happened to all actors, but I couldn't help being pissed at how we'd bungled it.

All I wanted to do was crawl backstage, change, and go home. It had been the worst ending to a seriously shitty day. I caught Betty glancing at me, but I was already greeting audience members.

A few of the season ticket-holders walked up and praised us. They were being overly kind.

"Fabulous job, son!" My mother stepped up and hugged me.

"Thanks, Mom."

I could've walked out drunk on stage, split my pants, and

vomited in a potted plant, and she would've told me the same thing. She was my mom.

"That was fucking hilarious," said Hale.

"Watch your language," Mom hissed at him, checking to see if anyone overheard.

My father looked around, brooding, probably wishing he was at home in his office, calculating some bullshit.

"Wasn't it great, Peter?"

"Yeah, yeah. Good job," he added, obviously begrudgingly.

I glanced to my right, seeing Betty standing too far away from me, obviously beating herself up over freezing on stage and skipping a part of the scene. I grabbed her hand and tugged her over. She frowned but came anyway.

"Mom and Dad, I'd like you to meet Betty Mouton."

"It is so nice to meet you," my mother gushed, practically floating on air.

I hadn't brought a girl home in a long while, and it was no secret that she wanted me married and settled.

"So nice to meet both of you." Betty smiled tightly and shook their hands, but I could see the anguish behind her politeness. "I hope you liked the show. Even if I screwed up the last act."

"Oh, we didn't notice a thing," Mom assured her. "You were amazing, so beautiful up there. You both were too adorable on stage."

Betty smiled at my Mom, but I could tell she was upset.

"Well, you need to come to the house soon," Mom told her. "Maybe for a Sunday dinner."

Betty nodded her head, playing shy. She wasn't shy.

"So nice to meet you," she said again.

Then my stomach dropped as I saw the next person maneuvering through the crowd toward me. Mandy. Of all the people to be in the audience tonight, she was the worst.

"Hey, Mrs. Broussard!" She patted my Mom's arm and went in for a hug.

Of course, Mom hugged her right back. She knew Mandy from all the shows we'd been in together.

"Hi, Mandy. So good to see you!"

While they exchanged pleasantries, I glanced at Betty whose expression was a mixture of pain, anger, and misery.

Mandy turned to me and gripped my bicep, giving me her sexy smile. "Great performance, Ben."

I hated it when she used that nickname. Only my family ever used it.

"Thanks. Glad you could come," I replied coolly.

Mandy's smug expression said it all. She enjoyed watching us fuck up on stage. It only proved to her that she should've gotten the part, which was bullshit of course. Betty had one bad night. She was still the perfect person as the lead.

I backed up toward Betty and moved my arm so Mandy was forced to let me go. But that only brought her attention to Betty.

"Nice job, Betty," she said then leaned in and whispered secretively, "don't worry about ruining Act Three. I'm sure not many people noticed."

"Shut up, Mandy," I ground out. "Like you haven't ever missed a line."

Before I could say anything else, Betty had pushed past both of us toward the side curtain and hallway that led backstage.

I hurried after her and grabbed her arm in the backstage corridor, pulling her to a stop. "Hey. Don't listen to her. She's just being a spiteful bitch."

"I'm going to take off," she told me, looking away, brow pinched tight. "I need to get out of here."

This wasn't the Betty I knew. She was a fighter, not a runner.

"Seriously, don't listen to Mandy."

Her gaze shot to mine, anger tightening her features. "I don't want to talk about fucking Mandy Harper."

"You're letting her get to you. So you fucked up on stage. So what?"

She scoffed with disgust. "Yes, I fucked up on stage, Bennett. I'm sorry I'm not as perfect as you. Or Mandy!"

"Whoa, whoa. What the hell? Who said I was perfect? Or that you had to be? And she sure as hell isn't—"

"I can see it in your face. You're mad that I embarrassed you on stage."

I scoffed. "Now you know what the fuck I'm thinking?"

"It's obvious."

"I'm thinking I had a seriously shitty weekend at work, and yes, I'm pissed we didn't perform well on our last show of the weekend when my parents were here. So what?"

"You mean that *I* didn't perform well." Her cheeks flamed with fury, but I couldn't figure out how all her anger was directed at me. "I was the one who screwed it up. And to have her see—" She gestured toward the curtain where the audience still milled around on the other side.

That expression of anguish tightened her features before she turned and stomped down the ramp that headed to the dressing rooms.

"No way." I stormed after her into the dressing room, where she was undoing the side zipper of her dress.

"Get out. I need to change."

"Betty," I tried to tamp down my own anger rising by the millisecond. "There isn't anything under there I haven't seen."

"But I don't want you to see it right now."

"What the fuck is happening here? You're making way more out of it than it is. Sure, you screwed up and dropped some lines."

"I dropped *pages*," she snapped back with disdain. "Obviously, I'm not ready for a role this big. I'm sure that's what you're thinking. That sure as hell is what Mandy's thinking."

"Who gives a shit about her? And you don't know what I'm thinking."

"Then why don't you tell me," she huffed, her cheeks flushed pink with anger.

"I think you're being absolutely irrational about this."

"Irrational?"

Fuck. I shouldn't have said that.

"That's not what I meant."

"Yes, you did. I'm sorry that I embarrassed you in front of your family and—" she bit out with disdain. "But I want to be alone right now. Then you won't have to be around your *irrational* girlfriend."

"I never said that you embarrassed me. But you sure the fuck *are* being irrational."

"Get out." She pointed to the dresser door. "And don't come over tonight."

"Are you serious right now?"

"As a matter of fact, don't come over this week." Her chest rose and fell with the fury feeding her temper. "Maybe," she was visibly shaking, "maybe we need some space."

I took a step closer. She took a step back. I stopped, inhaling a deep breath before speaking again, my own temper hot as hell.

"This isn't about what happened on stage and you fucking know it."

She propped her hands on her hips. "What the hell are you talking about?"

I scoffed. "This is because of the other night." She knew which night, the night she cried in my arms after sex and let me pet her to sleep because she was feeling too much. "You're finally starting to feel it, and you want to run."

She stared at me, fuming and refusing to respond, her lips tightening.

"This little tantrum here," I waved a finger between us, "is because I love you. And you're scared shitless that you *could* love me." I swallowed hard, shaking my head, my pulse racing erratically. "But you don't want to."

"You don't know what you're talking about." Her voice cracked, her sapphire eyes bright and glassy with unshed tears.

"No, Betty. You don't know what you want. You've been afraid from the start." I lowered my voice, trying to keep my emotions in check. "I understand you've got issues trusting because of your dad—"

"Oh, nice, Bennett. Accusing me of Daddy issues? You're such a bastard."

"For telling you the truth?"

She snorted and crossed her arms, turning as she swiped the back of her hand across a cheek. "It's obvious that we don't get along as well as we'd thought," she practically whispered.

"This is a fight, Betty. One fucking fight. This is what happens in relationships."

I took a step closer. But she stepped away from me again, tilting her chin up defiantly, her eyes swimming with so much emotion it cracked something open inside my chest. I didn't want to hurt her, but fucking hell, she was eviscerating me.

"If some *space* will help you figure it out, then fine." Clenching my fists at my sides, I said words that scraped jaggedly against my soul. "I'll go away and leave you alone. I'll give you space."

I turned and strode for the back exit, slamming the door into the parking lot. I needed the quiet dark of my bedroom, a Zoloft pill, and sleep. Deep, deep sleep. Where I could forget how insanely wrong this night had been. Where I could forget the look of fury and pain on Betty's face and this agony in my heart and feeling of wrongness as I walked away from her.

Chapter Twenty-Nine

~BETTY~

"HIM AGAIN?" FINN TOOK A BITE OF HIS SANDWICH.

I glanced at my phone, reading Emma's text asking if I was still coming by for dinner tonight.

I shook my head. "Emma." I opened my texts, scrolling to Bennett and the ones he'd sent me yesterday and today, which I almost answered every time. But hadn't yet.

MONDAY MORNING...

Him: I'm sorry about how I spoke to you on Sunday but not about what I said. Can we meet?

Monday afternoon...

Him: I know I said I'd give you some space, but I'd like the chance to talk to you when we aren't angry.

Monday night...

Him: I miss you.

Today before sunrise...

Him: Good morning. Can we meet after school today?

Today, mid-morning...

Him: Be mad if you want, but at least talk to me. Don't shut me out.

Today, an hour ago during fourth period...

Him: Fine. You win.

It was lunch, and I was so nauseous I couldn't eat. I was miserable but also still confused and hurt and angry. But mostly at myself.

I wanted to answer every single text, but I stopped myself each time I started to.

Was I overreacting?

Yes. Probably so.

But also, how could he say that? And not even understand how utterly humiliating it was to screw up so bad on stage. In front of Mandy Harper! I remembered her words during the audition, telling me I wasn't right for this role. Basically telling me I wasn't good enough for the lead. When I'd ruined Act Three, I thought she was right. All of those feelings of not being good enough rushed to the surface.

Even though I wanted to slap that smug smile right off Mandy's face, I was also drowning in feelings of inadequacy. I just wanted to get away from it all. Even from him.

But why did I want to get away from Bennett? He hadn't done anything wrong.

I swallowed the lump in my throat, remembering what he said to me. What he accused me of. Those were the words that hit me the hardest. I'd reacted in anger, refusing to believe him, but the truth was starting to sink in. And that hurt even more.

His last text kept haunting me, my stomach flipping for the hundredth time with a sinking fear.

Was he done with me?

"Figures," I muttered.

"What figures?"

"You know?" I snapped to Finn. "Just because Bennet and I had mind-blowing sex and I happened to let him in my back door doesn't mean I'm in love with him."

Finn coughed on his bite of sandwich, eyes watering as he picked up his water and took a swallow. "Jesus, Betty. Give me some warning next time." He wiped his mouth with a napkin. "Now, what are you babbling about?"

I hadn't told Finn the entire conversation I'd had with Bennett after Sunday's show. Only that we'd fought about my fuck-up on stage, and I'd told him we needed a break.

"I was just thinking about our last night together." I dropped my face in my hands. "I cried after sex, Finn."

"That bad?"

"No." I huffed a sad laugh. "That good." I swallowed hard, remembering how overcome I'd been. I couldn't even put into words what I'd felt that night. "Nothing had ever felt so good."

"Get it, Bennett."

"Shut up. It wasn't the sex."

He dropped his half-eaten sandwich. "I'm so confused."

"Fine. I'll tell you." I heaved out a sigh. "Bennett accused me of pushing him away not because of our fight about the play but because of my—" I air quoted— "*daddy issues*. Because he loved me and I was afraid of loving him back." I snorted. "Can you believe that?"

Finn sat back in his chair, watching me far too closely. "He's right."

"Finley Fontenot. You are my best friend. You're required to take my side in everything."

"I am taking your side."

My gaze snapped away from my phone to him. "No, you're not. You just said—"

"Betty." He stood up and walked around his desk to sit

beside me on the loveseat and took my hand in both of his. "Honey, listen to me. You obviously love him. And you're pushing him away because that scares the shit out of you."

"That's not true," I said half-heartedly, staring down at where he held my hand.

"Bea. Look at me."

I did, clenching my jaw against whatever he was about to say. I still wasn't prepared.

"You do have some hang-ups because of your dad." His eyes softened and he pulled me against him. "You've always strived for perfection because you thought you needed to be perfect in order to be loved. Because your father was a dick and abandoned you and your mom and your sister."

I heaved in a breath. "Ow, Finn."

"Just listen to me and actually hear what I'm saying to you." He stroked his palm over my head then pulled back and gripped my shoulders, giving me his serious Finn look. "You are not perfect and you are *so* worthy of love."

A boulder-sized weight shifted to the tipping-point edge of my heart.

"Finn. I know I'm not perfect."

"I'm sure you do. But you're also afraid you're not enough because of it. Because that dick of a father made you feel that way." He cupped my cheek as I held everything in, barely breathing. "You're more than enough. I know it. Your mom and sister know it." He brushed his thumb across my cheek, his voice dipping softly. "And Bennett knows it."

I stood abruptly and blew out a shaky breath, the weight on my heart rolling back, settling heavier, threatening to crush it. "I'm not saying you're wrong," I managed to say.

"Because I'm not. I'm right."

"I'm just saying that's a lot of heavy psychobabble to swallow on my lunch break."

Finn stood and propped his hands low on his hips, watching me, not letting me make light of this.

"You were the one who told him you needed space. Use it wisely, Bea. And face this like the grown woman that you are. It's time to say goodbye to those fears and let this man into your life."

"I've got to go." I packed my half-eaten lunch. Well, I'd eaten three grapes and taken a bite of my sandwich, so technically, a quarter eaten, maybe. I don't know. I hated math. Hated everything right now.

Even myself. Especially myself.

"Bea—"

"I'm fine. I just need to go."

I hurried out of his office and back to my classroom, clutching my blouse at the chest, finding it hard to breathe. I didn't want to agree with Finn, but his words played on loop in my head for the rest of the day and they sunk deep.

I could barely concentrate enough to teach my classes, the weighted sensation worsening as the day wore on. I went zombie-like through my last two of the day and headed straight to my car when the final bell rang.

I avoided Lily because I couldn't talk to anyone else and hurried out to my car, deciding to go straight home and drink a bottle or three of wine.

Why can't I breathe?

Rolling my windows down, I turned onto Acadian Trail Road toward my house, unable to clear this agonizing feeling that made me feel so wretched and heartsick I could barely focus on the road.

The Tractor Supply Company was coming up on my left. I veered into the lot, shoved my car into park, and pressed my forehead to the steering wheel, my head spinning with Finn's words. Taking a few minutes to settle down, I finally snatched my phone out of my purse and checked my texts to find there were still no new ones from Bennett. My fingers hovered over the letters.

I reread for the thousandth time his last message.

You win.

"He gave up on me."

My heart plummeted. I sucked in a shaky breath, refusing to cry. But the twisting pain inside my chest was almost unbearable. The thought that he was letting me go felt like being smothered slowly. I was breathless with longing and soul-shaking sorrow.

A strange, wailing noise came to me then. At first, I thought it was my imagination, my soul screaming like a forlorn banshee across the sugarcane field behind the Tractor Supply store. But then I heard it again.

Opening my car door, I realized it wasn't a wail but more like a hoarse squeal. I followed the sound up to the edge of the cane field, where I realized it was coming from the ditch on the side of the road. Taking a few more steps to the ditch, I gasped.

"Marigold?"

The giant pig was stuck in six inches of water and a thick slough of mud at the bottom of the ditch. Hoof marks scraped along the side, slicking the walls of the ditch around her. She'd tried to get out but had tired and was now firmly embedded in the mud.

I couldn't even see her legs, the mud reaching up to her wide belly.

She made that near-soundless squeal again, her body visibly quivering. From shock or the cold, I wasn't sure. The temperatures had dropped into the forties this past week, and there was no telling how long she'd been stuck here. She had apparently gone hoarse crying out for help. It was tearing at my heart.

"Hang on there, baby!"

I punched in 9-1-1 and paced along the ditch's edge till someone finally picked up.

"Beauville Police Department, what is your emergency?"

"The pig! She's in the ditch over here."

"Excuse me, ma'am? Can you repeat that?"

"The Facebook pig. Marigold. Mr. Guillory's pig that went loose."

"And where was she spotted, ma'am?"

"No, she wasn't spotted. I'm looking at her. She's stuck in the ditch by the Tractor Supply. I think she's hurt."

"I see. I need to get your information, ma'am Your name?"

"You need to get someone down here. I think she's in shock or something."

"I have an officer on the way. Let me get your information now, please."

I spat out everything she needed for whatever crazy-ass reason. I wasn't lying and I wasn't going to vanish before the cops got here. I could never leave her alone. By the time I hung up with the dispatcher, I could see the police unit approaching in the distance.

Marigold made that pathetic cry again.

"Someone's coming to help. Just hang on, girl."

While I was waving frantically, there was no need. The officer swerved into the lot and came straight toward me, parking right next to my car.

When he stepped out, I recognized him. It was the same officer who let me off that speeding ticket the morning of Bennett's grand opening.

Bennett.

My heart twisted.

As the officer approached, I saw recognition in his gaze.

"Miss Mouton," he said with a nod and headed straight over to the ditch in long strides.

"Officer Dugas. You remember my name?"

Because that was an excellent memory.

"Dispatch," he replied dryly. "But yes, I remember you."

"Oh. Right."

Marigold made a loud keening wail. My chest tightened.

"You've got to get her out of there," I told him, desperation and urgency in my voice. "See how she's shaking. She's cold and scared."

"I see that."

"Her voice is gone." I stared down at her, pathetic and shivering. "She's been all alone out here. No telling how long."

Then something highly unexpected happened. I burst into tears, a shaking sob making me hiccup and suck in a shaky breath.

"You can't just let her keep crying like that," I said through tears, the words barely understandable. "You've gotta hurry."

The frown on the officer vanished, replaced by an expression of both alarm and confusion. "It's alright, Ms. Mouton." He raised a hand in a calming gesture like I was a wild animal. "We're going to take care of her. We've got Mr. Guillory on his way with a trailer and another officer en route."

"It's just not fair," I sobbed again, wiping the arm of my sweater across my cheeks. "She doesn't deserve to be alone. No one there to help her and comfort her"—I blinked away more tears trying to fall—"she's just been left and abandoned here."

Silence from the officer next to me, then, "Ma'am? She isn't abandoned. You're here. I'm here."

I hiccupped again; the only sound was the wind through the sugarcane and Marigold's hoarse squeal.

Then the earth-shattering shift of the boulder fell, a stone of crushing self-doubt and self-loathing rolling right off of me. Realization dawned with frightening clarity. Finally.

I turned to the officer, his piercing blue eyes concerned.

"I am here, aren't I?"

He nodded, puzzled. "You are."

"Except I wasn't. I mean, I haven't been. Not really. Not the way Bennett was. The way I should've been."

He blinked, his bewilderment turning to deep concern.

"I'm sorry." I swiped at the tears on my face, partially laughing. "It's my boyfriend."

"Oh. I see. I think. You broke up?"

"Not really. Sort of. But he was there for me. It was me. I was the one."

"Excuse me?" Officer Dugas looked so lost.

"I thought he was leaving me, but it was me." It hit me like a sledgehammer. "I left him."

I'd abandoned Bennett. Not the other way around. Finn was right. A fresh wave of tears poured down my face.

Officer Dugas produced a handkerchief from somewhere on his person. Though I didn't know anyone still carried a handkerchief, I took it gratefully all the same.

"You love him," he stated as a fact.

"I do." I wiped my cheeks.

He nodded knowingly. "That doesn't come often." He finally looked my way, eyes ocean-blue and sharp. "Best hang on to it if you can. Never know how long it'll be before it comes along again."

I nodded and sniffled, wiping my face while trying to swallow the heartrending realization that I loved Bennett. And I'd pushed him away.

Right now, I had to pull myself together.

I took a deep breath and gave Officer Dugas a grateful smile. "Thank you."

"Not sure I did much, but you're welcome."

Observing him more closely, I realized he may be a little older than I'd initially thought. He wasn't classically handsome like Bennett. Few men were. But he had that rugged beauty and confident swagger. And eyes that could see right through you.

There was also something in his words that rang of a truth he had learned the hard way, from life experience. I checked his left hand, but he wore no ring.

"You got a wife or girlfriend?"

Those blue eyes widened with surprise.

"Not for me," I told him. "I'm taken. Even if my boyfriend hates me right now. I was thinking I could introduce you to my sister. She's about to graduate college."

One side of his mouth barely tipped up into a semblance of a smile. "I appreciate that, but I'm not looking. Least of all, someone so young with the world in front of them."

"You can't be that old."

"Old enough." He sighed, staring out across the cane field. "Feel like ninety some days."

Then another police unit swung into the lot right in front of Mr. Guillory's truck pulling a big trailer.

"Well, thank you, officer." I handed him back his handkerchief, which he shoved in his back pocket.

"It's Griffin. And you're welcome, Miss Mouton. Now, why don't you come step out of the way so we can see Marigold home?"

"Oh." I hurried far off to the side but refused to leave.

A tow truck arrived with a pulley system of straps that lifted a squealing Marigold out of the muck.

"This is what happens when you wander away," said Mr. Guillory from his position close to the ditch, speaking in soft but harsh tones to Marigold. Though his voice was somewhat scornful, worry knitted his brow.

He loved Marigold just like I loved Bennett. Well, not exactly the same way. I hoped. I snapped a few pictures and shot a video of them pulling her out of the mud for Lily.

Swallowing the nauseous feeling that Bennett might not forgive me, I opened my texts, trying to figure out what to say. It was Tuesday night. He'd be working late at the store with inventory. But I'd see him tomorrow at the theater for our next performance. We had a Family and Friends Night to kick off the last weekend of the show.

I'd hurt him. Badly.

I squeezed my eyes shut tight against the awful words I'd told him last Sunday. God, he had to forgive me. He had to.

Once Mr. Guillory and Marigold were on their way, I waved to Officer Dugas. It wasn't until I pulled into my driveway and walked into my dark, empty house that my smile slipped and fell away, that my heart pinched in a grieving sort of pain.

It wasn't that I was alone. I'd been living alone for a long time now. It was that I now knew what it felt like to have someone to come home to, to have love warming every corner of my house. Of my heart.

It was the absence of something beautiful that gouged me in the chest. A sense of loss that made my whole body ache, right down to my soul.

Sighing heavily, I tossed my phone and purse aside, poured myself a glass of wine, and planned what I could possibly say to make Bennett forgive me and take me back.

Chapter Thirty

~BENNETT~

Knock, knock.

"They're ready for mic check, Bennett," said Brittany through the closed door.

I opened it, keeping the door shut since I'd gotten to the theater. I couldn't handle even looking at her right now, couldn't handle her ignoring me right in front of my fucking face.

"Thanks, Brittany."

"I can help you," she offered, grabbing the mic tape off my shelf.

"I can do it. Thanks."

I took it from her and went about putting the mic on, threading the wire up the back of my shirt and taping it to my jaw.

After mic check, Peter would want to do our pre-show cast meeting where I wouldn't be able to avoid her any longer. Hands on the countertop, I let my head fall, wondering how the hell I was going to do this. The stage kissing and holding and laughing, pretending she was my wife and life was wonderful when I wasn't even sure she wanted me anymore, was going to be the most difficult performance I'd ever have to give.

Every text I sent that she left on read shot another piercing sting through my chest. I wasn't sleeping or eating. I could barely think straight. After three days with absolutely no response, I knew it was worse than I thought. I figured she'd realize she was overreacting and that what we had was worth fighting for.

But now, I was fairly sure I was wrong. Maybe I'd pushed her too hard when she wasn't ready and ruined it.

Unable to hide in my dressing room any longer, I opened the door and headed up the ramp and through the door that acted as the apartment bathroom to go on stage. Right as I swung it open, Betty jumped back.

"S-sorry," she said, her blue eyes wide and so beautiful, my stomach sank.

I stepped aside, staring at the floor because I couldn't stand to look at her. I held the door so she could get past me, unable to even say a word.

She walked part way through then turned to face me. "Bennett?"

Heart hammering with desperate longing, I clenched my jaw and met her gaze.

She gave me a sad sort of apologetic smile. Of course, she would. She wasn't a monster. She was sorry for hurting me since she didn't feel the same way I did for her.

"Bennett, I—"

"Look, I don't want to talk about anything before the performance. This isn't the time or the place," I snapped. "It's hard enough to concentrate as it is." There was no way to hide the harshness of my tone or the anger riding me hard.

But how else was I supposed to fucking feel? She'd broken my damn heart and was standing there all doe-eyed and apologetic but still seemed perfectly able to function and smile and act like she hadn't destroyed my world.

She dipped her chin, glancing away. "Right. Of course. Can we talk after the show? Please?"

"I doubt it."

Then I rushed on stage for the mic check and to get ready for the show. Peter congratulated us on having a big crowd tonight with family, friends, and board members. I didn't hear whatever else he was saying. I was trying too hard not to look at her and run through my lines in my head.

I focused on burying my head in the show and the performance, trying hard to forget about her. Which was impossible since I'd be acting with her for the next two hours.

"Okay, what's our lucky word for tonight?" asked Peter.

"How about *shama, shama* said Trish?"

I grimaced as everyone put their hands into the huddle. When Betty's finger brushed mine, I jerked away like she'd stung me.

"Shama, shama!" shouted our cast, but I didn't.

After we broke, I strode directly up the ramp stage right to get into place. I felt her before she came into my line of sight, then I smelled her. That citrus scent mingled with warm woman that made my knees weak. I swallowed against the pain, focusing on the apartment door entrance.

Then she was standing right beside me, ready to go on.

Fuck.

How was I going to make it through this?

"My family's here tonight," she whispered softly. Sweetly.

Like we could just stand here and pretend that she hadn't cut me open and gutted me.

"I'll try not to fuck up my performance for them," I bit back, refusing to look at her.

"You won't," she said sadly. "You're always amazing on stage."

I couldn't help it. My gaze slid down to her. "Only on stage, though, right?"

"Okay, Mike," said Brittany. "We're at places. Ready for the house lights and transition in one minute."

The pain reflected back at me should've made me feel better because I was intentionally trying to hurt her. To make her feel a fraction of my agony these past few days. Instead, regret burned a hole in my chest.

Then the theater music died and the stage lights brightened beyond this partial wall.

"You're on," snapped Brittany, since Betty was still standing there looking at me with the saddest fucking expression I'd ever seen.

She stepped up to the apartment door with her grocery bag in hand, opened it, and swept on stage.

"Fuck," I muttered.

"Everything okay?" whispered Brittany.

I waved her off and waited for my cue.

Everything was most definitely not okay. Everything was fucked up beyond reason.

Muttering my opening lines to myself, I remembered back to the dozens of times I'd done this scene with Betty. Savoring the way she smiled at me as Corie as she welcomed her beloved husband home. Remembering only stabbed the dagger deeper, but I had to recall those moments so that I could make it through this fucking show.

By some miracle, I was able to detach myself as Paul and let the character take the lead through the opening Act. Even when Betty sat on my lap and brushed a welcome-home kiss to my lips, I somehow didn't lose my shit. She remained in character for all but a flicker of seconds when I couldn't help myself and brushed a parting kiss to her lips before the buzzer sounded, signaling her mother's visit. Her gaze went soft and sad, feeling sorry for me because I was obviously still holding onto hope.

When Act One ended, I rushed backstage and into a storage room that no one used then pressed my palms to my eyes, willing myself not to actually start crying.

"Fucking hell," I hissed, breathing hard and fast.

I loved her so fucking much, and this was absolute pure hell.

I don't know how long I stood in the dark trying to get my shit together, but Brittany yelled, "Two minutes!"

"Thank you, two," Frank said as I exited the storage room. "Hey." His brow pinched with concern as he tapped my arm. "You okay?"

"Yeah. Gotta change jackets for this next scene." Then I hurried away.

By the time I'd changed and got back into places off stage, Betty was staring at me hard. But I never met her gaze.

Then we were in Act Two, Scene Two, where we'd come back from our night out with Mr. Velasco, the big fight scene between Corie and Paul.

Corie accused me of always doing the right things.

"You're very close to being perfect!" Betty yelled as Corie, her voice breaking.

She was acting the scene flawlessly. Only, the anger raging between us wasn't fake. Not at all. I couldn't control it when she mentioned wanting a divorce. I let her have it, the scene escalating as it was supposed to until they bickered back and forth that divorce was the best option. That they'd saved years of misery finding out how wrong they were for each other before the marriage had even gotten started. The parallels between Betty and me were excruciating.

"I thought you weren't going to cry!" I shouted

Then Betty burst into tears. Real tears. There was a heart-breaking pause, a moment hanging in the air when she couldn't say the lines. The audience held its breath. Not a sound but her sobs. She simply stared at me with all the hurt in her eyes. I towered over her as Paul, breathing hard. Finally, she snapped out her last line and stormed off stage.

When the scene ended and the curtain was drawn, I headed backstage to find her. I couldn't do this anymore. If she wanted to end this, I'd let her. I couldn't punish her anymore for not loving me the way I so desperately wanted. Despite everything, I wanted her to be happy, and it's obvious I was making her miserable. It was killing me inside.

She wasn't in her dressing room. Meredith was there, powdering her cheeks.

"Where's Betty?"

"She didn't come back here."

I walked around, trying to find her. Brittany was busy moving some props around for the final Act.

"Have you seen Betty?"

"No, sorry, Bennett."

By the time I found her, we had one minute left of intermission and Brittany was ushering us back into places.

"Betty," I whispered, standing right beside her. "Let's talk after, okay?"

"Fine," she said, having wiped her tears off, ready for the final Act. Now it was her refusing to look at me.

"Shit."

Then the curtains opened and we were on.

The scene was going fine. This was my big finale scene where I got drunk and climbed outside the apartment skylight in an effort to prove to Corie that I was the spontaneous, fun-loving husband she wanted.

Hale had done a great job creating a plexiglass window that leaned at an angle above the apartment so that the audience could see us clearly for the final make-up on the rooftop.

I was singing the "Shama, Shama" song drunkenly as Betty shimmied onto the makeshift rooftop until she grabbed hold of me. We were both standing on the precarious rooftop together, Betty staring into my eyes, not Corie.

"I'm sorry," she clutched my shoulders, facing me, "It wasn't your fault."

She was off-script, and my heart took a nosedive right out of my chest.

"I was wrong." She shook her head, blinking away a tear. This was Betty, not Corie, speaking to me. "So wrong. You were right…about everything." Her hands slid up my shoulders to my neck. "I love you."

I couldn't breathe, my hands holding her about the waist. "What do you mean?"

Now I was off-script! But this was Betty talking, and I couldn't wait a second longer to find out if what I hoped was happening was actually happening.

"Say it again," I said.

"I love you! And I don't care about anything else. I want to spend the rest of my life with you." She swallowed hard. "If you can possibly forgive me."

I gave her the only answer I could. I swept her up into my arms, her feet off the ground, and melded my mouth to hers.

The audience roared in applause as I kissed her for far too long. So long that Mike started the closing music to end the show. We were obviously off script and weren't veering back. I couldn't think beyond the sheer bliss lighting me up inside.

Whistles and hollers continued while I bit her lips and kissed her again like a ravenous animal. She made a sound then started to laugh as the curtains closed then pulled away.

"That wasn't a stage kiss," she said, grinning like mad.

"You're fucking right it wasn't."

I still held her against my body off the ground, and she was beaming, her eyes midnight stars. "You really forgive me?"

"Don't ever push me away like that again," I growled.

"I won't." She shook her head vigorously.

"Don't ignore me for days."

"I won't," she repeated breathlessly. "I'm sorry."

"If we get into an argument, then we fight it out. We don't walk away, you understand?"

"I know. You're right."

"Damn straight I am." I kissed her quick and bit her a little harder. "I love you, Betty. That means something."

"It means everything," she whispered against my mouth as another tear slid down her cheek.

Then I swept my mouth against hers again before she pushed back suddenly. "Peter's going to kill us."

"Yeah." I laughed. "But I don't care."

"Curtain call!" hissed Brittany from the wings of the balcony. "Hurry!" She was waving us to get off the damn stage.

I set Betty down but grabbed her hand and didn't let go. We ran, practically flying all the way down the stairs, Betty's laughter following me. The elation was indescribable.

All I knew was that I couldn't control myself as we ran out to thunderous applause and a standing ovation and took our bow. I picked her up, my arms bracketing her thighs as I spun her around and let her slide down, kissing her as she came. More whistles and cheers erupted from the crowd.

Cupping her sweet face, I pressed my forehead to hers. "You love me."

"Very much." She smiled, gripping my wrists. "Sorry it took me so long."

"Better late than never, Ms. Mouton." I trailed my thumb down her cheek. "Does this mean you finally forgive me about the glitter booby bomb?"

She laughed. "Yes. As long as you forgive me."

"Absolutely." I leaned forward close to her ear, "Now I'm ready for make-up sex."

"Come on, break it up, lovebirds," said Frank, still wearing his fedora in full Velasco character. "One more bow."

We clasped hands with the rest of the cast, looking out at the audience. Betty's Mom and sister Emma were clapping and yelling. Her friend Lily from school stood next to Finn, smiling and applauding as well. Peter and Trish were standing in the aisle, shaking their heads but smiling. I even saw Hale and his buddy Reed from the construction company bracketing their mouths with their hands and hollering up at the stage.

"Get a room!" yelled Hale, winking at me.

Holding Meredith's hand on my left and Betty's on my right, we took our final bow, ending the best show of my life. The show that brought Betty into it who became the best part of my world.

Epilogue

Four months later...

~BENNETT~

"There's a goat wandering around on your porch," my dad told Betty as she set another platter of hors d'oeuvres on the table, his expression a mixture of confusion and disgust. He turned to me, "Does she own a goat?"

"No, that's just Gilbert," I told him. "It's her neighbor's goat that gets out a lot."

"No one feed him," warned Betty with wide eyes. "Rich food makes him sick."

"Great wine," said Frank, balancing a plate of cheese, crackers, dip, and finger sandwiches.

"Thank you." I'd insisted on providing the food and alcohol for Betty's housewarming party.

Like Betty said, what was the point in owning a bougie grocery store without using the perks?

It seemed her housewarming party had turned into a little reunion with our cast from the show as well. Meredith and her husband stepped up next to us.

"Your house is so lovely, Betty," she said.

"Thank you. Glad y'all could come."

"Say, are you doing *Sound of Music*?" asked Frank around a bite of sandwich. "Auditions are next weekend."

"No. I'm going to sit this one out. Take a little time off from BPAL."

Betty was busy adding a fruit platter to the buffet table, but I caught her quick smile over her shoulder.

"Time off?" asked Peter, having just walked up. "Since when do you take time off from musicals?"

"Since I have better things to do with my time." My gaze remained on Betty.

She turned to us and rolled her eyes. "You can audition if you want to. I don't care."

I already knew Mandy was gunning for the lead and though Betty and I were in a solid relationship, I didn't want to spend hours every day with Mandy at rehearsal. I wanted to be with my girl.

"I'll go for the next straight play after that."

"Wonderful!" Peter's eyes lit up. "I'm doing *Odd Couple* in the fall."

"Another Neil Simon?" Betty's smile brightened.

"Yep, and there's a part in there for you." He winked at her.

"Sounds like fun," she said, hooking her arm with mine and giving it a squeeze. Just as quickly, she let me go. "I'm going to go say hi to your parents."

I nodded and glanced around the room, happy to see that Brittany was flirting it up with Mike from the sound and light crew. She'd realized I was a hopeless cause. It probably had to do with the fact that during the curtain call of our first performance, after our break-up and make-up, I'd hauled Betty into my arms and kissed her soundly in front of the entire audience.

I grabbed a glass of wine from the buffet table set along the wall as Peter sidled up to me.

"We had record-breaking sales on *Barefoot*, you know," he said, smiling triumphantly. "Never before has BPAL had a straight play do so well," he added.

"That's awesome to hear," I told him.

"You guys should be proud of the job you did."

"So should you."

He laughed and tapped his wine glass to mine. "The board members are convinced it was the stage chemistry between you and Betty that caught fire. After the first weekend, every show was sold out. People must've told all their friends and family in Beauville."

It might've also had something to do with our real chemistry beyond the stage, but I didn't bother telling him that. It was a special kind of thrill to play opposite the woman you loved on stage. I had no idea how fun, how exhilarating, how fulfilling it would be. Almost as much as playing with her off stage.

Almost.

My dad appeared at my side out of nowhere. "Dad, this is the director of my last show, Peter Thompson."

They shook hands then Peter said, "Your son is quite an asset to BPAL. He's a great actor."

"Yes, he is." Then he turned abruptly to me and clapped me on the shoulder. "I'm proud of him."

While Peter said he agreed and started chatting away with my father, I stared at him like I didn't know him.

Sure, we'd called a truce where he promised not to overstep into my business, but he'd never complimented me so openly. Especially about theater, which he'd always thought was trivial.

My gaze strayed to Betty standing next to my mother, who

was saying something to her with a smile. But Betty's knowing expression caught me and held me captive.

"Thanks, Dad," I said casually, as if we had these sorts of exchanges every day. "Excuse me a minute."

Setting my glass of wine on a side table, I maneuvered toward Betty and grabbed her hand, "Sorry, Mom, I need to steal her."

As she laughed, I tugged Betty through the kitchen, where Lily was slicing up the cake and serving pieces on plates. I led Betty out to the back porch.

Swooping her into my arms, I pressed a deep kiss to her sweet mouth, tasting and lingering, nipping at her bottom lip before angling again to sweep my tongue along hers. The intimacy of it penetrated straight through me, to kiss my lover. My love. It was beautiful. And I was grateful for it. To have her.

"Thank you," I murmured against her lips.

"For what?"

"You know what. For sending my dad over to congratulate me on the show."

"I didn't send him," she protested. "Well, maybe, I nudged him. He said he was proud of you to your mother. So I butted in and gave him a little nudge."

"What did you tell him?" I asked, grinning wide.

"I said, 'Well, what are you waiting for? Armageddon? Go tell him.' Then your mom laughed and said I was right."

I squeezed her tighter as a rumble of laughter vibrated in my chest. "I bet she did."

"I like your mom. She's a no-nonsense woman."

"She is. A lot like you." I kissed her again. Softly this time. Sweetly. "Thank you again."

"I'd like to be thankful for my multiple orgasms later on. Sooner rather than later. Please and thank you."

"We should probably wait till the party ends."

"Probably so." Then she winced. "Ow." She looked down and pulled out of my arms. "No, Gilbert!"

"*Baaaa*!"

"Bad boy!"

He was wearing his new red collar with a bell on it. My idea so we knew when he was breaking and entering on the porch.

"What did he do?"

"He nipped my thigh." She rubbed at the pink spot right below the hem of her dress.

No skin was broken, though. Gilbert wanted attention.

"I completely empathize with Gilbert. I know what it's like to want to bite your thighs and not be able to."

She arched a brow at me. "Stop taking his side."

"Betty!" Lily shouted as she peeked out onto the porch. "Your mom and Emma just got here. They're looking for you."

"Coming," said Betty.

"Well, I think my dad was right," I told her, pulling her back into my arms, hands squeezing at her waist.

"About what?"

"That *is* your goat."

"Maybe. Just don't tell Gretchen." She laughed, the sound falling through my body like summer rain, refreshing and necessary.

"We'll need to get him a woman so he'll stop trying to steal mine."

She took my hand and walked ahead toward the door. "Not a good idea. Then we'd have a bunch of baby goats."

"What's so bad about that?" I stopped her in the kitchen and pulled her back to me, whispering into her hair, "Having babies sounds like a great plan to me."

Her breath hitched, and she looked over her shoulder at me, blue eyes wide. "I'm not ready for babies right now, Bennett."

"Of course not now." I brushed my lips against her cheek. "But one day?"

"One day." Her eyes went warm and affectionate. "Besides, we're not even married yet."

"I can fix that."

She laughed, a flush of pink filling her face as she grabbed my hand and hauled me toward the living room.

"Why don't you surprise me?" she asked, stopping in the hallway.

"Deal." I smacked her ass, which got her moving again.

I was proud of my acting skills. While my heart rate had tripled in a matter of seconds during that conversation, I'd managed to play cool and calm. Testing the waters had worked. I knew she loved me, but I wasn't sure if she was ready for that big of a step.

Her eager response and the light in her eyes when the conversation had strayed to marriage and children was all the encouragement I needed. Still, I wasn't going to tell her I had a princess solitaire diamond set in platinum in her size stashed in my dresser drawer at home.

Not yet.

But someday soon, I was going to make the love of my life Betty Broussard.

I smiled at the thought that she'd share in the name splashed on the sign of the most bougie supermarket in Beauville. That would likely irritate the hell out of her.

"What?" she asked as we made our way into the party.

"Nothing. Just happy," I told her honestly.

She wrapped my arm around her waist and leaned back into me.

"Me, too," she said, sighing against me. "Perfectly happy."

"Perfectly."

~

THANK YOU SO MUCH FOR READING! IF YOU LIKE PARANORMAL romcom that's heavy on the relationship and romance and light on the PNR, try WOLF GONE WILD, book 1 in my New Orleans-based STAY A SPELL series.

YOU MIGHT ALSO LIKE MY MOST RECENT SMALL-TOWN, ENEMIES-to-lovers romance, PARKS AND PROVOCATION, about Betty's college roommate, Lola Landry.

Author's Note

As a long-time supporter, actor, and assistant director for my own community theater, it was such a joy to write this book.

I want to commend all members of community theater—actors, directors, assistant directors, board members, stage managers, prop coordinators, costume designers, choreographers, tech personnel, set designers and builders and anyone I accidentally omitted—for volunteering so much of your own time and talents to bring joy to your communities.

I know the amount of work that goes into putting on a show, and I just want to say, thank you. You're more appreciated than you know.

And to the non-thespians out there, if you have a community theater, be sure to go out and see a show and applaud the local talent in your town. And as we say in Cajun country, *pass a good time*!

Also by Juliette Cross

GREEN VALLEY HEROES SERIES:

- *Parks and Provocation* (#2 in Smartypants Romance series)

STAY A SPELL SERIES:

- *Wolf Gone Wild*
- *Don't Hex and Drive*
- *Witches Get Stitches*
- *Always Practice Safe Hex*
- *Resting Witch Face* (October 2022)
- *Grim and Bear It* (May 2023)
- *Walking in a Witchy Wonderland: Holiday Anthology*

NIGHTWING SERIES:

- *Soulfire*
- *Windburn*
- *Nightbloom*

VALE OF STARS SERIES:

- *Dragon Heartstring: Prequel*
- *Waking the Dragon*
- *Dragon in the Blood*
- *Dragon Fire*
- *Hunt of the Dragon*

THE VESSEL TRILOGY:

- *Forged in Fire*
- *Sealed in Sin*
- *Bound in Black*

VAMPIRE BLOOD SERIES:

- *The Black Lily*
- *The Red Lily*
- *The White Lily*
- *The Emerald Lily*

DOMINION SERIES:

- *Darkest Heart*
- *Hardest Fall*
- *Coldest Fire*